"Now you're stuck here...."

"No one could have gotten through that storm." Anna brushed snow from her thighs. "I'm sorry."

"You may as well come inside," Tyler said gruffly. He couldn't let her freeze to death.

"Thank you," she said. "I know you wanted to be alone, and I swear I won't be a bother. I'll just keep to myself and not talk at all, and I'll even cook for you. I feel terrible about imposing like this."

"Do you always talk this much?"

"Sorry. I'll try to be quiet."

Suddenly a snowflake drifted down to her mouth, and Tyler watched it melt into a silvery bead on her red-rose lip. A vivid image of his tongue against that bead and the plump flesh below sent dancing heat over his nerves.

Frustrated, Tyler turned away. "Try harder," he said.

JANET DAILEY
AWARD
WINNER

Dear Reader,

It's summer. The days are long…hot…just right for romance. And we've got six great romances right here, just waiting for you to settle back and enjoy them. Linda Turner has long been one of your favorite authors. Now, in *I'm Having Your Baby?!* she begins a great new miniseries, THE LONE STAR SOCIAL CLUB. Seems you may rent an apartment in this building single, but you'll be part of a couple before too long. It certainly works that way for Annie and Joe, anyway!

Actually, this is a really great month for miniseries. Ruth Wind continues THE LAST ROUNDUP with *Her Ideal Man,* all about a ranching single dad who's not looking for love but somehow ends up with a pregnant bride. In the next installment of THE WEDDING RING, *Marrying Jake*, Beverly Bird matches a tough cop with a gentle rural woman—and four irresistible kids.

Then there's multi-award-winning Kathleen Creighton's newest, *Never Trust a Lady.* Who would have thought small-town mom Jane Carlysle would end up involved in high-level intrigue—and in love with one very sexy Interpol agent? Maura Seger's back with *Heaven in His Arms,* about how one of life's unluckiest moments—a car crash—somehow got turned into one of life's best, and all because of the gorgeous guy driving the other car. Finally, welcome debut author Raina Lynn. In *A Marriage To Fight For,* she creates a wonderful second-chance story that will leave you hungry for more of this fine new writer's work.

Enjoy them all, and come back next month for more terrific romance—right here in Silhouette Intimate Moments.

Leslie J. Wainger

Leslie J. Wainger
Senior Editor and Editorial Coordinator

Please address questions and book requests to:
Silhouette Reader Service
U.S.: 3010 Walden Ave., P.O. Box 1325, Buffalo, NY 14269
Canadian: P.O. Box 609, Fort Erie, Ont. L2A 5X3

HER
IDEAL MAN

RUTH WIND

Silhouette®

INTIMATE™MOMENTS®

Published by Silhouette Books

America's Publisher of Contemporary Romance

This book is for Lord James, also known
as my little brother, Jim Hair.
With love from Queen Anne.

 SILHOUETTE BOOKS

ISBN 0-373-07801-3

HER IDEAL MAN

Copyright © 1997 by Barbara Samuel

RUTH WIND

is the award-winning author of both contemporary and historical romance novels. She lives in the mountainous Southwest with her husband, two growing sons and many animals in a hundred-year-old house the town blacksmith built. The only hobby she has since she started writing is tending the ancient garden of irises, lilies and lavender beyond her office window, and she says she can think of no more satisfying way to spend a life than growing children, books and flowers.

Excerpt from the diary of Louise Forrest...

I have to do something about Tyler. That boy is so lonely, it's breaking my heart. I hate to think of him growing old all alone on that mountain of his. Sure, he has Curtis now, but sooner than he expects, his toddler son will be grown and gone.

Tyler's got so much love to give. He's my romantic son—as noble and steady and passionate as a knight in one of those fairy tales Curtis is always begging Anna Passanante to tell him. Anna already thinks Tyler hung the moon—probably because he's so old-fashioned and brooding. But now that I think about it, she's the only woman I've seen him notice. Of course, it's hard not to notice Anna, but Tyler gets that look in his eye when she's around....

Hmm.... Maybe I'll just send Anna up to his cabin on some errand. And if things don't work out, no harm done.

It couldn't hurt to try.

Chapter 1

Anna Passanante cursed herself. There were some things no mortal should ever undertake, and this was one of them.

Driving. In the mountains. In a blizzard.

Snowflakes the size of crystal balls fell from a sky so low it swallowed the tops of the pines growing in dark abundance on the mountainside. The higher she climbed on the twisting, narrow gravel road, the lower the sky fell. She could see almost nothing beyond a few feet ahead of her brand-new Jeep, which had proved almost—but not quite—equal to the task of navigating the mountain.

A tank, now, might have been up to the task.

She wrapped her leather-gloved hands around the steering wheel more tightly, inching up the road at five miles an hour. Overconfidence. That was her problem. Misplaced exuberance and overconfidence. After twenty-five years, she thought, a person might have learned better.

The Jeep lurched in a pothole as big as Montana, tossing Anna against the door. A jagged bolt of fear tore through

her lungs and belly as the car hovered just this side of
control, then settled evenly on the other side of the hole.

"Insane," she said aloud. She would have turned back
twenty minutes ago, but there had been no place to do it
on the narrow road. She was stuck going all the way.

Just as the first threads of alarm started winding through
her veins, the road abruptly leveled and ended in a clearing
set amid the dark, snow-laden pines. Anna stopped the
truck and turned off the ignition, staring in wonder.

The woodcutter's cottage.

Crouched close against the forest that towered behind it,
the cabin was small, crafted of weather-darkened logs.
Snow drifted in thick swirls around it, making Anna think
of the glass globes sold in tourist shops. Smoke came from
a stone chimney, and neat piles of wood of various sizes
were stacked under a small shed.

Anna smiled. No wonder Curtis loved fairy tales so
much. He lived in one.

Curtis. The four-year-old grandson of Louise Forrest
was the whole reason Anna had agreed to this wild quest.
Far from her enormous family, Anna had taken a special
liking to the motherless Curtis, who raptly listened to
Anna's endless store of fairy tales for hours on end.

Thinking urgently of the drive back down the mountain
and the teddy bear Curtis could not sleep without, she
opened the door.

Before she had made two ungraceful steps in the thick
snow already piled on the ground, a figure emerged from
the log-framed doorway. Curtis's father, Tyler. Anna
halted at the furious nonwelcome she read in his posture.
An enormous muslin-colored dog with bright black eyes
stood next to him.

"What do you want?"

Defensively Anna called, "Your mother sent me!"

He only stared, his arms crossed, his face thunderous.

On three occasions she had met Tyler Forrest. This was

the fourth, and her reaction to him had not changed one bit. Although he lived in the woodcutter's cottage, Tyler was the enchanted prince of every fairy tale ever written.

In the soft gray light, he was hauntingly handsome. Snow caught in his long hair, hair the color of sword gilt—not quite gold, not quite silver, but some ethereal color in between. Thick flakes clung in airy stars to the dark blue corduroy of his shirt and landed in tufts on his lean, broad shoulders. Snow melted on the heat of his elegantly sculpted face, a face molded to capture the hearts of a thousand maidens, with its high brow and aristocratic nose and high, sharp cheekbones. Only his mouth marred the elegance, for it was wide and full, a sensual mouth formed perfectly for the shape of kisses.

It was foolish, this besotted sense of fate Anna felt every time she looked at Tyler Forrest. A prickly loner who lived alone up on the mountain with his son, miles from town, he'd never said more than three words to her directly. He never spoke to women at all, if the truth were told. He was as unattainable as a myth.

And yet, she could never seem to stop the quick, yearning ache of her heart whenever she saw him.

He lifted his chin now, that gorgeous mouth flattened to a tight line. "Did she send you to rescue me?"

Rescue him. Anna clutched her hands together. He certainly *needed* rescuing, but a blue-collar woman from Brooklyn didn't have the tools to break the spell holding him in his lonely world. He needed a princess with golden hair and dreamy blue eyes.

"Something far more prosaic, I'm afraid," she called, forcing a smile. "Curtis forgot his teddy bear, and you know he can't spend the whole weekend without it, even with his grandmother." She felt her face get warm as she babbled, and clamped her lips together. She took a breath and dared to take another step forward. "If you'll just get it for me, I'll be on my way—before this storm gets any worse.''

As if he'd only just noticed, he looked up at the sky. ''All right.'' His mouth tightened. ''You may as well come in while I get it.''

Anna made her way through the thick snow in the clearing, thankful for the fur-lined boots and her parka. He waited for her, his face blank, and when she got to the porch, he held out a hand to help her up. ''Watch your step.''

The hand was lean and very strong, with smooth oval nails. Small nicks and scratches, likely from his carpentry work, gave it a manly aspect. Anna allowed him to haul her up to the porch. For one minute, he looked at her hard, as if he were angry, or maybe disappointed.

His dog whined up at Tyler, his tail wagging, his feet restless in the snow. ''No, Charley,'' he said firmly, letting go of Anna's hand.

The dog, still very young by the look of him, looked crestfallen. ''I won't bother him if you're training him as a watchdog,'' Anna said, ''but I'd love to greet him, if it's okay.''

''Go ahead. Be careful. He thinks he's supposed to kiss you.''

Anna bent down to rub the dog's enormous head. Exuberantly he leaped up and put his paws on her shoulders, giving her chin a lick. His thick, short hair was well brushed. ''What kind of dog is he?'' she asked, softly admonishing him to sit.

''A greyhound mix. Probably a little golden Lab.'' He scowled at the dog. ''No, Charley! Sit.''

Charley did, licking his chops as he waited for the pat Tyler gave him. ''Good dog.'' The scowl returned when Tyler turned his attention back to Anna. ''My mother sent you, huh?''

''Yes.''

"How did that happen?"

Anna shrugged. "She called and asked." Uncomfortable, she felt compelled to point to her Jeep, glossy with factory-fresh paint. "She knows I like any reason to drive my new truck."

He looked at the Jeep, then at Anna. His eyes were as unusual as everything else about him. Pale gray, with a dark ring around the iris. The eyes of a mage, somehow clear and opaque at once. Standing so close, she could see that his eyelashes were a light brown tipped with gold, as was the shadow of beard on his narrow jaw.

She laced her fingers together and looked away. For once in her life, she would act with decorum and dignity.

Or try, anyway.

He led her inside. Anna stopped just beyond the door to let her eyes adjust to the dimness after the blazing snow light. She smelled a heady combination of spicy pine and wood smoke and apples, and heard Tyler moving away over a wooden floor. Charley padded over to the hearth and plopped himself down with a sigh.

Slowly, her vision cleared, and Anna was staring at a hearth with a low fire burning orange and yellow. The mantle was made of native stone, and the only decoration was a picture of a pretty young girl, blond and smiling, in front of the cabin on a summer day.

Conscious of the mess she'd make, Anna stayed close to the door. The cabin looked to be mainly one large room, with a kitchen at one end, a living area in the center and a bedroom at the other end. A ladder led to a loft that was dark and appeared to be unfinished—she assumed it held a storeroom of some kind. Tyler had gone through a doorway below the loft, probably a bedroom for Curtis.

She had expected something primitive, but it wasn't. Braided rugs covered a floor made of wooden planks, and the furniture was all of an elegantly simple design, the fabrics in warm hues of dark red and blue. In the kitchen, copper and iron pots hung from hooks. The bed was neatly made with a Pendleton blanket in a Native American pattern.

It made her feel better, somehow, to think of Curtis living here in this warm, pleasant place. For all his aloofness, Tyler had made a good home for his son.

Which she really should have expected. She'd rarely met such a bright, adorable, loving child. Neglected children were never that sunny and giving. They were afraid to be.

Tyler returned in a moment with a bedraggled teddy bear in his hands. "Anything else?"

"I think that's it. Thanks." Anna clutched the bear close to her tummy and turned to open the door.

"Look," he said roughly. "I don't mean to be rude. It's just that my mother knows I want to be alone this weekend, and she doesn't like it, so she's meddling."

Anna looked up in surprise. "I swear, I—"

He lifted a hand. "Understood. She means well, but everyone has to grieve in their own way, and she won't stay out of it."

He wanted to be alone to commemorate the anniversary of his wife's death. Anna knew that much, because Louise had told her. "I know," she said. "She told me she wants you to get over it and get married so Curtis will have a mother."

At his hard look, Anna realized how that sounded, and hastily backtracked. "I mean, not that she meant I should be...um...not that she sent me to be your—" She broke off, feeling heat in her face. Nothing like making a complete fool of yourself in front of the most gorgeous man in the universe. "Never mind." She spied the photo over his shoulder and seized the distraction. "Is that her? Your wife, I mean?"

Tyler glanced over his shoulder. "Yeah."

"She's pretty."

He crossed his arms.

Anna took a breath and reached behind her for the door handle. "I gotta get out of here before the storm gets worse."

He followed her out to the porch, and frowned. "This is one hell of storm," he commented, almost to himself. With obvious reluctance, he asked, "Are you sure you'll be all right? I can follow you down, if you like."

In spite of his lack of relish for the job, Anna seriously considered the offer. She had only been inside ten minutes, and already a new layer of snow had collected in thick wet flakes on her windshield. It seemed to be coming down even harder now. If that were possible. Thinking of the narrow, heart-stoppingly twisting road, she hesitated. What if she got stuck somewhere?

But going down was easier, and wouldn't take as long. "I'll be fine," she said with more confidence than she felt. "What's the worst that could happen? I have to walk out?" She pointed to her boots. "I'm dressed for it."

He looked at the sky, and the road. "Maybe I should follow you, at least to the frontage road."

"It's not necessary. Really." She smiled. "I may sound like a tenderfoot, but I've done my homework. I know how to drive in the mountains."

He lifted one shoulder. "All right. If you think you can handle it."

Anna scowled. "I can handle it." Without giving him further time to question her, she jumped in the Jeep and slammed the door. As she turned the vehicle around, the tires skidded a little, renewing her fears. It had been a bad trip up. Maybe she *should* let him follow her.

No. She clutched the wheel and leaned forward. She could do this. She didn't need some snotty native to laugh at her all the way down the mountain. Much as she loved Colorado, the superior attitude of the born-and-bred locals could be extremely annoying. And it was especially true

in Anna's case. Her accent labeled her a New Yorker—
and the mountain people seemed to think New Yorkers
were all fast-talking, clueless tenderfoots.

Or would that be tenderfeet?

Whatever. No native could love Colorado more than she
did. It had been the land of her dreams from the time she
was fifteen years old and her family took a two-week va-
cation here. Those two weeks had changed her life irrev-
ocably, giving her a glimpse of a world she had never even
dreamed existed.

More than ten years later, Anna could still remember
the way she had felt the first time she stepped out of the
car in Colorado Springs and she really saw the mountains
in their astonishing scope and power for the first time.
There had been a wild, intense pull on her heart at the
sight, a soul-deep cry of such joy and wonder that she
forgot she'd been needing to find a rest room for sixty
miles, forgot the bruising pinch her brother had given her
when she wouldn't give him a dollar, forgot the squabbling
noise of her siblings. She'd simply stood there, drinking
in the view as if it alone could sustain her for the rest of
her life.

When they got home to New York, she bought a poster
of Colorado and hung it on her bedroom wall and announced to the world in general that she would one day
make the mountain state her home.

No one believed her, of course. Not her friends at school
or her sisters and brothers or her parents or grandparents
or cousins. No one could understand why she'd want to
go so far away, how she could survive out there in the
world without the comforting bulwark of family. They
snorted and chuckled and said she was an incurable romantic. "That's our Anna—such a dreamer."

She stopped talking about it. But she didn't give up her
dream. Previously an indifferent student, she became possessed, achieving such high grades that she graduated early

from high school, and, at the urging of a kindly teacher, took her degree in museum studies. There were a lot of little museums all over Colorado, and as soon as she was eligible, she joined the Colorado/Wyoming Association of Museums. Twice, by working nights as a tutor, she had saved enough to fly out for conventions to network with the group.

And on the second trip, Lady Luck at last smiled upon her. Anna met Louise Forrest, who had single-handedly won support for a full-time curator for the Tacker House museum in Red Creek, and wanted someone who wouldn't decamp after one winter. Anna was overjoyed at the opportunity. To live not only in Colorado, but actually in the mountains, was more than she had ever dared hope.

Her family had been utterly aghast at her announcement. They had never believed she would really leave. Even as she packed her belongings and got ready for the cross-country drive, her mother had been dropping by her tiny apartment to bring her news of a birthday party that would be held the following week. Swarms of well-meaning emissaries had visited the days before she drove off, but none of them had swayed her even the smallest bit.

They still expected she would be home at any moment. But Anna *was* home.

At last.

She missed her family, but in a good many ways, it was a relief to make a new life for herself here, away from their loving, intruding ways. Louise had practically adopted her, anyway.

As she made her way carefully down the mountain, Anna understood Tyler's frustration with his meddling mother, but she wondered if he realized that Louise was only a busybody out of love and worry.

On the road ahead loomed the gigantic pothole. Just in time, Anna swerved to avoid it, taking a long breath when the wheels clung to the outer rim and she stayed on level ground.

She realized she was perspiring. Two more hairpin turns, and the rest of the trip would be a cinch. Maybe. She swallowed, leaning over the steering wheel to peer out the small pocket of windshield the wipers managed to clear.

Visibility was poor, even worse than before, because the wind had picked up. It blew through the hollows and open passes with alarming gusto, shaking the Jeep, turning the huge snowflakes into a whirling, blinding whiteout.

She stopped after one bad gust made it impossible to see. Gnawing her lip, she peered out the window at the uniformly white world and wondered at what point a native would give up and walk the rest of the way. It was still about six or seven miles to town. A long way to walk in a blizzard.

And this had undeniably become a blizzard. It snowed a lot in Red Creek—which was one of the reasons Louise had been looking for a curator. Few people were enamored enough of the mountains to put up with almost two hundred inches of snow every winter. Anna loved it. The dry, crisp cold made her feel energetic. She was dressed for it, in layers, with her insulated boots and leather gloves and heavy down parka, with its functional hood—so she could walk a long way if necessary.

But this was a bad storm, even for Red Creek. If she could just get around the next two turns, she would be all right. Gripping the wheel hard, she inched forward, praying aloud to Saint Christopher, who might have been officially disqualified, but still comforted her at times like this. If he could see her safely through the subways, she figured he could help with a blizzard.

The first turn was coming up—a sharp, almost ninety-degree angle that hugged the mountain on one side and plunged hundreds of feet into a valley on the other. As she approached, her tires skidded on the piled-up snow. Just a little slide, but a knife went through her heart.

A sturdy guardrail protected the edge of the drop, but Anna wouldn't trust it to keep her on the road if she hit it. With a deep breath, she pulled the truck over as far as possible out of the road, grabbed the teddy bear and got out. Much safer to walk. One thing a native knew was when to say when. It wasn't as if she could get lost, after all. The road led right into town, and it was all downhill. It would only take her an hour or so to hike the rest of the way.

Relieved, she settled into a comfortable gait, following the faint path her tires had made in the road on the way up the mountain. Aside from the wind, it was quite beautiful—only the snow and the sky and the graceful, arrow-shaped trees. When the wind stopped its periodic blustering, the world was utterly silent, broken only by the squeak of her boots and the moist puff of her breath through her wool scarf. She lifted her head and breathed in the cold, unsullied air, tasting winter and sky and—

She halted abruptly, and swore profanely. It was a habit she'd largely given up—it had only been a rebellion, anyway—but there were times a good Anglo-Saxon curse word summed things up better than any other choice.

This was one of those times. Just below the second turn, a gigantic tree, along with two good-size boulders, a couple thousand gallons of snow and half the mountain, had fallen across the road, clear to the edge of the guardrail. A reddish slash of newly bared earth showed where the tree had once stood, forty feet above the road. Obviously the wind had knocked it down.

Two things crossed her mind. The first was a sick sense of relief. She had been on this road only a little while ago. The avalanche might have buried her.

The second was a sense of panic. How was she going to get back to town? The road was completely blocked.

On one side was the sheer, dizzying drop to the valley a thousand feet below. On the other was a steep mountain that looked none too stable. Anna didn't fancy starting a second avalanche.

Going over the top of the mess was impossible, though she seriously considered it for a moment. The tree's broken, spiky branches, combined with the treacherously unsettled earth and snow, would make it a dangerous undertaking. One she wasn't willing to risk.

She had no choice. Taking a deep breath, she turned around and began to walk up the hill, trying hard not to imagine the reception she would receive from the prickly Tyler.

Chapter 2

Tyler felt restless. Each year on the anniversary of Kara's death he made arrangements to be alone, and this year was no different.

Except for Anna's invasion. Unsettled and uneasy after she left, he prowled the cabin end to end, over and over, trying to dislodge the disturbance she'd left behind.

He scowled. Damn his mother. She was prodigiously meddlesome and undeniably canny. Each time he met the little museum curator, Tyler had been surprised by his attraction to her, and somehow, Louise had noticed that.

Desire had become an almost alien emotion to him the past few years, but if he was honest with himself, he had to admit that Anna kindled something. It was an odd sensation. Kara was the only woman he'd ever loved, the only woman he'd ever made love to, the only woman he'd ever even looked at. It was old-fashioned, and his brothers had teased him unmercifully about it, but Tyler was a one-woman man, and when that woman died, he had had no interest in finding another.

But something about Anna had caught his attention the first time he met her, at his mother's house for a Fourth of July celebration last summer. He'd never met a woman made of such vivid colors. Curly black hair as glossy as Chinese lacquer, cherry-red lips, dancing black eyes. There seemed to be a field of snapping energy around her, so much so that it was a surprise to look at her and see that she was actually rather small.

Whenever she appeared, he found his reluctant gaze drawn back to her, to those colors and that vividness, and felt stirrings of—

Need. Pure, simple, animal lust. It was as if his body had a will of its own and it wasn't about to listen to any rational, logical or moral reason a man didn't have to have sex. He saw Anna and every nerve in his body went on alert.

But Tyler felt bound to remain celibate. Love and sex were sacred treasures, and he could not betray what he'd had with Kara, or be a good example to his son, by indulging in a casual fling. Love was out of the question, so celibate he would remain.

Until Anna appeared, there had been no conflict. Now he had to fight this struggle he didn't want and hadn't asked for, the old fight a man faced between his body and his mind. If he hadn't been so lonely these past months, the struggle wouldn't have seemed so intense, but watching both of his brothers fall in love and get married in the past year had been hard on him. Their happiness reminded him of everything he'd lost.

Annoyed with his thoughts and his restlessness, Tyler threw on a coat and went outside. On the porch, he halted, surprised at the increasing ferocity of the storm. This particular spot was protected from the wind, but he could see whirlwinds of blinding snow over the trees. The sheer volume was incredible, even for the mountains. In the hour since he saw Anna off, another foot had fallen.

With a frown, he glanced down the road, wondering if she had made it safely to town, and if Curtis would have his teddy bear. Worried, he flipped open the cellular phone and tried to get a line, but it was as dead as it had been the last three times he tried.

There was no help for it. His mother had known Anna was coming. She'd also known his line was dead, or Anna wouldn't have had to drive all the way up here for the bear. If Anna didn't come down off the mountain in a reasonable amount of time, Louise would send a search party out for her.

He frowned. If worse came to worst, he'd try the ham radio later on.

For now, a good stint of woodchopping would do a lot to improve his mood. He was used to being alone, used to being trapped on the mountain—sometimes for weeks at a stretch. It was just the storm and the unexpected appearance of the museum curator, combined with the anniversary of Kara's death, that was making him feel so unsettled. Hard physical exercise would ease that.

He'd cut a quarter cord when Charley started barking fiercely in warning of an intruder. Tyler straightened, brushing snow from his face, and turned to see a bright figure emerging from the storm. Anna, as bright and startling against the uniformly gray-and-white world of the mountains as a toucan. He straightened, feeling a strange, thick dread at her appearance. Carefully he put the ax aside and waited for her.

Judging by the crimson of her nose and forehead, she'd been walking a long time, and genuine concern overrode his dismay. He stepped forward. "God, Anna, are you okay?"

"Oh, I'm fine." The words, given coppery edges by her New York accent, were breathless. "I had to park the Jeep and start walking to town, but then a tree caused an avalanche down below that nasty turn—you know the one right beyond that grove of aspens?—and I couldn't get over it." She paused to catch her breath, and clasped her hands in front of her nervously. "I didn't know what else to do but come back here."

Shards of some strong emotion needled through his lungs. A mixture of things—regret and worry and anger. "So now you're stuck here," he said harshly.

She bowed her head. "I didn't do it on purpose. Even if you had followed me, it wouldn't have made any difference. No one could have gotten by that mess. A whole tree, and half the mountain, came down." She brushed snow from the front of her thighs. "I'm sorry."

"You may as well come inside," he said gruffly. He couldn't let her freeze to death. "Let's get something hot into you."

"Thank you," she said softly. "I know you wanted to be alone, and I swear I won't be a bother. I'll just keep to myself and not talk at all, and I'll even cook for you, if you want. I just feel terrible about imposing like this."

Tyler halted and turned. "Do you always talk this much?"

She widened her eyes. "Mostly," she said despairingly. "It's worse when I'm nervous, and now I'm kind of pumped from the walk. It was really beautiful, but I'm tired and cold, and I know you didn't want anybody around and that's why you took Curtis to his grandmother's." She seemed to realize what she was doing, and closed her mouth. Then: "I promise I'll try to be quiet."

Snow caught in her hair, sparkling against the blackness. One fat flake drifted down to light upon her mouth, and Tyler found himself watching it melt into a silvery bead upon her rose-red lip. A vivid image of his tongue against that bead and the plump flesh below sent dancing heat over his nerves. Before he could halt it, the vision expanded, showing him the slick taste of the inside of that mouth, a mouth a man would gladly plunder for hours at a time.

She stared at him, waiting for his reply. Furiously, Tyler turned away. "Try harder," he said.

Inside, Anna shed her parka and boots and gloves, putting them by the door so that they would dry. Discomfort prowled her spine, making her want to chatter. It was her usual response, but this time, she bit down her words with effort.

Tyler moved around the kitchen area smoothly, lighting a small kerosene camp stove on the counter, and drawing water from an old-fashioned pump at the sink. She touched it, charmed, and wanted to ask questions about the way the water got to the cabin, and if there were any other niceties of modern life—like electricity or gas—but she didn't. She simply settled on a stool at a high counter and folded her hands as if she were in Sunday school.

As she watched him, admiring the shine of his hair and the breadth of his shoulders below blue corduroy, the full scope of the situation sank in. She was stuck, alone, with a man she'd been having fantasies about for months, and just sitting in his kitchen, looking at him, made her thighs tingle. The whole cabin smelled of him, too, although she had not known before what gave him that earthy scent. He smelled of wood smoke from his fires, and pine from his mountains, and herbs from the fragrant tea he gave her.

"There's sugar in the dish over there. A spoon in the drawer."

"It smells heavenly."

"Ramona makes it—she told me what it was, but I don't remember. Lemon something. Maybe some chamomile."

Ramona was his sister-in-law, the town doctor, who had the biggest herb garden in the county. Anna nodded. "Thank you." She added sugar and drank the tea gratefully, letting it warm her frozen insides. Her hands ached and her nose tingled as feeling came back to them, but her toes were still little blocks of ice. "Do you mind if I sit by the fire to drink this? My feet are frozen."

A trace of concern broke through his stoic expression. "Do you think you might have been frostbitten? Maybe I should see your toes."

"No, I didn't mean literally frozen, you know."

"How about your hands?"

"Tyler, I'm fine. I swear."

But Tyler took her free hand and examined the tips of her fingers carefully. "It wouldn't have taken much longer. Didn't anyone tell you leather doesn't keep you dry?"

A flush of heat rose in her cheeks. Stiffly she pulled her hand back. "They have rabbit-fur lining."

"Which also gets wet."

"I didn't really intend to be cross-country hiking today."

"Well, you should know you have to be prepared for anything up here."

Anna, stung, lowered her eyes. "I do try."

"Damn, I'm being an idiot," he said suddenly. "I'm sorry. But you really might have been killed in this storm, and it would have been my fault for letting you leave here by yourself. I knew better."

"But I did fine!" She'd been so proud of herself for getting back here, for making the right decision. "Except my gloves, maybe. I would even have been okay if I'd had to build a snow fort."

The faintest gleam of amusement lit those gray eyes. "Is that right?"

"Yes. I learned how at a winter survival class last fall. You have to find a sheltered place, and build the cave with the door facing away from the wind, and you can sleep on pine boughs."

This time, he almost smiled. She saw the quirk of his lips before he caught them, and the knowledge warmed her.

"You're right, Miss Anna. I'm very impressed. Will you still let me look at your toes to make sure they aren't frostbitten?"

She sighed and put her tea on the counter beside her. What would it hurt, after all? "Fine," she said, and stripped off her sock before she remembered her nail polish.

He grabbed her foot. "Interesting color choice," he commented mildly.

Anna blushed. It was purple, with gold glitter. Way too obnoxious for everyday wear on her nails, but the garishness pleased the little girl inside. "My mother always said I have gypsy blood."

"And do you?"

He still held her foot, and when he raised his eyes, Anna was a little overwhelmed by his nearness. For a moment, she thought she saw something like heat, way back in the depths of those crystal-colored irises, and against her arch, his hand tightened the faintest bit. It was oddly arousing to have him touch her bare foot like that.

For one long moment, she contemplated the forbidden fantasy of leaning forward to kiss those perfect lips, to put her hands on his princely jaw and pull him into her. A ripple of imagined pleasure rushed up her spine, and she lowered her eyes hastily, afraid he would see too much. "Maybe."

He let her foot go. "I think the toes are fine. Are you hungry?" He stirred something in a heavy black kettle on top of the potbellied stove in the corner. "I've got stew for dinner. I'd planned to eat at dark, but if you're hungry, you can have some now."

Anna shook her head. "I can wait."

"All right." He picked up his coat. "I want to make sure there is plenty of wood. This storm might take a day or two to blow itself out."

"Okay. Do you want me to do something?"

"No. There are things to read over there on the shelf."

As he put on his coat, Anna realized there was one more thing she required. "Tyler, I hate ask, but do you maybe have some sweats or something that I could wear? My jeans are soaked."

The cool gaze flickered over her body, and without a word, he crossed the room to a bureau against the wall, tugged open a drawer and pulled out the requested sweats, a shirt and a pair of socks. He put them on top of the dresser without looking at her, and before Anna could even frame her thanks, he was out the door.

Left in the silence, with only the howl of the wind and the crackling of the fire, Anna let out her breath. She carried her tea over to a small, low table made of unvarnished pine that sat nearby the fireplace. Her jeans, heavily wet, made her thighs feel clammy, and she carried the neat pile of clothes into the small bedroom she'd glimpsed earlier. Gratefully, she peeled off the wet jeans and damp sweater. A low fire burned in a second potbellied stove, and she stood in front of it for a moment, warming her cold legs and hands.

The sweats were way too big, and the extra length pooled in a clump around her ankles, and the flannel shirt wasn't much better. She had to roll the sleeves up four times to find her wrists. Padding back out to the other room, she imagined how she must look, and grinned wryly. So much for the femme fatale.

Not that she had the qualifications, anyway.

Warmed by the fire and tea and dry clothes, she wandered over to the books to see if he might have something for her to read. A knot of anticipation or excitement or worry made it hard to concentrate. Alone with Tyler. For days, maybe. How would she avoid making a fool of herself?

For months she'd entertained vague, dreamy fantasies about him. About his long, gilded hair and his sensual mouth and even some other parts of him she wouldn't admit. Just being in the same room with him made her a little giddy, made little nerves on her legs and the inside of her arms lift in anticipation.

Classic crush. It happened. She'd seen her sisters go through it dozens of times.

Anna had thought herself immune. Both of her sisters had gone boy-crazy the minute they turned thirteen, and spoken of little else forever after except this boy and that boy, and who would take them to what function. Anna, the youngest in her family until her last brother was born, when she was ten, had watched them with more bewilderment than anything else. She'd dated sometimes, and gossiped with her girlfriends over the phone for hours, and dreamed of the perfect man, waiting out there for her, somewhere.

But mostly, her goal had been to escape to Colorado, and to do that, she'd known she had to have a good education and a skill that would provide her with employment when she got there. There had not been much time left for boys. Her only relationship—if you could even call it that—had been a man right after college, a director at the Metropolitan Museum. He'd been too demanding and snobbish about her desire to leave New York, and she'd let him go after a few months of dinner-and-show dates, with no regrets.

It was a surprise to find herself awash in a crush at the age of twenty-five. She didn't exactly know how to handle it, particularly when the object of that crush was about as attainable as a movie star.

It was just plain silly, a ridiculous fantasy born of too many fairy tales.

Practicality had never been her strong suit, but for this bit of time stranded in Tyler Forrest's cabin, Anna would try hard to employ it.

She bent her head sideways to read the titles of his

books—and smiled. There were several books on the Crusades, and serious historical examinations of European history, and the expected books on woodcraft and carving and renovation. As a carpenter, Tyler was unequaled, and he was much in demand for his handmade banisters and railings, for the hand-carved doors and window frames and baseboards he made in the old way. Louise said he could make a fortune if he charged what he was worth, but he didn't.

He also had children's books, no doubt for Curtis, and a collection of serious novels. Very serious novels—Hermann Hesse and Willa Cather and Jerzy Kosinski. Ugh. Not only serious literature, but very dark books, as well. Anna fingered Hesse's novel *Narcissus and Goldmund,* and remembered the tale of an aesthetic priest and a sensual artist with some fondness. She pursed her lips. Tyler had both in his nature, but she'd have bet a large sum that he fancied himself the aesthetic priest—while she had always identified with the sensual man.

Finally she found a row of paperback fantasy. Something readable, anyway, though most of it, too, was of serious nature. She doubted Tyler allowed himself anything frivolous. Choosing a retelling of the Tam Lin ballad from the shelf, she settled by the fire, covered up with a thick cotton throw, and settled in to read.

Charley, apparently pleased, padded over to lean against the couch next to her. She chuckled. "What a good companion," she said, scratching the pup's ears. Gratefully, he licked her wrist, then, as if to give her permission to ignore him, curled into a surprisingly compact ball and fell asleep.

Tyler had escaped outside more to put his thoughts in perspective than out of a need for wood. The cabin had no furnace, only the big fireplace, the potbellied stove in the kitchen and another in Curtis's room, so woodchopping was something he didn't neglect. There was a small generator to augment the solar panels he had installed last summer, but they would still have to be very careful with lights until the storm was over.

He wondered with a frown if Anna understood how much she would be roughing it here. Because of Curtis, he had installed a septic tank last year, and water was no problem, but the cabin was still rather crude, as modern conveniences went. And she was a city girl.

Unlike Kara. Out in the storm, with snow lighting on his face, he called up a memory of his late wife. She had loved the snow, and especially loved fierce storms like this one, when they would be trapped for days or weeks alone together. Kara had sewed one of her many quilts, and hummed to herself, while Tyler contentedly carved wood. At night, she'd drunk one of her specially concocted herb teas while Tyler sipped at a snifter of blackberry brandy, and they'd talked until the fire boiled in them, at which point they would drift to bed and make love for long, slow hours.

A sharp pain cut through his belly. Not only over the loss of his wife, but over the loss of his ability to commemorate their time together in his usual way. Today, she had been dead four years. He had planned to drink brandy and carve wood tonight, and remember her, honor her memory. He'd done so every year, and now Anna would be in his way.

"I'm sorry, Kara," he said aloud, as was his habit. "I'll find a way to make it up to you."

Only the wind, howling down from the mountaintops, answered him. It made him feel hollow.

It was bitterly cold, and his earlobes and nose were burning within minutes. Recognizing the foolishness of lingering outside to avoid his guilty attraction to the woman in the cabin, he gathered an armload of wood and carried it inside.

Snow-blind for a moment, he made his way toward the fire. When he straightened, his vision clearing, he saw that Anna had fallen asleep on the couch. Deeply asleep.

The picture she made snared him with unexpected fierceness. He found himself standing still as stone, his hands hanging limp at his sides, melting snow dripping from his coat to the floor, the fire hot against the back of his knees.

Her black hair spilled in curls around her face, one spiral lying over her white jaw as if to point to her rosy red lips. Sooty lashes, as long as a doe's, lay against her cheeks, and at the hollow of her throat a slim gold chain glinted against her flesh. The throw outlined her small, neat body, swelling sweetly at breast and hip.

Immobilized by a wave of sharp desire, Tyler simply drank in the look of her. One part of his mind, that rational, moral portion, cried out in warning, *Flee!* But the rest of his brain—and his chest and belly and loins—were so awash in the splendor of all those colors, all those unfamiliar textures of which she was made, that he simply could not move. He let his eyes travel over the length of her. Since the moment of their first meeting, he'd fought the visions those colors kindled, but now he simply had no more will. He gave in and let the tempting visions swirl over him, visions of a naked back, the flesh heated by the fire, of his mouth devouring hers, of the taste of an inner elbow and the feel of her hair against his body, the delectable weight of a loose breast against his palm.

It had been so long. So very, very long.

And for one yearning moment, he was tempted to simply kneel at the edge of the couch where she slept, and kiss her into an aroused and drowsy wakefulness. He did not think she would turn him away.

Unaccountably, he thought of the purple-and-gold nail polish on her toes. He had once had a baby-sitter who painted her nails with glitter, a bright butterfly of a teenager who popped her gum in the most glorious way, and wore sticky red lipstick that left marks on his cheeks and read him stories for hours if he wanted her to.

Marlene. He had adored her. It had been years since he thought of her.

The connection between Marlene and Anna eased some of his guilt. No wonder he found Anna so appealing. Bemused, he wandered into the kitchen to get supper on the table.

He made biscuits, quickly and efficiently. Even making the connection between Anna and Marlene didn't address the quandary he found himself in. He was deeply attracted to her, and she would be stuck here for several days at the very least. He wasn't quite sure how to resist the lure of her in such tempting circumstances.

The only answer was simple discipline. No need to get complicated about it. He could be attracted all he wished, but he could not allow her to realize it, and he could not allow himself to act upon that attraction.

Simple enough. The best answers usually were the obvious ones. Yeah, he wanted her. Yeah, he wanted to get laid.

Tough luck.

Anna pattered in, blinking, just as he was about to go wake her. Darkness was falling in thick shrouds beyond the windows, and she stretched unselfconsciously. "I must have slept quite a while."

"More than an hour." He gave her a box of wooden matches. "Will you light those candles?" Realizing that sounded like an invitation to seduction, he ducked his head and added hastily, "We have to conserve electricity."

Anna made a face. "I'm a lot more interested in other facilities, if you know what I mean. Do I need to put on my shoes?"

"No." He smiled and pointed to a door behind the kitchen. "Right through there."

"Thanks."

Tyler lit the candles, and a lantern in the other room. As Anna came back out, a shrill noise ripped through the room, as unexpected and shattering as a charging bull. "What is that?" she asked in alarm.

"My phone. The cloud cover must have shifted a little." Hastily, he tugged it out of his shirt pocket and answered it. "Mom?"

The connection was a bad one. Static drowned all but one word: "Anna?"

"She's here!" he shouted. "She's safe! Can you hear me?"

"Anna is there?"

"Yes!" he yelled. "She's stuck."

A large crackle of static swallowed everything. "I can't hear you, Mom. Yell, will you?" He could never get it through her head that cellular phones were not the same as direct lines.

"I *said*," she cried, "tell her not to worry!"

"Okay." The line crackled very loudly. "She's safe."

The static popped louder, and whatever Louise said was lost in the roar of the bad connection. Then the line went dead again. Tyler shrugged and flicked the receiver closed.

A small noise caught his attention, and he looked up to see Anna giggling helplessly, her hand over her mouth.

"What's so funny?"

"You just don't know how many times I've been at the other end when she makes those calls." She mimicked Louise holding a phone to her face. "'Can you hear me?'" Her black eyes danced with mirth, making him think of elves.

"She thinks they're some weird invention, not fit for civilized people."

"I know."

"At least she got through. I was worried about that. Now all we have to do is wait it out."

She bit her lip. "How long do you think it will be?"

"It's impossible to know. Too many variables." He cocked his head toward the kitchen. "It'll be at least a few days. You'll have to do your best to get through it."

Chapter 3

After supper, they shared the chore of the dishes, then went to sit by the roaring fire in the living room. Tyler lowered his long-legged form to the simple couch. "There isn't much to do here. And evenings are the worst. I have some cards and games, if you want to do something."

"Please don't think you have to entertain me," Anna protested. "Do whatever you'd ordinarily be doing."

His jaw tightened, and he stared hard at the fire for a moment. "That isn't possible."

"How rude of me. I'm sorry—I'm in your way." She hopped up, taking her tea and book. "I guess I'm sleeping in Curtis's bed, right, so I'll just take my book and read. It's so rarely I get the opportunity to just read anymore. Do you have a lamp? I can—"

"Anna."

She stopped. "I'm sorry. I do feel terrible about this. I should have let—"

"Sit down, Anna."

She clamped her lips together to keep any more words from spilling out, and sat on the edge of the couch cushion.

Tyler eyed her, a small light of amusement in his eye. "You are a talker, aren't you?"

"Afraid so."

"Only two words in answer?"

"I'm sure I can come up with more, if you like."

He held up one hand. "Two words are fine." The amusement faded from his face, and he ducked his head. "I don't mind your company, if you want to stay. But I spend a lot of time alone. You won't find me the best conversationalist."

"That's okay." She grinned. "I'm plenty capable of talking for two."

His answering smile felt like a huge victory. "I bet."

She inclined her head. "What do you usually do in the evenings, Tyler?"

"Curtis and I read together, then I get him ready for bed. By then, it's usually almost time for me to turn in, too, so I read or something for a little while." He lifted a shoulder. "Exciting, huh?"

"Sounds peaceful."

"Yeah."

"And how about when you're alone? What were you going to do tonight that I interrupted?"

"That's personal," he replied. But his gaze strayed to the photo of Kara on the mantel. The expression on his face was yearning and hopelessly lost.

"You loved her very much."

He seemed to return to himself from very far away. "Yes." He picked up a smooth piece of wood with faint markings and a remarkable grain, and began to whittle.

Anna watched his beautiful hands touch and smooth and carve, with the clean, certain movements of long knowledge. "What will that be?" she asked.

"A recorder for Curtis." He held it up, and Anna could

see the vague outline taking shape. "He saw one at the Renaissance Festival last year and thought it was one of the coolest things he'd ever seen."

"He is such an adorable boy. I really enjoy spending time with him."

Tyler only nodded. The actions of his hands seemed to ease him, however, because after a moment he said, "You're from New York?"

Anna suspected he was only making polite conversation, but she jumped on the opening. Anything was better than sitting there in awkward silence. "Queens, actually."

"You have family back there, I guess?"

"Oh, yes—I have family." She chuckled, tucking her feet under her comfortably. "Seven brothers and sisters, three hundred cousins, forty aunts and uncles, the usual number of grandparents, minus one, an even dozen nephews and nieces, and a jillion assorted relatives like second cousins and great-aunts and godparents." She widened her eyes for effect. "A whole army of family."

He looked up. "No hyperbole in there, huh?"

"Well." She smiled. "Maybe a little. I only actually have eighty-three cousins, and thirty-three aunts and uncles. I really do have an even dozen nieces and nephews. Eight boys and four girls."

"Eighty-three cousins?" He stared at her. "You're kidding."

"Eighty-three *first* cousins," she said. "Amazing, isn't it? I've never met anyone who had a family as big as mine. And they all live in New York State. Most of them live somewhere in the boroughs of New York City."

Tyler blinked. "I can't even imagine what that would be like."

"It's just like you think it would be. You think your mother is a busybody?" She chuckled. "You have no idea."

"Is that why you left?"

"No," Anna said honestly. "I mean, they do drive me crazy sometimes, but New York is a big city. I can get away when I need to, and it's nice to know there's always somebody there for you if you need them." She lifted a shoulder. "I just always wanted to be in Colorado."

"Has anyone else left?"

"My second oldest brother went into the marines, but he came back after his tour."

"I can't even imagine it." He coaxed a curl of pine from the stick in his hand. "Even just having my mother and two brothers around sometimes gets insane."

"I've seen that." She nodded. "I love them, but everybody in big families gets stuck with a label, you know? Like my sister Mary Frances is the pretty one, and my brother Joe is the math whiz. Everybody divides all the possible virtues and character flaws between them, and then you're stuck with it for the rest of your life."

An honest laugh slipped out of his throat. Looking up in surprise, Anna thought it was a wonderfully sensual sound, as rich and dark as café mocha. "Which one are you?" he asked, his pale eyes glittering. Then he held up a hand. "No, let me guess. You're the gypsy, so that means what? Wild?"

"No, unfortunately. I could have lived with wild, but my sister Teresa got that before I was old enough to claim the title." She lifted her eyebrows. "She actually hot-wired a car when she was sixteen."

"Ah. So what were you?"

"The romantic one. History, and stories, and too much color all the time."

His smile this time was gentle. "I can see that."

She shrugged. "The trouble with labels is that they usually stick like tar."

"Let's see," he said, counting on his fingers. "You're the romantic, Mary Frances is pretty. Teresa is wild. Joe is the math whiz. Right?"

"Very good."

"Who else? You said seven, plus you."

"Jack is the charmer, Sal is the bad boy, although he's put that to work for him and runs this great club near Flatbush." She paused. "Um, Catherine is the practical one—she sews and does money better than anyone—and Tony, the youngest, he's the pious one. He says he's going to be a priest." She spread her hands. "See, all divided up neatly."

"I see."

Feeling more comfortable, Anna straightened. "You can see it in your family, too."

He frowned. "You can?"

"Sure. Lance is the charmer. Jake is the intense one. And you are—" She halted, embarrassed.

"Come on, don't leave me hanging. I'm the what?"

She raised her eyes and met his curious gaze head-on. "You're the lost one."

It pierced him. She saw the arrow go straight through him, its smooth shaft burning as it moved through his body. The pale gray irises flickered, bright and dark and bright, and Anna was only a little sorry to see that awakening pain. "I'm not lost," he said at last. "I'm just alone."

"No, you're the lost prince, cursed by some evil sorcerer in the woods to wander alone until you find your quest."

"The quest," he said roughly, "is already lost."

Wisely, she stood, sensing he needed to be alone. "It's never lost, Tyler. Not until you're in your grave."

"You really are a romantic, aren't you?" His tone said he did not consider it a particularly appealing characteristic.

"I'm afraid so."

He lifted his head. His eyes were haunted by pain, and Anna felt an answering cry. She wanted to put her hands

on his lean face and press a kiss to that weary brow. She
wanted to find the good witch in the forest and ask for a
potion to heal his heart. There was always a price for healing magic, but Anna would gladly pay it, whatever the
cost.

Her wish must have shown on her face, for he said,
"Don't look at me like that, Anna. Don't cast me as a
prince in your fairy tale. I really loved my wife. I won't
betray her memory by taking another lover. Not ever."

Curiously, the words did not wound. "I know," she
said. She remembered suddenly the way her grandmother
had always talked of her grandfather after he died, and
how uncomfortable many people in the family had been
with that. Impulsively she said quietly, "Tell me about her,
Tyler." "I'll listen if you want to talk."

His eyes were opaque, showing nothing. "Why?"

"Why not? It's a good way to remember her, isn't it?"
Anna jumped up and grabbed the photograph. "Tell me
about this day," she said, putting the frame in his hand.
"Tell me how you came to be standing here."

He held the frame loosely in his hand, but his gaze was
on Anna. His expression was faintly perplexed. "I'm not
sure I've ever met anyone quite like you."

"I doubt it." She sat on the couch and leaned forward.
Using the same sort of words she had used to help get her
grandmother talking, she said, "Tell me the first time you
met her."

Still he was silent. Anna had just about decided he
wasn't going to speak when he said quietly, "We met on
the first day of sixth grade. She had just moved here from
Wisconsin, and she didn't know anybody." He paused
abruptly. "I don't want to bore you with all this."

She inclined her head. "You know, my grandparents
were married fifty-six years. After he died, my grandmother liked talking about him more than anything else.
She just really wanted to think about him, this man she

spent so much of her life with. She just wanted somebody to listen to her, but it made most of the family uncomfortable. They were afraid that she was living in the past.''

Tyler bowed his head abruptly. ''So you listened?''

''Yeah. And not just because she wanted to talk.'' She twisted a curl in her finger, remembering the long, cold afternoons in her grandmother's kitchen, drinking tea. ''It's nice to hear stories. Real stories or not real. Doesn't matter. I enjoyed listening to her. They met the day before they got married. She came over from Sicily to marry him.''

''That's amazing.''

''They were happy, you know?'' She smiled. ''So—tell me a story, Tyler. Tell me about Kara and the day you met. She came to sixth grade, and why did you notice her?''

His smile was reluctant, but she sensed his relief as he began to speak. His family probably worried that he was obsessed. They probably wanted this young, healthy man to take a new wife and get on with the business of living, but he was obviously just not ready. Maybe he never would be, and he would always want to tell stories of the wife he had loved and lost.

All women should be loved so well.

''She had a picture of a wolf glued onto her notebook,'' he said. ''I thought she was pretty, and she sat down in the desk next to me, so I tried to think of something to say.'' He half smiled, gazing backward in time. ''I wasn't the smoothest guy around. Kind of a loner, you know, and I never had the same interests as the other kids, so I didn't really know what to say.''

Anna imagined a classroom with large windows and a view of the mountains beyond, with sunlight shining on a young girl's blond hair. She envisioned Tyler at twelve. Probably tall and too skinny, and maybe all wrists, the way some boys were at that age. "How did you wear your hair in those days?" she asked.

"Real short—and it was very uncool at the time. But my dad—" His mouth tightened briefly. "He gave us haircuts every Saturday morning."

Anna knew a little about Olan Forrest, by all accounts a real good old boy, a man's man who'd made a fortune in construction by working eighty hours a week and showing up at home only long enough to verbally assault his three sons. All three brothers bore the scars to some degree or another. "So what did you think of to say?"

His grin was rueful. "Oh, I was brilliant. I leaned over and pointed to the wolf and asked her if she knew that it was *Canis lupus.*"

Anna chuckled.

"The thing is, she knew. She flipped open that notebook quick as a wink, and inside were all these pictures of mountain animals. Birds and foxes and bears and wolves. She knew all their names."

He talked for a long time, and Anna simply listened. The young Tyler and Kara had become fast friends, spending their afternoons and weekends bird-watching and catching insects—which they always let go after a decent period of examination.

By Christmas break, they'd been best friends. By the end of seventh grade, when everyone else was pairing off and breaking up with their first crushes, Tyler and Kara had been acknowledged to be the most mature and stable couple around.

By high school, it had been common expectation that they would be married, and they had been, two days after graduation. They had already started building this house, on the land Tyler had inherited from his grandfather.

He stopped. "I have some brandy. Do you want some?"

"Sure." She hopped up to follow him to the kitchen. "You aren't going to stop there, are you?"

From a high cupboard, he took the bottle and two glasses. For a moment, he seemed to hesitate, holding those glasses in his hands. Then he put one down on the counter in front of Anna and poured in a generous measure of plum-red liquor. "It isn't such a happy story after this," he said, and poured some for himself, as if for fortification.

"I knew it had to be sad at some point."

He gave a soft, humorless laugh, his head bent at an angle. In the low flicker of candle flame, his hair shone like moonlight, and Anna allowed herself one moment to admire it, and the long, strong column of his brown throat. "I guess that's plain enough."

Settling on a stool, Anna sipped the fiery liquor. "So what happened then?"

He took a breath, let it go. "Kara was a diabetic. She lost one kidney when she was fifteen, and they told her then she should never try to have children." He took a full draft of brandy and swallowed before he continued. Even after he swallowed, his face held a closed expression. "She didn't listen."

Anna felt tension radiating from him in great waves, and she recognized that he barely knew she was there now. He was lost in the past, in the relief of being able to talk.

"A friend of hers, who was also diabetic, had a baby with no trouble, so Kara got it in her head that it would be okay for her, too. She wanted one so badly." He shook his head. "I used to get upset with her for not just being happy with what we had—which was a hundred times better than what most people get. I told her we could adopt, but she was afraid of all those cases where the birth mother comes back to get her baby. So I suggested we could go to South America or China or someplace, but she wanted her own baby, *our* baby."

Anna saw signs that the story was knotting up inside him, and she sensed that it was somehow important that he say this part, too, that he remember all of it. "Did you give in?"

His jaw went hard. "No. I was with her when she lost that first kidney, and a baby wasn't worth it to me. But she lied to me about birth control, and got pregnant anyway."

"I'm sorry."

"I should have realized sooner that she would try that, that somehow it would be okay in her head. I should have realized she might try it." His jaw grew very tight. "It was terrible. She was sick all the way through, and went into labor a month early, and it was too late." Flatly, he said, "Her kidney failed and she died."

"So she didn't even get to be with her son."

"Yeah, she did. For three days. We were hoping for a transplant, but..." He sighed. "No organs were available."

Something clacked against the window, thrown by the wind. Both of them jumped, and Tyler leaned forward to peer out the window. "One hell of a storm tonight."

Anna could see the dark tops of pines swaying against the gales, bending and whipping against a night sky so bright with snow and clouds that it looked like twilight. Tyler whistled softly.

"I wonder if it's hitting Red Creek like this," he said.

"I hope not," Anna replied, accepting the change of subject. It was enough that he'd emptied himself. She would let him retreat now, to whatever world he needed now. "Your mother really hates storms."

"She was raised in tornado country," Tyler replied, without turning. "But she has Alonzo there now. That'll help."

He didn't look at her, and Anna stood up, realizing it was time to leave him alone. "I guess I'll turn in," she said. "Shall I just sleep in Curtis's bed?"

"Sure."

"Okay."

"Do you need anything?" He turned, finally, the polite host.

Anna smiled. "No, thanks. Good night, Tyler."

He said nothing until she was nearly at Curtis's door. "Anna," he said.

She turned.

Tyler crossed his arms. "Thank you."

"Anytime."

Chapter 4

After Anna went to bed, Tyler took his snifter of brandy back to the fire. Kneeling, he carefully fed the low, hot flame bits of small wood and two thick logs, poking the ashes to heat things up for a minute. It was going to be one cold night—he hoped Anna would be warm enough. He should check the fire in the stove there a little later, but first he'd give her a chance to fall asleep. He'd grown adept at doing it silently while Curtis slept.

Curtis. Tyler picked up the teddy bear from one of the chairs and clasped it to his chest as if it were a child. He missed his son tonight, and wondered how he was doing. Probably fine. And it would be nice for Louise to have the boy there if the storm really was this bad in the valley.

Of course, she did have Alonzo now. Sort of. With his courtly manners and twinkling eyes, he was the man Louise should have had a long time ago. Although Tyler didn't think anything had really developed between them yet, he didn't think it would be long. And finally, maybe, his mother would have the mate she deserved.

Which would leave Tyler the odd man out. As he always had been, except with Kara.

He looked at the picture of her on the mantel. She had been his best friend for more than twenty years. With Kara, he had been free to be himself, as he never had been with anyone else.

Familiar melancholy descended, a hollowness he had finally realized would never go away. She had been more than his wife, more than his lover. She had been his best friend, the other half of him. He was thirty-one years old, and had spent more than half his life with her.

He lifted the brandy and toasted her picture. "To you," he said softly, and sipped.

But the ritual left him oddly cold. With a frown, he looked into the red-amber liquor in his glass and wondered why he'd felt numb about this all day. Usually, he awakened on this anniversary with a sense of anticipation, as if he would be actually seeing Kara again. In some vague part of his brain, he knew it was foolish, and he also knew he had to contain his ritual to one night a year or he'd end up as crazy as a rabid dog.

If Curtis had been here tonight, they would have played games, simple card games and board games such as Candyland and Chutes and Ladders. They would have had hot chocolate and maybe baked cookies, and Tyler would have had the comfort of that small, plump body next to his own.

Instead, Tyler had consigned himself to the habitual, now empty ritual, in an empty house, in a raging storm that would trap him with his melancholy, miles away from the rest of the world.

And who had the heavens sent to keep him company? A gypsy magpie with a Queens accent, who had more earnestness than good sense and a suspicious shine in her eyes when she looked at him.

He scowled. The lost prince. Right.

With a sigh, he got to his feet and extinguished the

candles and lamps. Quickly he shed his clothes in the dark and climbed under the covers, thinking with some embarrassment of the way he'd spilled his guts tonight. She was a good listener.

But he'd left parts of the story out. He had left out the furious anger he had felt toward Kara throughout her pregnancy. It had been fury fueled by love, but it had seriously strained their previously solid relationship. To make matters worse, he had vowed that she would never trick him again like that, and had had a vasectomy in her third month. Kara had wept for days over it.

A knot of disgust settled in his belly. He'd been so arrogantly certain of his decision, so sure she had no say in the matter if she was going to be so foolish as to risk her life. There had been times through that pregnancy when they spoke only in the politest of terms for days and days on end. His mother had counseled Tyler to be more understanding, to have faith that things would work out.

Now he knew that Kara had hidden her worsening condition out of a desperate need to see the pregnancy end in a live child, because it was her only chance to have his baby.

He would live with that guilt the rest of his life.

He would also live with the time he'd lost by being angry all those months. The truth was, he just had not expected her to die. He was waiting for her to come home and take care of Curtis, and then they could get back to the business of mending their marriage.

But they never got the chance.

Guilt and sorrow welled up in him, an acid burn that seared away everything else. "I'm sorry, Kara," he whispered. "I'm so sorry."

Only then did he remember he had to check the fire in the stove in Curtis's room. Swearing mildly, he pulled a robe over his naked body and padded to the closed door. He knocked softly, and heard a faint answer.

"I just want to check the fire. Are you decent?"

He heard her laugh, throatily. "Come in," she called.

He opened the door, carefully ignoring the womanly shape on Curtis's little bed. A line of soft orange glowed around the edges of the stove door, and when he opened it, he saw that the fire was not quite out, but was burning pretty low. He stirred the embers vigorously. "Be right back," he said.

From the stack in the living room, he gathered a few healthy chunks of pine and carried them back to the stove. Wind clattered and howled around the windows, and a hard crack struck the west pane. "Damn," he said, kneeling to feed the fire, "I meant to cut that branch last week."

"Don't you worry that Curtis will get burned on that stove?"

His mother had worried about the same thing. "I think kids figure things out pretty fast if you don't overprotect them. Curtis put his hand on the one in the kitchen when he was two, and blistered himself pretty badly, but he hasn't touched one since."

She made a sound of pain. "How could you stand to let him hurt himself?"

Tyler looked in her direction. Cold pale light from the storm fell through the uncurtained window and caught in the tumble of black curls. Firelight made of her eyes two luminescent pools. One hand was tucked under her cheek. "We're not here to protect them from everything," he said. "We're here to guide them, give them the ability to think for themselves and make good decisions. Letting him burn himself once means he won't have to do it again. It works a lot better than me telling him over and over."

"Makes sense, I guess." She shifted to one elbow, and Tyler tried not to notice the way his too-big flannel shirt revealed the top of one round white breast. "But surely you have to protect him from some things. What about wild animals and getting lost in the forest and things like that?''

Tyler lifted a shoulder. "Sure I have to protect him sometimes, just like I have to feed him and love him and help him learn to keep himself clean." His leg was going to sleep, and he shifted to sit on a stool, carefully pulling his robe around himself. "Bears are a real problem around here, and kids think they're like Yogi, and Goldilocks and the three bears, so we've talked a lot about them. He knows what their tracks and spoor look like, and he knows you never, ever come close to a baby bear." With a distant part of his mind, he realized he hadn't spoken so many words to anyone in one day in literally years. "Not too many other animals around here would be dangerous. If he saw a wildcat, unless it was trapped somewhere, it would just run away."

"Bears don't run away?"

"Sometimes, but not like a lot of other wild animals. They're curious, and they're hungry, and with the development in the mountains, there are fewer and fewer places for them to hide."

"That's sad."

"Yeah, it really is." The fire behind him was quite warm now, as flames caught on the new wood. Tyler could go back to bed. He told himself he should.

But it was warm, and Anna was so pretty and earnest that he couldn't find the motivation to leave. "Bears and wolves pay a big price for humans falling in love with wild places."

She sucked her lower lip into her mouth, as if in thought, and narrowed her eyes faintly. When she looked back at Tyler, letting go of the lip to speak, it glistened with moisture, and the sight sent a hard, leaping life through his loins. He swallowed, trying not to think—

"I worried about that," she said soberly. "That maybe it would be bad for the land for me to come here, like everybody else running to Colorado. Another pair of feet to trample all over the forest, another body to drink the water.''

It surprised him. "You really thought about it?"

"All the time."

He leaned forward. "How did you come to terms with it?"

She lifted one shoulder, and the gesture caused the shirt to slip off the shoulder on the other side. She grabbed it quickly, but not before Tyler saw the whole of one white shoulder, unbearably feminine and alluring, below the fabric. She wore no bra, which was only normal, since she was in bed, but the knowledge sent a new level of heat through him.

He needed to get out of there, but instead he stayed where he was, perversely enjoying the vicarious thrill of imagining her breasts naked beneath flannel he'd worn against his own skin.

"I didn't really solve it," she said, and Tyler was lost for a minute. Solve what? "Don't laugh, but I gave it to the saints. If I should go, somebody would give me a job. If I shouldn't, nobody would."

"The saints, huh?" He found himself smiling gently. "Does that mean you're a good Catholic girl?"

Her smile was not good. It spread sensually to show her even white teeth, and glinted wickedly in the limpid pools of her black eyes. "There is no such thing."

For one purely sensual moment, Tyler forgot everything as his blood heated and tingled, and lust as narcotic and forbidden as opium pulsed through him. It would be easy, so easy, to move forward and touch her. And she would be the kind of woman he had sometimes wanted, free and wicked—

He heard the traitorous thought and abruptly stood up, catching his robe around him so that she would not know what she'd done to him with that throaty laughter and wicked smile. "I'd better get to bed."

"Good night, Tyler," she said softly.

He backed out quickly and shut the door safely behind him, tugging the fabric of his robe around that ridiculous flesh that had tried to leap between the folds of fabric to freedom and woman.

He scowled. That was the trouble with biology. It was so damned undignified. With a sigh, he climbed back in bed and covered his face with a pillow, trying to blot out the past and the future, and the sweet curves of a woman who smelled like hope.

The storm intensified during the night. Anna awakened several times to hear the wind howling and screaming through the trees. It slammed against the little cabin with rocking blasts, rattling the windows and throwing things around. Twice she heard something hit the house with a fierce thump.

The second time, she listened carefully, wondering if it might be a bear, instead of the wind. Then she remembered that bears hibernated, and it was likely just broken tree branches and deadwood being tossed around in the ferocious wind.

It made her think of hurricanes, those storms that had sometimes swept up the Atlantic coast with fierce destructive power, and although she didn't know what a hurricane's Colorado counterpart was, it made her nervous. She had a little trouble going back to sleep. Surely they were safe enough here. Tyler knew these hills intimately, and he was acknowledged to be one of the best carpenters around. Anything he had built would be made to last. She drifted off again.

Only to be shattered out of sleep by a loud crash. She bolted upright, blinking, holding the cover to her neck in protection from a wild animal. For a moment, she stared at the mess without truly understanding what had happened, even when a sharp wind began to pile snow in drifts over her covers.

The door to the other room flew open, and Tyler swore. "Anna, are you okay?"

"Yeah." Blinking, she realized that there was a whole long pine bough on the floor. "What happened?"

"I told myself to get that branch cut off last week and didn't do it. The wind put it through the window. Don't move. Let me get some shoes."

Anna simply nodded. Shivering, she drew the covers around her and kicked off the snow collecting on the bed. The branch was at least ten feet long, and thick. The force of the wind had shoved it through the window and into the middle of the floor, amid piles of broken glass and the drifting snow. The torn, jagged edge of the bough rested against the demolished window frame.

In a moment, Tyler was back, clad in his thick, long robe and a pair of unlaced work boots. "Where are your things?"

"I have everything on." Which was not quite true, but she would deal with her underthings tomorrow. She did not think she could bear to have Tyler Forrest handling her bra.

"Okay. Grab the covers and pillow, and put your arms around my neck."

"You don't have to carry me!" she protested in alarm.

"I'm afraid I do, kiddo. There's a lot of glass on the floor." He bent and slid one hand under her knees and the other around her shoulders. A quick smile showed in the darkness. "Don't worry. I'm stronger than I look."

It wasn't that. Anna clutched the covers close and put the pillow in her lap hurriedly, then put her arms around his neck just as a blast of wind sent fistfuls of snow through the window. She gasped and turned her face away, bumping into Tyler's shoulder.

He lifted her as easily as if she were a child. Anna closed her eyes, aware of every millimeter of his body that touched hers: a biceps against her back, his hand firm around her shoulder, his belly against the side of her hip. And against her forehead, she felt an electric tingle at the press of her skin against his neck; a neck that smelled of Ivory soap and pine and wood smoke. Against her fingers was his long, pale hair, brushing her sensually with his movements. She could barely breathe, so awash was she in the dizzy, narcotic pleasure of touching him.

Touching Tyler.

It took only a moment to carry her to the door, and then he bent to set her down, but not before Anna felt the unmistakable thrust of aroused male against her hip. With a jolt of surprise and desire, she looked up, reluctant to let him go, and in the low light, she saw the moment he realized she had felt him. The clear gray eyes flickered, and she saw him look at her mouth, and for the most fleeting seconds, his hands spread open on her, as if he would allow himself to explore.

Then he swallowed and let her go. "Sorry about that. Haven't had a woman around in a long time."

She smiled, tightening her cocoon of blankets. "They never do behave themselves, do they?" she said lightly, and hobbled toward the couch before she could give herself away.

His laughter, surprised and warm in the darkness, told her she'd said the right thing. "No kidding." A pause. Anna didn't look at him, just put her pillow on the couch. In a moment, he said, "Let me put the fire out in there, and I'll be back to get you settled."

Anna, wide-awake now, pulled the big quilt around her and sat down by the fire. She wondered what time it was. The storm was howling and moaning and screaming outside; she couldn't even imagine what it would look like come morning.

Tyler came back, stomping his feet and trying to brush his windblown hair back into place. "Whew. That's a mess in there. Curtis is going to be at Grandma's house a little longer than we planned, I think."

"That was a pretty big branch. Is the wind that bad?"

"The worst I've seen in about ten years." Casually he tugged at the leather thong holding his hair back. The long, pale hair spilled free over his shoulders as he wandered toward the kitchen in his big work boots. "You want some hot chocolate or something? That woke me up."

Anna smiled at the picture he made. "Sure."

He caught her grin. "What's so funny?"

She couldn't help it. A throaty chuckle escaped her. "Your very elegant attire."

As if he hadn't given it a thought, he looked down at his robe and his bare legs, stuck into the unlaced work boots. His hair slid forward like a length of moon-colored silk, and Anna wanted very much to touch it.

Touch him. Touch that slice of golden chest, and the exposed shins, with their dusting of gold-sparked hair. The longing made her ache for all she would never have. This was the man she'd been searching for all her life. Silly as it was, she'd known that the instant she first saw him.

Now he looked up with a wry little smile. "I'm not used to having visitors." He inclined his head. "You should see yourself, anyway. Not exactly ready for the castle ball, are you?"

Anna laughed. "Touché." She got to her feet and hobbled over to the long counter that divided the kitchen from the rest of the living space. "Can I help?"

"Light some candles." He tossed her some matches. Self-consciously he combed his fingers through his hair. "Better?"

"Beautiful," she said with a smile, and let the blanket pool around her waist so that she could finger-comb her own hair. "How's mine?"

His smile was genuine, and so natural Anna found herself amazed that such a change could be wrought in the man in a few short hours. This Tyler was far more approachable, far more real and comfortable, than the prickly loner who had glared at her from his porch this afternoon. He reached over the counter and, with one broad palm, smoothed a patch of hair over her ear. "Now it's okay."

"Thanks."

Watching him draw water from the pump and set the kettle on the stove to boil, she asked, "Don't you ever get tired of not having all the modern conveniences?"

He raised an eyebrow. "If I tell you the truth, you have to swear you won't tell a soul."

"I swear. Cross my heart—" she made an X over her heart "—and hope to die."

Tyler dropped to his elbows. The counter was wide enough that it wasn't really an intimate position, but it was much more open than his former body language. "I would kill for a microwave," he said, sotto voce.

"Gasp!" Anna said.

"Not only that, I'm dying for a television and a VCR." One side of that wide, sensual mouth turned up in an ironic expression. "Pitiful, huh?"

"If this got out, it could ruin your reputation forever."

"Tell me about it." He straightened to take some cups down. "I have a lot invested in being the mountain-man loner type. Years."

Anna inclined her head. "It fits, you know."

He measured powdered cocoa into the cups. "I worry about Curtis. He needs more than he's getting up here."

"Oh, no, Tyler, don't ever think that. He's such a wonderful, bright, imaginative child. He hasn't been all filled up with mass culture, so he thinks in very original, wonderful ways."

"You think so?"

"Oh, I know so." Earnestly, she leaned closer. "He

tells magnificent stories—and he uses the old archetypes, like dragons and spirits and witches and quests, instead of Bugs Bunny and Ninja Turtles.''

"Hey, now," he said mockingly. "Nothing wrong with Bugs."

"No, of course not. But most kids have to work hard later to understand the underlying myths of our literature, and our culture. Curtis hasn't been distracted, and he won't have to work so hard. It hasn't hurt him to live in an unusual way with you like this. He's a great kid."

"Thanks. He thinks you hung the moon, you know."

"He does?" Anna felt oddly touched.

"He talks about you all the time. About the stories you tell him, and the presents you bring him—that PEZ dispenser was about the coolest thing he ever saw in his life. You must like kids a lot."

Anna shrugged. "Lots of practice." She grinned. "Don't forget my family."

He poured hot water over the chocolate and, to Anna's surprise, came around to sit on the stool next to her. "You want to play some cards, or chess, or something?"

"Sure. What do you have?"

"You ever play Pente?"

"No. What is it?"

"I'll show you." He fetched a long cardboard tube from the bookshelf and came back. "It's like go, the old Japanese game," he said, pulling out a soft mat printed with a grid, very pretty, and two bags of what turned out to be glass stones. "The idea is to get five stones in a row, kinda like tic-tac-toe."

In the candlelight, the blue and red glass pieces glowed like precious gems, and Anna was entranced. "It's pretty."

"Don't let it fool you. It's harder than it looks."

Companionably, they played several games. Anna, a fan of both backgammon and chess, was able to pick up the need for strategy very quickly, and managed to nearly beat

him twice. The last game, she actually pulled it off, and
chortled happily. "I won!"

"Good game." He pulled his stones to his side of the
board. "You want to play again?"

"No, thank you. I think I'll quit while I'm ahead." She
touched her stomach. "Actually, I'm getting hungry. It is
almost morning?"

He glanced toward the window. "Probably. I have a
watch, if you want to know the real time."

"No. It's not like we have an appointment or anything."

"Exactly." He started gathering the stones and dropping
them into their little suede bags. "I'm hungry, too, now
that you mention it. I have some eggs and bread."

"Cheese?"

"Mmm. I think so."

Anna stood up, grasping the blanket around her waist.
"I'll put on my sweats and make some omelets, then.
What do you say?"

"Sounds good. Where are your sweats?"

"In the other room."

He swung himself around on the stool, and Anna tried
not to notice the length of bare, hair-dusted thigh his gaping robe exposed. "I'll get them. I need to get dressed,
anyway."

Chapter 5

Anna would not allow Tyler to help her cook. He finally contented himself with sitting on a stool and giving her verbal guidance into the slightly tricky world of cooking on a woodstove. Outside, the wind died down as the sun rose. More or less. The light only revealed that snow was still falling, and showed no signs of letting up.

It made him feel restless. No way could he stay trapped inside with Anna for hours and hours without sooner or later succumbing to his wish to have her. Another man, in the same circumstances, might have settled for a long, lazy seduction to pass the day. Even Tyler was tempted—who would it hurt? And more than that, who would believe they hadn't indulged in a nice, entertaining round of sex while trapped together? But aside from his own resolve to remain celibate, there was a funny kind of innocence about Anna that he'd rather leave undisturbed. She was a sweet, honest young woman, and she'd probably been very fiercely protected by all those older brothers.

No, in order for the pair of them to indulge in sex simply

for the sake of entertainment, they would both have to be different people.

Those sensible thoughts did not necessarily ease his attraction to her, that ridiculous thrust of his body when she moved around his small kitchen. She'd washed and dressed, pulling the black curls into a loose, high ponytail. Her black sweater was cut like a dance leotard, to a V in both front and back, and as she grated cheese, Tyler found himself eyeing that back V covertly, the smooth, almost pearlescent skin, the tiny rise of the bones in her spine. Once he wondered aimlessly what she would do if he simply kissed her there, in a nice, sliding line up those bones to the delicate nape, where tiny whirls of hair curled against her neck.

He also figured she didn't know that he knew her bra was ruined, littered with broken glass and splinters and mud when the branch came through the window last night. When he went in to nail a board over the broken window, he'd seen it among the pine needles on the floor, torn in two. She'd been lucky that she'd hung her clothes on a peg behind the stove in Curtis's room, or they'd have suffered the same fate.

Even if he had not seen the actual clothing, he would have known by the way she looked. The sweater was not tight, but the fabric was something furry and soft, and it clung to her, illuminating the sway of unfettered breasts in a way that made it hard for him to keep his mind clean.

Restlessly, he shifted his focus to something less dangerous, and picked up a yo-yo from the counter. He had to think of something for them to do to while away the hours of the day. Preferably something physically exhausting, so that he could work off some of this tension—and then, maybe, given the short night last night, they'd be able to just sleep until morning. Maybe by morning the storm would have blown itself out.

Maybe.

The perfect solution popped into his head. "Have you ever used snowshoes?" he asked.

"No. I've always wanted to. Is it hard?"

"Not at all." He was warming to the idea. She'd be bundled up, those sweet curves hidden below her heavy parka, and the activity was strenuous enough they'd be worn out when they got back. "You'll love it."

"I'm game."

After breakfast, Tyler filled a backpack with a thermos of hot coffee, sandwiches, oranges and cookies. Anna's outerwear was in general very good. She had worn long underwear under her jeans, and the parka was a high quality hooded variety. He loaned her a pair of gloves, and scrounged up an extra scarf to tuck around her throat. "We'll work hard enough that the cold won't be a problem unless the wind kicks up again."

"Better to be prepared, anyway." She grinned at him. "Every Girl Scout knows that."

"You were a Girl Scout?"

"My mother ran the troops. I had no choice."

Tyler grinned. "Did you make s'mores in Central Park?"

"No, silly. We went out of town for that, just like everyone else. Just because you live in a city doesn't mean you can't leave it." She tied her parka hood. "You know, New Yorkers have some very strange ideas about the West, but you guys have just as many about us."

"Do we?" He tucked his jeans into his boots and tied them. "Like what?"

"Like what you just said, for example. The city is only the city. You don't spend your whole life in concrete canyons. We went to the beach on the weekends, and out to Long Island to visit my aunt Viola. It's not like there are walls around the city, making sure you never leave. It's just a place."

Tyler lifted his eyebrows in concession. "I guess I never thought about that before."

"I'll tell you something else. Everybody always says New Yorkers are mean, but they aren't, really. Not once you scratch the surface. Out here, everybody acts like they're all friendly and warm, but they're really prickly underneath."

At that, he had to laugh. "We're sick of all you guys coming out here, telling us what to do."

A brief, wounded flash crossed her face. "I wouldn't do that."

"I didn't mean it like that. You seem very sincere." Taking the snowshoes in one hand, he opened the door and gestured her in front of him. "Not everybody gets to learn to snowshoe, after all."

Her wild gypsy smile flashed with genuine happiness. A twist caught Tyler's lungs. Hadn't anyone ever shown her how to hide anything she was thinking? It made her too vulnerable, the way everything showed on her face. "Thank you," she said.

Outside, the snow was falling lightly, but there was no wind. As long as it was still, the air would not be too cold, and he hadn't exaggerated when he told her the exercise would keep them warm. He illustrated the basics, and they set off across the open meadow fronting the cabin. Charley leaped along beside them for a few feet, but even his long legs were no match for the depth of the snow. With a brief, sad whine, he cat-jumped back to the porch to wait for them to return.

"Shouldn't he be in the house?" Anna asked.

"He won't go in until I'm back. If he gets cold, he'll go behind the woodshed. It's warm and dry back there."

He led the way up the mountain, without any real aim in mind at first. Because breath was needed for exercise, conversation was sporadic, and limited to comments on footprints in the snow and nature's wonders and the obvious effects of the windstorm the night before. Not only his tree had been broken. Dozens of branches littered every clearing.

It wasn't until they'd been out for a couple of hours that Tyler thought to lead her to the summit of a particular hill. Even on a cloudy day, the view of the back valley was one she wouldn't forget. First, he paused at a stream, still running in trickles in spite of the weather, and offered her the thermos. "You holding up okay?"

She drank gratefully, then nodded. "It's wonderful." Her ruddy cheeks showed the bloom of exertion, but it wasn't a dangerous color, just the clear, rose-red blush of health. It made her eyes look even blacker. "When I first got here, I could barely cross the street without resting, but I guess my lungs have adjusted now."

"Good." He tucked the thermos back in the pack. "We can have a snack and rest at the summit, then go back."

"How do you rest in the snow?"

"On pine branches, Miss Winter Survival."

She grinned, and just that swiftly, Tyler had an uneasy feeling. He was not acting like himself, not at all. He should have sulked through all this. Unpleasant as it was to admit, it would have been a lot more in character. But somehow the snow and the gypsy-colored Anna and the forced proximity had caused a shift in his thinking, in his attitude. Maybe it was her earnestness, or the magpie way she chattered so easily, but it wasn't hard to talk to her. He felt comfortable with her, and that had led to an unconscious lowering of his guard.

He had a feeling he would be sorry.

Anna thought the whole thing was glorious. The gray of the skies over the frosted Ponderosa pines and blue spruce, the utter stillness of nature, the evidence of creatures that had been about this morning. She loved the heat in her muscles and the crisp sight of her breath hanging in the air.

Most of all, she loved being with Tyler. Especially this new, approachable version. She'd always known this side of him existed; she had glimpsed it when he teased one of his brothers, and when he herded Curtis and his cousin Cody from one place to another downtown.

But he'd never dropped his armor in her presence before this, and she found that it was very easy to like him. He had an ironic turn to his quick mind, a quick glitter in the pale eyes, and more—a rare, wry self-honesty that was surprising. If he would allow it, they might be friends after all this. He struck her as a man who could use a friend.

Falling into the rhythm of the snowshoes, Anna wondered what he had been like as a boy, as a four-year-old, like Curtis. Louise, naturally, had spoken often of all three of her boys, spinning tales of their childhood as she and Anna performed the dozens of physical tasks required by the old house museum—window work and dusting and the arrangement of exhibits. Anna, always ready to hear a good story, had listened happily.

Lance had been the wild one, even as a little boy. Full of mischief and trouble. Jake, the oldest, had been competitive and driven toward success, and had nearly destroyed himself.

Louise loved all her boys equally. Anna could see that. She worried over them, and fussed, and meddled, and bragged shamelessly about each of them in turn.

But Tyler, this tall, strong, silent man at Anna's side, was the child of Louise's heart. By the time he came into her life, she had been savvier about protecting her children from the hard ways of their father, and Tyler always had been different—quiet and introspective, but also fiercely intelligent and sensitive. Louise had shielded him in order to allow him to be whoever he became—and she was very proud of the man he had grown to be.

He paused next to her. "One really tough ten-foot stretch ahead," he said, breathing hard. He blew out, and tossed the hood off his head. "Then we can rest."

Anna nodded, unable to find enough breath to even frame the words. She'd be glad of a break, actually.

The last stretch was steep, but when Anna stepped out to the clearing behind Tyler, she gasped aloud at the wonder of it. "Oh!" she exclaimed, and was rewarded with a rare, deep smile from Tyler.

It was not a big space, perhaps only thirty feet square, at the pinnacle of the mountain. A few jagged rocks climbed skyward behind them, and a ring of trees clung to one side, so they weren't quite above the timberline.

But the true wonder lay to the southern end of the small mesa. The mountain fell away to reveal a deep valley stretching as far as Anna could see. Mountains rose in burly grandeur on either side, sweatered in blue and spruce and white. Clouds of slate and pumice and blue clustered densely over the peaks, pillows and feathers breaking free to drift over the valley. Starry clusters of snow danced in the still air.

Closer in was a neighboring slope, and Anna pointed urgently, grabbing Tyler's arm in a hard clutch.

There, perched calmly on a rock, was a gray wolf, its paws crossed, its nose lifted to the air in a lazy manner. Anna's heart hurt at the sight. He looked as if he'd been made from the sky itself, his fur the same melding of grays and whites as the clouds, the black markings only lending him a greater drama.

The valley between the mesa where Anna and Tyler stood and the mountainside where the rock lay was steep and unbreachable, and Anna thanked the saints for the stillness of the air, for the wolf seemed unaware of them as he looked out over the valley serenely, a wild creature in his wild world.

Tears sprung to Anna's eyes, and she simply drank the

sight in, knowing the rarity of it. As long as she lived, she would likely never see such a thing again.

In an awed, low voice, Tyler said, "There aren't supposed to be any wolves in these mountains."

"And yet," she said softly, "there he is."

"God, he's beautiful. I can barely breathe."

Anna nodded, squeezing her fingers on his arm where she yet held on to him.

A sound in the woods behind the wolf alerted him, and in a flash he disappeared into the trees, whether in pursuit of prey or to avoid being prey, they would never know.

Tyler turned to look down at her, and his eyes were the same colors as the wolf and the sky, grays all mingled together, a color as rare as the wolf itself. And this once, they were unguarded, and shining with rare happiness.

Her heart gave a hard squeeze, and she knew with certainty that she could easily fall all the way in love with him, that her crush could slide from something superficial, based on a fantasy, to something as deep as the valley, if she wasn't careful.

But she was not cautious by nature, and there was a fierce joy in her that she had shared with him such a rare and beautiful thing, that for once she had glimpsed true joy in his eyes. "Wow," she said, and grinned. "When you welcome a person to Colorado, you don't mess around, do you?"

Fine lines, made by wind and weather and bright mountain sunlight, fanned over his cheekbones as he grinned. "Well, I do what I can." With a perplexed expression, he glanced back to the place where the wolf had lain. "I really didn't think there were any wolves here anymore. It might be a mix or something."

"Don't analyze it," Anna said. "You'll ruin it."

His smile was rueful. "Good advice." He swung the pack from his shoulder. "Let's eat something and head back down. I don't want to get stuck up here if it starts to get windy.''

"Should I get some branches to sit on?"

Amazingly, Tyler actually chuckled as he pulled a small plastic tarp from the pack. "No, I was teasing. This is a hell of a lot easier.''

They ate the sandwiches and drank coffee. Without the wind, it was not terribly cold, and the view nourished something inside Anna, something that had yearned for exactly this for as long as she could remember. "You know," she said quietly, her gaze on the blue mountains, "I used to lie in my room, and outside there were sounds like cars and sirens and people talking as they walked by. Even in the quiet, it was never really quiet, you know?''

He nodded.

"So I'd lie on my bed and remember the way the mountains smelled, that kind of spicy smell, and I'd think about sitting on a mountain, with all the Colorado sky above me, and all the colors, and most of all, the quiet.'' She lifted a shoulder with a smile. "And here I am. It's like a miracle.''

"I have to be honest," Tyler said. "I'm one of those natives who hates outsiders coming in. When I was about fourteen, we used to be pretty obnoxious to tourists. Rude, actually.'' He paused to sip from the thermos. "And it really irritated me that my father built houses for them.''

"Is that why you don't work for your brother?"

"I do some work for Lance. But that isn't why I didn't work for my father.''

"What's the difference?''

"Lance just loves building things. When he was a kid, he built things out of straws, and rocks, and toothpicks— whatever he could get his hands on. My father just wanted to make money, and he didn't give a damn about the land. Lance does. He's not going to overbuild.''

Anna felt a little hurt that he was still classing her with

outsiders. Technically, she was one, but—she just wanted his respect. "You can't stop it, you know, all the people coming here."

His jaw was hard. "I know. But it's sad. Don't you think it is? I mean, look at that—" He gestured to indicate the view. "How can we let that be ruined? How can we let people build on it, and chase the animals away?"

"Not everyone is coming in here to change it, Tyler. Most people want to be here for the very thing you're talking about. We want to—" she frowned, trying to find a way to put it into words "—become part of it, let it teach us. It sounds so silly, but I swear, Colorado claimed me the minute I stepped out of the car when I was fifteen. It was like I couldn't *not* come here. You know?"

Unexpectedly, he covered her hands with one of his own. "I didn't mean you, Anna."

"Yes, you do. You mean people like me. I hear the natives talking about easterners coming and changing things, and I hear how bitter they are about it."

"Yeah, there's a lot of bitterness. But you're not doing what a lot of them are. They come from big cities and from California, and they come to be part of the wild, open West, where everybody is supposed to be an individualist, and free to make his own way." His brows lifted. "And then they start agitating to change the laws so things are just like the places they left. Like the damned PTA is running the world."

Anna laughed outright. "So you moved up to a mountain where they can't tell you what to do."

He slapped his leg mockingly. "Damn right, missy. Man's gotta be free." He shook his head. "Sorry. I'll get off my soapbox now."

"Well, console yourself with one thing," she said. "I happen to know all of that valley is national forest, so it's protected. And I also know that more of Colorado than almost any other state is either national park or national forest, so it's safe from the kind of development you're talking about."

He sobered. "Don't count on it, Anna. Money talks."

She looked out to the wilderness, and listened to the stillness, and tried to imagine it being lost. It gave her a hollow, lost feeling, and she could only imagine how much worse it was for Tyler. "How do you stop it?"

"That is the twenty-thousand-dollar question." He stuffed sandwich wrappers back in the bag and offered her another sip of coffee. "We'd better get back down the hill. Hear that wind?"

Anna stood, listening closely. "No."

"Low, like a moan."

And suddenly she could hear it, a distant rustling. She looked at Tyler and grinned. "I do hear it!"

He was facing her, his hair shining bright in the dark day, his eyes warm. Anna felt a shift in him suddenly, a softening, and he seemed to sway closer. For a fleeting second, she thought he was going to capture her face in his hand and kiss her. And he did touch her face, lightly, just the barest brush of a thumb over her jaw, a feathering of fingers near her ear. Then he seemed to catch himself, and straightened, pulling himself upright, away from her. "We're going to have to make quick time," he said gruffly, stuffing the thermos into the pack. "Can you handle it?"

The deliberate push wounded no more than his warning last night about his love for his wife. Anna calmly pulled on her gloves. "Sure. Lead the way, Captain."

He didn't bother with even a semblance of a smile. He simply tossed the pack over one shoulder, pulled up his hood and led the way back down the mountain. Just before she followed, Anna spared one more glance for the vista behind her, and touched the memory of the wolf. Not even Tyler could take that from her.

Then, steeling herself, she followed him down the hill.

Chapter 6

Tyler had been right about the hard exercise. When they got back to the cabin, both of them stripped off their coats and gloves wearily. Anna sank to the couch, where her pillow and the neatly folded quilt were waiting, and without even taking off her socks, she tipped over sideways. "Quite a workout," she said. "Thanks."

Her eyes were already closing. Tyler turned his back and stoked the fire and, without allowing himself to look at her again, stretched out on his bed. Charley trotted over, licked his hand, and sank down with a little groan next to the bed.

It felt good to stop moving, to let himself be enveloped in the warmth of the room. His body tingled with exercise and warming skin, and he felt enormously sleepy.

But his jeans were clammy and uncomfortable, and if he let himself fall asleep like this, he'd be miserable when he woke up. The same was true for Anna. Reluctantly he dragged himself upright and over to the couch. He leaned over the back to nudge her shoulder.

She barely stirred, making a low, muffled noise that meant nothing at all. He grinned to himself as she tucked her face more closely into the pillow. "Anna," he said, poking her again. "Don't go to sleep yet. You need to take off those wet clothes."

This time, she opened one eye and looked at him in confusion. "What?"

"Take off your jeans before you go to sleep."

"Oh." She shifted. "Oh, yeah."

"You can change into my sweats again, if you want. I'll leave you alone."

She nodded, and Tyler left her. In the small bathroom, he shed his jeans and shirt, leaving on his boxer shorts for the sake of modesty, then donned his robe for the short journey to his bed. It was odd to have to think about modesty. It had been a long, long time.

To his relief, she was already changed and covered and, by all appearances, asleep when he came through. He checked the fire in the stove and put the old cast-iron tea-kettle on the back so that they would have hot water when they woke up, added one more log to the fire and fell into the comfort of his bed.

He wasn't a napper, and didn't like sleeping in the day-time hours, but he did fall into a restless sleep, never very deep, filled with strange dreams about wolves and castles and chasing something vaguely frightening into the woods. He was not quite conscious, not quite asleep, and his sub-conscious coughed up strange, fragmented images: Kara in a red cloak, Curtis as a baby, Anna bare and beckoning.

The last one dragged him to full wakefulness. It was nearly dark, and he lay in the tangled mess of covers, star-ing at the ceiling, feeling unrefreshed and cranky. Flick-ering shadows from the fire played between the wooden beams, creating images that all too soon took shape and form, just as his dozing dreams had done. He saw the wolf on the mountain, so wild and free and noble, and Anna's shining eyes as she'd stared at him in breathless awe.

She could not know, of course, that Kara would have killed to see a wolf in the wild, and never had. Of all the things he wished he could have given her, that was high on the list. A wild, free wolf, in his own environment.

It bothered him that it had been with Anna that he saw it. He was not a superstitious man, but he did live close to the land, and he had a special love for wolves. They were what some might call his totem animal.

Silly. He knew it was—the legacy of his superstitious Irish Texan mother who read signs into everything that happened, and saw in feathers and rocks the answers to prayers.

And however he tried to ignore it, his gut said there was a reason he'd seen a wolf with Anna.

Quietly he disentangled himself from the covers and slipped on his jeans. He didn't bother to button his shirt, or put on socks. He simply rounded the couch and settled before the fire. Very deliberately, he faced the sleeping woman. Until he faced her, acknowledged what he needed to know from her, or learn from her, or learn about himself, he would have no peace.

A pretty face. Not beautiful, as Kara's had been. Only pretty, with soft features that would both sharpen and blur as she aged. Her coloring was the riveting thing—the black hair and white skin and rosy cheeks made him think of her fairy tales, of Snow White.

She lay half on her side, the covers thrown off against the warmth of the fire so close by, her posture far too open for a woman asleep in a stranger's house. Silky black curls spilled over her cheek, around her neck. The V-necked sweater revealed the curve of one unbound white breast, and he had to take a breath against the power of the yearning that simple sight roused in him. A man didn't forget the way a breast yielded to his hand. He didn't forget how good that felt, or stop wishing for it, even if there was no possibility of experiencing it again. He would have liked to brush his hands, and his face, and his chest over that supple white flesh.

So much.

Resolutely, he moved on. The dip of her waist, her small, neat legs. Her stocking feet that were so small her boots looked like kid shoes.

Now that she was quiet, he was able to think about her more calmly. Her awakened self was exuberant and bright and chatty; it gave her an aura of great sexuality he was sure she didn't even know she possessed.

The fire heated his back to burning, and Tyler shifted a little closer to Anna to escape it. Now he was close enough that he could simply stretch out a hand and touch her, if he so chose.

Instead, he consciously called forth a vision of Kara. Kara, with her long blond hair, glittering all over her bare shoulders and much lusher breasts; Kara with her blue, blue eyes and clear, evenly cut features. He narrowed his eyes to focus and tried to transpose the ghostly image over the sleeping figure of Anna.

But it didn't work as well as he'd hoped. The perfection of Kara's Nordic clean blond looks could not compete with the vividness of the flesh-and-blood woman breathing in sleep on the couch in his house. The memory of long golden hair held no power over the lure of lively black curls. The faintly remembered lushness of Kara's figure had no power to rouse him as did the promise of Anna's sweet body and uptilted, nubby-tipped breasts.

The detail caught his attention. Through her sweater, he could distinctly see the peaks of her breasts, standing straight and tall. Heat touched his cheeks, and he looked to her face, to find her gazing at him with heavy-lidded awareness. She did not move even a little, only held his gaze steadily, and Tyler found he could not quite bear it. He bowed his head.

He wondered how long she had been watching him mentally undress her. He felt foolish sitting here cross-legged like a simpleton, hungrily eyeing a woman as if she were some exotic and unusual being newly come to his world. She would think he was the strangest man alive.

And yet, his gaze had roused her. The thought struck him with a fresh wave of yearning, this one so intense it flooded his thighs and chest and hands with an urgent, compelling need. He looked at her again. "I was trying to—"

Her fingers, pressed to his lips, stopped him. "Don't explain. I liked it."

"I don't want you to like it," he said harshly, raising to his knees. "I want you to push me away."

"I know."

"Please, Anna," he said, and yet his hand was reaching for her, falling into those black curls. And he didn't know if he meant please stop him or please meet him halfway.

Her eyes were sultry black pools, their expression as old as woman as she looked at him. Tentatively, she raised a hand and touched his chest. "You are the most beautiful man I have ever seen, Tyler Forrest. From the first time I saw you, I wanted to touch you." Her fingers drew tentative marks on his chest, dragging over a flat nipple, and trailing down his belly.

He felt his heart thudding in a thick, aroused beat, and every nerve in his torso leaped alive. He swallowed, his hand moving almost of its own accord over the delicate, elfin ear, over her smooth cheek, back into the allure of her hair, hair as silky as rabbit fur. "Your hair is so soft." He trailed his fingers over her neck. "And your skin."

As if his touch wounded her, she closed her eyes, and it sent something hard and bright shattering through him, the sight of those long black eyelashes falling on her cheeks, as if to hide her vulnerability. What she didn't know was that she couldn't hide, even by closing her eyes. Her lips, so red and full, were parted slightly, as if in readiness for what he would offer—his tongue, his flesh— and the faint, restless way she arched her back told him she wanted his hands on her.

One word, whispered, undid him. "Tyler," she said, a whisper as yearning and pained as a ballad.

He swore softly. "This is a mistake," he said—the last, lost protest of his rational mind as he fell under Anna's spell.

He swayed toward her, feeling his hair come free as he bent over her and very delicately kissed her. Just the lightest brush of lips, that was all he meant to do, but in an instant, he was lost. He sank deep into the seduction of that mouth, fell into the velvety promise of sensual, slow pleasure. She made a small, soft noise and her hands slid under his shirt, over his bare skin, and Tyler shuddered at the stunning response of his body after so long a drought.

Braced with one hand on the couch, the other on her face, Tyler kissed her. And kissed her. And kissed her. She tasted of the earth, of the sky, of all things made by goddesses, and her full lips fit his own as if they'd been made together, something he'd never experienced. Lost, he plunged his tongue deep and drew hers back, and Anna met him fully, completely.

He lifted his head, dizzy, and looked at her. Struggling to be fair, to halt the forward tumble before it could damage them, he said, "There won't be anything but this, Anna. I don't have anything else to give you."

The black eyes were sober and somehow shining, all at once. "I know," she said, and, impossibly, smiled. "I know."

And she pulled him down to her again, deep into the passion of her kisses, into the wonder that was a gypsy as free as the wolf to wander where she would and take what came, with no thought for tomorrow. And just this once, Tyler, too, would let go of everything but now. Now, in this minute, with Anna.

The position was awkward, and Tyler grabbed the quilt, and spread it on the floor before the fire, letting go of her to spread it out. She sat up, watching, and he thought, now she would come to her senses. But when he settled atop the quilt and shed his shirt—his offering to her—she came to him, and knelt before him, and put her arms around his shoulders, pressing her breasts close, putting her mouth on his jaw.

She straightened suddenly to look at him, a frown on that smooth white forehead. "What about condoms? A baby would be a disaster."

"I'm fixed," he said, and there was a strange, distant sorrow in him over that.

A fleeting shadow touched her eyes and was gone, and then she was against him, pressing herself close. "Don't hurry," she whispered. "Let me really touch you."

"No hurry," he said roughly, pulling her tightly against him. He rubbed his hands up and down her spine, feeling the sweater bunch and grow moist with the heat of his palms as it slid over her skin. Her hands moved on him, on his back and over his waist and into his hair and, finally, she held his face between her hands, touching his brow and eyelids and mouth before she tilted her head and kissed him.

Roaring built in his blood, a pounding, furious need that threatened to engulf him. Tyler pulled back, gasping and holding on to her shoulders, and held her at arm's length. She settled easily on her bottom, reaching to put her hands on his thighs. Firelight gave a gossamer covering of orange light to her form. It swept along her cheek and jaw and the edge of her neck.

He held her patient gaze for a long moment, and realized she wanted to look at him in this fine light, too. He forced himself to be patient, to wait while the dark gaze touched him, crown to lips to chest.

But then the need grew in him, ragged in its ferocity, and with one smooth gesture, he reached for her sweater and skimmed the edges of the V downward, slowly revealing the smooth white shoulders, the sweet upper swell of her breasts and the slimness of her upper arms. His hands shook a little, and he paused in anticipation and an effort to make himself take things slowly.

She shifted, putting her hands on his thighs as if in encouragement, and Tyler found his touch steady, and resumed the exquisite torture of disrobing her. The sweater slid easily over her breasts, and she freed her arms, letting it pool at her waist, then simply lifted her eyes, utterly comfortable with her breasts bared to his gaze, to his touch, as if she knew it was too much for him, that each little step of this was no simple thing for him.

He would make it last, he told himself. So first he filled his eyes with her. He'd never seen a woman with such colors, not even in the forbidden pictures his brothers and he had smuggled out of the construction offices. Her skin was white as alabaster, and took the colors of the fire like some rare pearl, luminescent along the surprisingly rich curve of a breast, the deep-rose nipples. Her shoulders and rib cage were small, but when he lifted his hands, her breasts fit his palms exactly—a sensation like no other, that oddly weighted flesh nestling in his lifting palms.

It roused her, Tyler saw, looking back to her face. Her eyes were aflame, limpid luminosity sparking higher as he caressed her there, explored the curves. When he stroked his thumb over her nipples, once, lightly, her nostrils flared and her lips parted. Tyler swayed forward to nip those parted lips, and slid his tongue between them hungrily.

She gripped his shoulders, and he felt the sharpness of nails against his skin, a sensation that sent his sex into screaming arousal. He gasped and pushed her backward, shifting his hands to her wrists, which he pulled over her head. Madness filled him, a madness born of the war of his sensual nature with his chosen celibacy, and he knew which side was winning. The animal had broken free.

Nestling one thigh hard between her legs, Tyler bent over her and opened his mouth on her throat, sucking hard once before he moved lower, and nipped her lightly on the top curve of one breast.

She arched against him, her arms straining against his grip, her hips arching into him. With the very tip of his tongue, he touched the very tip of her nipple, and Anna cried out softly.

And then, oh, the taste of her was too much. He tumbled entirely into a consuming hunger, feasting with decadence on the pleasures of her, the nubby taste of her nipples, the nectar of her cries as he suckled her deep, rolling her flesh in his mouth so that he would not forget just this texture, just this huge ache of thrusting want where he pressed against her, where she pressed upward to him.

He tasted her belly, with the flat of his tongue and the suck of his lips and the nip of his teeth, and when he encountered the waistband of the sweats, he tugged them down to show pretty little lace panties. And he touched her, her thighs and the juncture between them, conjuring heat and damp cries and quivering from her. She clutched his hair in great handfuls and dragged his face to hers, and kissed him with almost violent need, and Tyler loved that she could be so wild, that her need seemed as insane as his own, that there was an almost unholy bewitchment upon them, a spell of passion they were helpless to resist.

Only then did he pause, and straddle her waist, so she could free him. With trembling hands, she unfastened the buttons containing him, and impatiently dragged the jeans from his hips. He helped her, shifting to rid himself of the clothing, but she wrapped her hands around his thighs and pulled him back to that straddling position.

And she touched him. Touched his belly and his sex with equal pleasure, her eyes following the path of her hands. But when her hands closed on his rigid sex, he groaned, and pulled away. "I can't..." he said, moving quickly before he humiliated himself. He lay against her for a moment, trying to think of something, anything, else. The firewood, the storm, the wolf—

But her hands moved with gypsy magic over his shoulders, into his hair. Her mouth teased his jaw, his neck, his ear. And he felt her shifting below him, spreading her legs, arching upward. Inviting him to join with her.

With a groan, he accepted the invitation, urgently catching her buttocks in his hands, lifting her closer to him and, at last, entry to the cavern, a slow, agonizing slide. A gasp tore from his throat at the deep, overwhelming pleasure of it.

She tensed against him, and Tyler felt a slight resistance. He lifted his head, puzzled. "You aren't a virgin?"

"Come to me, Tyler," she whispered, and the agonized passion in her throat would have sent him over the edge even if she had not gripped him, her heels digging close, and arched hard, sending him deep.

He was lost, his mouth hard on her neck, his member deep and tight in that glorious heat, and there was nothing but the passion of Anna all around him, pulsing and crying and sensually writhing, "Please," she sobbed against him, not a tearful sob, but that nearly overwhelmed sound of a woman who did not quite know—

He knew.

He knew. He gave her what she desperately wanted, and he loved it that her cry was feral, deep and guttural and all of her body shuddered around him, against him, in his arms. She bit his shoulder, like a cat, and her fingernails hurt his shoulders, and it was everything it should be, everything, as he pulled her violently to him and thrust with the madness until he could let go, until all of Anna and all of him were somewhere in the wild heart of the world, and he threw back his head and, silent, Tyler howled like a wolf at the welcome power of his release.

Chapter 7

Tyler collapsed against her, and Anna held him, her breath and his ragged and hurried, their skin slick with sweat. In that first, dazzling moment, she felt iridescent, as insubstantial and light-filled as a scene within a crystal ball. She loved the feeling of him all around her, his body heavy with release, his hair against her fingers, the sticky and slippery feel of their skin. His hand cupped her head, his fingers moving in her hair, and his breath fell on her neck, hot and moist.

And in her exuberance, Anna could not be silent. "Holy cow," she breathed, and heard the laughter in the words.

Tyler said nothing. Only pressed his face into her neck and kissed the column of her throat with a gentleness that nearly broke her heart. He kissed her chin, and finally lifted his head to kiss her mouth, his ethereal eyes open and serious. He took his weight on his elbows. "Are you okay?"

"I'm fine," she whispered. And, really, that was all she could manage. Caught in the beauty of his glorious eyes, her body pulsing and tingling, she had no desire for him to go anywhere. She touched the wings of his eyebrows and the clean line of the aquiline nose. He dipped and caught her finger, sucking it into his mouth, and a new wave of sensation moved through her. "Are *you* okay?"

"I'm dizzy," he said, lowering his head to murmur the words against her lips. As if her mouth contained some nectar, he drank again, deeply, and the powerful body moved against her, his chest brushing her breasts, his stomach pressed hard against hers. "I feel crazy with wanting you. Again. And again."

His hips moved aggressively, and Anna found a new sensation spreading through her loins. She had thought they were finished, but there he was, moving again, but this time slowly, sending rippling pleasure through her. Slow, slow, slow, and his lips moved on her, and one hand strayed to her breast and teased a nipple, and Anna felt the heat growing, thickening, until her breath was again small, panting cries that punctuated his movements.

And this time Anna burst into flames with him, shuddering as he let go, as he gripped her so tightly and the world swirled and spun and wild explosions rocked her body.

He fell over her, kissing her neck, her cheek. "Anna, you're wonderful, so free."

And at last they lay sated before the fire, bodies shining side by side in the firelight. Anna touched him lazily, letting her hands wander over the round of muscle in his upper arm, and over the actual ripples of his belly, and in turn his big hands touched her breasts and her hip and her thighs, wandering, learning. "I never imagined you to have so much muscle," she said quietly. "I thought you would be too thin, and you aren't."

A glint grew in his eye. "Does that mean you imagined my body naked?"

Anna blushed. "Well—" She stopped, realizing how

ridiculous it was to be blushing over what she'd thought after what she'd *done*. She raised her eyes. "Yes, actually, I did. Often."

With one finger, he traced the curve of her lip. "Your mouth drives me crazy. You can't imagine how many times I got hard just looking at your mouth."

"Tyler!" she protested.

"Sorry. See why I could never talk to women?" He sobered. "I really meant it as a compliment."

She smiled. "I'll take it that way, then."

A warm silence fell. Firelight made the hair on his thigh a red-gold glaze, and, idly, she stroked the long limb.

"Anna," he said.

Here it came, she thought, and raised her head.

"You were a virgin."

"It doesn't matter, Tyler."

"It does to me."

Firmly, she caught his hand. "Don't." She chose her words carefully. "Don't think it was some sacrifice on my part. It wasn't." It was hard to express what she meant, and she paused, trying to think of some way to tiptoe around the whole business.

In the end, she simply blurted out the truth. "When I opened my eyes and saw you looking at me like that, it was like this wonderful gift. Something to make up for all the chocolate cheesecake I never ate, and the nights I had to spend studying while my sisters went out, and all the dangerous, sexy boys my brothers chased off." Earnestly, she kissed his palm. "For once, I got to indulge myself with something I wanted."

His expression was grave, and he touched her face. "I needed you this weekend, Anna. You'll never know how much."

Yes, she did. But the moment was growing too serious, and that would ruin all of it, so she lifted up on one elbow saucily. "And what a trade! I got to learn a new skill."

That coaxed a genuine chuckle from his throat, and he reached for her playfully. "So you're using me, huh?"

She nodded brightly. "Is that okay with you? You do seem to have an understanding of the finer points."

The pale eyes went sultry, and that gorgeous, sensual mouth moved closer. "I know a lot more, if you want some more lessons."

"Oh, yes, please," she whispered, and let him kiss her again.

The night was enchanted, Anna thought later as Tyler dozed beside her. To one end of their makeshift pallet on the floor were the remains of supper—sandwiches made from saltines, cups of tea, cookies and cheese. Now, replete, Anna leaned against the couch and sipped blackberry brandy and admired Tyler.

In the general region of her heart was an ache, equal parts wonder and poignance. If she had felt she'd stumbled into the pages of a fairy tale before, the feeling was trebled now. It was as if some witch in the forest, seeing how the storm had trapped the two of them together, had cast a spell over the cabin, over Tyler. A spell that would last only as long as the snow.

It almost hurt to look at him. His long, lean body was sprawled on the quilt before the fire, his head was cradled on his arm, and he was splendidly, unashamedly naked. And to Anna he looked like an artist's vision, made of gold light and supple flesh and impossibly beautiful angles. She drank in every inch of him. His hair, the hair of a knight, so long and clean and shining; his arms, so surprisingly well-defined, a vein running visibly over the round of a biceps. She gazed at his long, smooth back, and at the curve of his rear end, so firm and round and high; down the length of his thighs, his calves; his elegant, long feet.

And then she looked again at his face, at his beautiful,

haunted, aristocratic face, and a pain went through her. She drew her knees up to herself, hugging them close to ease away the pain. Visions of that mouth on hers, those eyes so fiery with need, flickered over her imagination, sending remembered heat through her limbs.

"Oh, sweet Mary," she whispered aloud. How could fate be so cruel as to give and take in the same moment?

But that, she knew well, was the price of enchantments. The warning was always the same, wasn't it? Be careful what you wish for.

Fighting off the ache, she stared at the fire and sipped the plum-colored brandy. Surely there was some way to win her quest. Perhaps when the snow stopped, when they went again their separate ways, Tyler would find he could not do without her, after all. Perhaps through the very real, very intense magic of their physical attraction to each other, he would somehow be saved.

His hand fell on her foot, and Anna started. "Penny for your thoughts," he said.

Anna shook her head and, appallingly, felt herself close to tears. Hastily she swallowed them and lowered her eyes.

"Oh, hey." Suddenly, that long beautiful body was wrapped around her, and he dragged the quilt around them, making a cave of cloth and his body. He pulled her close, pressing her head to his chest, and kissed her crown. "Let me hold you, okay?"

It was ridiculous, this sudden emotionalism. "It's nothing," she whispered. "Just a sudden rush of melancholy."

"I understand." With a sweetness she would not have expected, he rocked her a little. "Don't be ashamed, Anna. This is beautiful, you know." His arms were fierce around her. "So beautiful I feel like I'm dreaming. Like I'm going to wake up and you will never have come for that teddy bear at all, I just dreamed it."

Against her cheek, his chest was warm and smelled of wood smoke and the essence of Tyler himself. "I'm not ashamed," she said quietly. "I'll never be ashamed of this."

"Good. I would hate that."

She shifted to look at him. "It's going to be weird when I see you after this, though. I have to admit that much."

A shadow crossed his face. "Anna, I don't want you to be hurt by this. I don't have casual sex." He paused and looked away, as if he were embarrassed. "I've never had a woman except Kara. I never wanted one." He touched her cheek with his fingertips. "But this is only for now. That's all. That's the only way I can bear to—" he looked away "—to allow myself."

"I know, Tyler." She found a smile. "Let's make a deal. I won't feel ashamed, and you won't feel guilty."

For a moment, he looked surprised. Maybe that she would know it was guilt that drove him. Then he nodded. Soberly.

"Let's also not think about anything but now," she said. "We'll forget there is another world, or a past, or future, until the snow stops."

"Deal." He kissed her, then shifted so that they were both facing the fire. "Tell me a story, Anna."

She laughed. "A story?"

"Yes. You tell Curtis stories. I've heard you. Tell me one."

"Okay, but you have to sing a song when I'm done. Fair is fair."

"A song? You sure you want to be tortured like that?"

"Oh, no, you don't. Your brother told me you sing ballads and things at the RenFair." She pulled back to look at him. "Is that why you have your hair so long? So you look right for the festival?"

He touched it self-consciously. "Is it strange, my hair?"

"No," Anna protested. "Not at all. It looks right on you. I just wondered why."

He said nothing, and Anna guessed this, too, went back to Kara. "No big thing. What kind of story do you want?"

He settled closer. "Anything you want to tell."

"Hmmm…" She tossed a few around in her head, then began, "Once upon a time, there was a very beautiful woman, a woman everyone in every village for miles around wanted."

"Of course."

She smiled. "You can't interrupt unless I prompt you."

"Got it." But he grinned, and she knew it wouldn't be that easy.

Anna told an old French folk tale about a king so jealous of his wife that he locked her up in a tower and only let her go to mass, and even then only in the company of her waiting women and several burly guards. Because of his jealousy and the secrecy under which the wife was kept, tales of her beauty spread all over the land.

"One day," Anna said, "a valiant knight came to the kingdom and heard the stories of the king's beautiful wife, and he hid himself in the church so he could see her for himself. He hid behind a curtain, and when the woman came in, he felt his heart stolen away in an instant."

"Why aren't there ever any ugly princesses?"

Anna shushed him. "Shhh… Do you want to hear the story or not?"

He sobered mockingly. "I do."

"The queen was very unhappy. She was young, after all, and longed to dance with the court, and laugh and feast, like everybody else, but she was always kept in her tower, all alone. Her ladies-in-waiting were jealous of her beauty, and so were not kind to her, and not one befriended her, but instead stayed out in the hallways all the time, flirting with the guards."

"Are you sure the story says 'flirting'?"

"More or less." She pinched him. "You asked for the story, now listen."

He jumped away. "Ouch!" But he laughed. "Go ahead. The lonely queen went to the chapel...?"

"This was a gray and gloomy day, and she felt especially lonely, so she knelt on the stones and prayed to Mary to send her a true companion to ease her days.

"Hidden away behind his heavy curtain, the knight was moved by the queen's deep sorrow, and he vowed to find a way to answer her prayer."

"Ah. He wasn't just a little bit swayed by her immense beauty?"

Anna turned her lips down. "I'm getting to that part." She took a breath and sat up straighter. "Every year for the queen's birthday, the king let her out of her tower and allowed her to attend a ball in her honor. When the ball came, the knight swore he would find a way to speak to her privately and tell her she was not alone, that he would be her champion.

"He waited in the great hall, dressed in his noblest tunic, and waited for the queen to appear. His palms were hot and his stomach was nervous and he feared that if his plan were discovered, he would be beheaded."

"Yeow."

"Exactly. At last, the full moon rose, and as if conjured by the light, the queen appeared on the dais, dressed in a gown of shimmering silver, her hair unbound and trailing black as the night over her back, all the way down to her knees. And the knight felt a knife through his heart, for indeed she was the most beautiful woman he had ever seen. No man could look upon her without feeling that faint, clear longing."

Next to her, Tyler was shaking with laughter.

Anna sighed. "Don't say it."

"I won't. I'm not. But I know where they felt it." He moved away as her pinching fingers reached for his thigh. "I'll stop."

"*Anyway,* it was not her beauty that snared our valiant knight. It was the deep sorrow in her sapphire eyes, and the way her ruby-red lips never smiled, even as she was toasted and music leaped around her and she danced with barons and knights from throughout the land, who had come solely for the pleasure of her smile.

"Now, he was not a rich knight, and his turn fell late in the evening, but at last he took the beautiful queen in his arms and looked deep into her eyes. He whispered that he had heard her prayer for a companion, and he would be her champion. He revealed his plan to build a tower nearby and a tunnel under the ground to her, and when it was done, they would run away."

She expected some light note from Tyler, but there was suddenly a faraway look in his gray eyes, and she went on. "The queen told him he should not do it, that if he were discovered, he would be killed and his head put on a spike on the town wall. But he was adamant. As long as it took, he vowed, he would devote himself to this task.

"And he was true to his word. He fought valiantly for the king, and asked for a parcel of land nearby the castle, where he might build himself a modest home. The king agreed, and the knight set to work.

"He knew the queen was still most desperately lonely, and sometimes he contrived to see her in the church for a moment, when all they could do was exchange a look. And each day at noon, he had learned, she sat by her tower window to eat her midday meal, so he always walked in the square where she might see him.

"Years passed, and the knight dug his tunnel through the moonlit hours, hiding the entrance from his servants and workers each morning. Each year at her birthday feast, she seemed only more beautiful to him, for the love she carried for her faithful knight made of her beauty a luminous thing. All remarked upon it, how her skin seemed never to age, how her eyes seemed ever more blue, her hair ever more lustrous, with each passing year. Which only made the king more jealous. He had noticed her happiness, and was sure she had found some lover, and forbade her to even go to mass any longer.

"At last the knight's tunnel reached the stone wall of the queen's tower, and it was with shaking hands that he carefully dug away the mortar holding the stones. And this task took him many weeks, the slow removal of those stones, for he had to make it appear as if they were all still in place, in the chance that someone might happen by.

"The king had grown suspicious of our knight's devotion, for he refused to marry, even when the king offered one of his own sisters, and he ordered a watch put upon him day and night.

"Finally, the day came when the knight had made so great a hole in the mortar and stones that he could slip through, and on the day he was to do so, he donned a fine velvet tunic and walked in the yard where the queen might see him. That night, he waited until the kingdom slept, and went through his tunnel, and at last crept up the stairs to the tower room of the queen."

Tyler rubbed her arm. "Go on."

"The queen was waiting, her hair unbound, her eyes shining, and she flew into the knight's arms, and he showered her face with kisses, and they fell to her richly appointed bed, where at last they could make love."

Now his attention was close upon her, and Anna sobered, looking into his eyes. "The guard who had been told to follow the knight everywhere had followed him to the tower, too, and he crept up the stairs behind him, and saw the knight take the beautiful, lonely queen into his arms.

"And the old guard, who had been in the king's service for many years, was touched with mercy. He left the knight and the queen alone to their love, and crept back through the tunnel to wait. Only at dawn, when they had had those long, long hours of love, did he go to the king and tell him what he had seen."

Anna paused, letting the crackle of the fire and the

sound of the wind fill her listener with the dread he must have. "The king, in a rage, stormed the tower room, and found the lovers, and thrust his sword through their hearts. But all who were present that day said the queen, seeing her husband in all his rage, only smiled, and gladly took his sword into her heart, and died in her lover's arms.

"The king, seeing what he had done, was stricken with remorse, that his jealousy had killed his beautiful wife, and he ordered the pair to be buried together on a distant hill, and they were laid together in each other's arms. It is said that upon that hill, the grass never fades, and the roses are so plentiful and the birds sing so sweetly that many a babe has been made there."

Tyler looked at her. "You don't tell that story to Curtis, do you?"

"No. He likes dragons and goblins and witches. Scary stuff." She grinned. "He hasn't learned to appreciate beautiful princesses, yet."

"I thought fairy tales were supposed to have happy endings."

Anna shook her head. "Only in the cleaned-up versions. The originals are bloody and sexy, and a lot of them are very dark." She leaned her head back on the crook of his elbow. "They were teaching tools."

Absently his hand moved on her thigh below the covers. "Like the old Indian legends, I guess. All those ogres and punished children."

"Exactly. They were told to keep children safe, or teach a wife or husband how to treat their spouse, or warn against some vanity or character flaw. "

"Why do you know so many fairy tales?"

"I like them. I used to check collections out of the library and read them to my nieces and nephews, and after a while, I just remembered a lot of them."

Under the covers, his hands moved more freely, over her thighs, up to her tummy, around an ankle. "That one gave me a lump in my throat."

"I know," she said quietly.

His hand slid under the shirt she wore and cupped her breast. An immediate jolt went through her, especially when he put his mouth close to her ear and said in a low voice, "I wonder what the knight and the queen did all night?" He pressed a kiss to her neck. "Do you think they talked?"

Anna closed her eyes. "I don't know."

He pushed her sideways, tossing away the quilt, and she glimpsed his beautiful long body, splendidly aroused, before he covered her with himself, tangling his thighs with hers, his hands on her face. "Or did they make love over—" he kissed her chin "—and over—" her neck "—and over?"

She could not find her breath to answer him. His full-cut mouth opened over hers and she was lost once again, lost in the pure force of his desire as he pushed aside the shirt that covered her, and kissed her body, all of it, as if he'd been starved.

Again he roused her slowly, fully, deeply, not so much by skill as with his devouring want of her, the pleasure he took in each taste, each brush of his mouth or his hands on any part of her—her arms and breasts and belly and thighs and throat, her mouth and eyes and wrists. And in turn, Anna touched him back, stroking the fine length of his torso, and the rounds of his arms. She explored every inch of his flesh, every sinew and swell, every sleek angle and sensual curve. She learned to tease, as he teased, by bringing him close, close, close, to his release, then ceasing, laughing as he tumbled her back and teased her in return, the ferocity of his need a wild aphrodisiac. And when at last they were both trembling with the force of that need, when their breath tore from them in ragged, burning gasps, and their skin was slick with sweat, only then did Tyler sit up and draw Anna into his lap so that they could be one.

It made her a little shy, and she hesitated, but Tyler

gripped her buttocks firmly and said, "So we can kiss," he said breathlessly. "So I can look at you." He swallowed, raising one hand to her breast. "So I can make you crazy."

He pulled her to him, guiding her hips with his hands, holding her hard till they were joined deep. And he held her there without moving, and they kissed and he touched her, and at last, when Anna thought she would come apart, he eased his grip and looked at her, and she knew, without prompting, how to move, what to do.

And all the world, all of time and space and the heavens, narrowed to this, to Tyler's pale eyes burning into her, his elegant face sheened with sweat, his hands on her face, and her breasts and her lower back, his body joining hers with a rocking, slow rhythm. All the world was in Tyler's eyes, all the sorrow and the love and the passion that had ever been, right there as they moved together, as he lost control no matter how he tried to keep it, right there as he gripped hard and pulled her hard against him, and pressed his face to her neck.

And in the lightning seconds before her own rocketing response burst through her, Anna shaped her hands to the dearness of his skull, below his hair, and tightened her thighs against the sides of his lean waist and stowed it all away for the time when he would not be with her, when she would not feel him this way. And when the violence of her response claimed her, she wrapped her arms around him and forced herself not to weep, because the words she could not say were on her lips.

Instead, she only whispered his name, over and over, and took comfort in the fierce, tender way he held her close to him and kissed her as if he knew he would miss the taste.

Chapter 8

Tyler was not sure what had awakened him at first. He had no recollection of falling asleep, only of holding Anna close in the warmth of his bed. Now he felt the silken brush of her calf against his foot, and opened his eyes.

She slept peacefully, deeply, her black curls scattered over the pillow and her shoulder and neck. She looked so young lying there like that, her face unmarked by time or sorrow, and he loved it, even as it made him sad to know that sooner or later the marks of living would fall upon her.

But would they ruin her? No. Those fine clear eyes would always twinkle. The skin would always be beautiful, even with a netting of wrinkles. The hair would likely go very silver, and he tried to imagine how silver hair would look with those lovely, deep black eyes.

In the morning light, he also saw with a little shock the littering of marks upon that flesh. A reddish bruise from the fierceness of his passion on her neck, another at the top swell of her breast. Her lips were pouty and faintly swollen. Absently he touched his own mouth, wondering if his showed the same look, and he became aware of the faint sting of scratches on his back. The night flooded back to him, in visual and sensual detail.

Wild. They had been so unbelievably wild, like two starving animals.

Suddenly, he lifted his head, realizing what the difference was this morning. There was sunlight falling through the uncurtained windows, vivid yellow sunshine that pooled on her body in sweet yellow bars.

And as if the sunlight carried some moral code with it, Tyler felt dread replace the drifting sense of arousal that had moved into his blood. He looked back to Anna's young, innocent face, and felt he'd been kicked.

What had he done?

He closed his eyes, and moved away from her quietly, so as not to disturb her, and when he stood up, the muscles along the front of his thighs protested. The remains of their picnic meal lay by the fire, along with a pile of discarded clothes and the sticky brandy glasses. Standing nude and stunned, Tyler looked at the room with the eyes of a man who had been very drunk and had indulged in shocking behavior.

But he hadn't been drunk. He didn't even have that excuse. He'd been horny and greedy and selfish and he'd seduced a virgin he knew had a crush on him.

Feeling sick with shame, he hid in the small bathroom, with its low-water shower. Ten gallons of hot water, period. He was sure Anna would want some of it and he stared at the pine-lined cubicle blankly, still reeling.

Over the toilet was a mirror, and Tyler saw that his own body was as marked as Anna's. His shoulders were littered with half-moon marks made by her fingernails. At the juncture of his neck and shoulder was a deep red mark made by her mouth, and even in his disgust, Tyler felt himself respond to that memory, and what had been happening when it was made.

Winded, he turned on the water and stepped under it. How could he have let himself go like that? Taken advantage of a sweet young woman who wore her heart on her sleeve? A woman who believed in fairy tales and lost princes?

It was more wrong than anything he'd ever done in his life. Worse because he knew she didn't believe he meant what he'd said about it being only for one night.

Quickly he washed and turned off the water, starting when a soft knock came at the door. "Tyler, I'm sorry to bother you, but the forest service is at the door and I need to get dressed."

He had only a small, threadbare towel that covered about a postage-stamp corner of his body, but even as he considered the problem, another knock came at the front door. He heard Anna call out, "Just a minute!"

Hell. They'd spent the past sixteen hours making love. It was a little late for modesty. Dripping, he held the towel over the most vulnerable part of himself and hauled open the door abruptly. "Come in."

"Thank you," she said in a small voice, squeezing past him. She was wrapped in the quilt, her sweats and sweater in her hand. She didn't look at him.

It was a very, very small room—if she inhaled, Tyler had to exhale. They both struggled with getting dressed at the same time, and finally Tyler gave up. Keeping the handkerchief-size towel over himself, he leaned against the door. "You go first," he said gruffly.

She looked at him miserably, a deep blush on her cheeks. "I'm too embarrassed with you watching me."

And Tyler realized he'd been hoping to watch. He'd been wanting that last, forbidden look at the flesh he'd explored in such detail last night. It shamed him even more, and he straightened. "Fine," he said, dropping the towel. "You watch me, instead."

A flare lit those dark eyes. Her chin lifted defiantly, that made-for-sex mouth tightening, but not enough to take away its appeal. Never enough. Proudly, her nostrils flaring, she dropped the quilt and stood there nude, her breasts upthrust and moving with the heat of her breathing.

Tyler clenched his fists against the roar of need the sight gave him, trembling as she shoved her legs into the loose sweats and lifted the black sweater from where she'd dropped it. It was twisted inside out, and she seemed to take forever to turn it right side out, standing only inches away with her bare torso and squared shoulders.

And he knew he'd be risking serious injury if he tried to reach out to her in this moment. She'd already seen rejection in his eyes, and Tyler would be insane to take it back.

But, heaven help him, he wanted to. He felt almost faint from the raging lust in his loins. And innocent though she might have been before last night, Anna was instinctive enough to know, to punish him with the slow, patient way she took first one sleeve, then the other from the sweater's tangled inside, the way she at last lifted her arms, and her breasts lifted with her, ripe and white and tipped with aroused points until the thin, soft fabric safely covered them.

She shot him a dark, knowing glance. "Excuse me. I'll go let them in."

It pricked his pride and his anger. He caught her arm, not ungently, and said, "Wait for me."

And he had the smallest sense of satisfaction in knowing she was as compelled to watch his body as he had been to watch hers. When his jeans were zipped but not buttoned, he took her arm and pulled her close. She resisted rigidly, but she was no match for him. "It's over, Anna, our one night."

"Don't worry about me," she said, coolly, but her breathing betrayed her.

He kissed her, hard, and let her go. "Go let them in. I'll be right out."

Anna fled the small bathroom. In the main room, she had to pause, fighting to control the tears of rage and pain and humiliation that swelled up in her chest, crowding her throat, flooding her cheeks with heat. On the floor were the remains of the meal they'd shared, and the bed was mussed, and she knew she looked as if she'd spent the night doing exactly what she had.

And now she had to open the door to those rangers, and look them in the eye and act as if everything were perfectly normal. Fat chance.

Only the sound of the bathroom door opening spurred her on. Smoothing her wild hair from her face, she hurried to the front door and opened it. "Hi. Sorry it took so long. I wasn't dressed."

The two rangers, one skinny blond man and a woman much taller and even skinnier, looked a little abashed. "Sorry, ma'am," said the woman. "We were told you'd been stranded here. Is that your Jeep by the avalanche?"

"Yes. I walked back here when I couldn't get through the road. It seemed smarter than trying to hike to town."

The man nodded. "You did the right thing."

Anna felt Tyler moving behind her. "Why don't you come in?" he said. "I've got hot water for tea."

"Thank you, but we can't stay. We just wanted to let you know we've got the road nearly cleared, and you can probably hike down there by noon and drive on out."

"That's amazing!" Anna exclaimed. "How did you get it taken care of so fast?"

"Storm blew itself out about midnight, and that's an access road to the communications towers for three counties. It's high-priority."

"Thank you."

She closed the door behind them, carefully avoiding Tyler's eyes as she moved toward the mess by the fire. Stiffly, she picked up the plates and brandy glasses and cups, trying very hard not to let any of it remind her of what had passed between them. Without speaking, she carried them to the sink.

Tyler stepped aside, careful to avoid letting their bodies touch, and the small avoidance pierced her. Emotions crowded into her throat again, and she turned away blindly, determined he would not see how she felt, how much it had all meant to her.

In a voice devoid of emotion, he said, "I saved some hot water, if you want to take a shower. There are towels in the closet."

"Thank you," she said politely, and was proud of the steady sound of her voice.

In the tiny pine-paneled room, Anna was glad of the chance to wash the night from her, wash away the sweat and the stickiness of lovemaking, wash the scent of wood smoke out of her hair and the taste of Tyler's kisses from her mouth. When she emerged, she was again just Anna, who had learned a valuable lesson about lost princes.

When she came out, the long main room had been restored to perfect order: the bed made with its brightly colored Pendleton blanket, the couch cushions straightened and the quilt from Curtis's room evidently returned. Even the dishes had been washed and were draining in a wooden rack on the counter. Tyler was nowhere to be seen.

The light was different now. Since her arrival, the skies had been dark and overcast. Now bright sunlight streamed through the windows, giving the room an entirely changed mood. No longer enchanted, just a simple, comfortable room where a man lived with his son.

The emptiness in her belly felt like the last day of camp. She'd gone every summer to a camp in the Adirondacks, and every year the last day of camp, with the mattresses stripped and the fires dead and the meadows where they'd sung songs all empty, had been a misery to her. There had always been a sense of precious things forever lost, things only lightly touched again when the photos came back.

But then, as now, there was nothing to be done. The idyll was over. This time she didn't even have pictures to remember, only the memories she'd tucked carefully into a secret box in her mind, to be reviewed later, when it wasn't all so raw and strange.

She picked an apple out of a bowl and bit into it, looking out the kitchen window. The house butted so close to the forest that there was no view of sky and mountain, as there would be from the front, only thick stands of old trees, their branches heavy with snow that sparkled in the bright sunlight penetrating in thin shafts through the dense growth. In summer they probably saw deer in that forest, she thought absently. Deer and raccoons and all sorts of other creatures. There would be blue columbines and those red bells and other wildflowers.

Now, into the snowy landscape, ran an exuberant dog— Charley, doing an awkward, bobbing leap into the trees after a stick. He dived after it joyously, coming up with his nose full of snow, the stick in his teeth.

And behind him came Tyler, laughing as she'd never seen him laugh. His long blond hair had been pulled back, and he looked vigorous, and healthy, and beautiful, as if the land itself had created him from sky and sunlight and the fast-running crystal waters. In response, her heart squeezed hard. He *was* a prince, she thought wistfully, a prince of the mountain.

Wistfully, she touched her messy black curls and remembered she was after all only a peasant from below, who'd wandered into his realm by mistake, and been given one enchanted night to love him. She'd touched the magic that was Tyler.

A vision of taking his angled, sober, hungry face into her hands and kissing him sweetly floated over her eyes, and another, of him pausing to look at her in perplexity and wonder and pleasure. Watching him dance in the snow with his dog, laughing as he never did with people, Anna realized she had touched him with magic of her own. The enchantment had come from her. She had been given a bittersweet gift, but she'd given one, as well.

The knowledge eased the thick sorrow she felt, and she tossed the apple core into a bag of trash. There had been magic afoot, but it wasn't hers to know what purpose it had served, and it would be churlish to ask for more than she'd been given.

But she paused, watching him through the window. "I think I love you, Tyler Forrest," she said aloud. Then she set about the practical business of getting ready to go.

Back to reality.

Tyler and Charley drove her down to her Jeep. The cellular phone was working again, and Tyler had called down to his mother to let her know he was going to fetch his son in a few hours. He told Anna he'd feel better following her down anyway, in case there were any problems.

Anna was anxious to get back home. Tyler had not spoken more than the absolutely essential words since they awakened this morning. He didn't look at her, or make polite conversation, or anything else. The awkwardness was driving her crazy.

The Jeep was parked right where she'd left it, a few feet away from what had been an avalanche. A bulldozer was still working on the lower levels, but a path through the tons of earth and snow and tree branches had been cleared.

Tyler whistled softly. "You're damned lucky you didn't get caught in that."

"Tell me about it." She scowled. "I'm not sure I'm

crazy about driving through that little tunnel, either. Is it safe, do you think?''

"You'll be fine. That's what all-terrain vehicles are all about.''

She pushed the door open. "Okay, then.''

"Anna.''

A sword of anticipation and worry went through her chest. She looked back.

Tyler looked at her very soberly, his pale eyes full of emotion. "I—'' He shook his head. He reached out and touched her cheek, very gently, with the backs of his fingers. She saw him swallow. "Drive carefully.''

"Tell your mother I'll see her tomorrow at work,'' she said, and got out, closing the door gently behind her. As if this were all perfectly normal, she lifted a hand in a casual farewell and climbed into her own truck. It started immediately, and Anna left it running while she cleared the windows of snow and shoved nearly a foot of snow off the hood.

Then there was nothing to do but climb in, and drive down the mountain. It didn't seem to take very long, and when they reached the main byway through town, Anna felt one more clutch of sorrow as Tyler turned one way and she turned another.

It was done.

Louise Forrest was dispensing chocolate chip cookies to her grandsons, Curtis and Cody, when Tyler arrived. In a fine fury, by the look of him as he stormed up the driveway. Smiling secretly, she put the cookies away and composed her face before he reached the door. "Curtis, baby, your daddy is here.''

"Oh, boy!'' The child jumped down and ran toward the door, hurtling into his father's arms the instant he walked in. "Daddy! I mithed you! Do you got my bear?''

Tyler growled. "I'm a bear," he said, and chomped playfully at the boy's shoulder. "Will I do?"

"No, my real bear!"

"Well, no, I didn't bring it, Curtis. I thought you were coming home with me. Aren't you?"

Curtis looked over his shoulder. "Gramma. You were thuppothed to tell him."

Tyler looked at Louise guardedly. "What?"

"Tamara and Lance have to go to Denver, and I told them I'd keep Cody for the weekend. Curtis wants to stay and camp in the basement. Remember how you boys used to love that?"

A dark flicker crossed Tyler's face, and she could see that he wanted the boy home with him. "I don't know—"

"Oh, Tyler Forrest, where is your sense of childhood? Honestly, neither one of these boys has a playmate, and they get lonely."

"Yeah, Daddy," Curtis said guilelessly, putting his hands on his father's face.

"Me, too," Tyler said.

"But you can't be lonely now," Curtis said. "Miss Anna came to play with you through the whole blizzard."

Louise stifled a guffaw at that, but not quickly enough. Hot color rushed into Tyler's face, and seeing it, Louise wanted to run into the privacy of the kitchen to do a little victory dance.

She restrained herself as Tyler put Curtis down. "You can stay, but you boys go on and let me talk to your grandma for a minute."

"Yippee!" they cried, and ran off to the bedroom.

Louise met her son's eyes. The stain of his anger or embarrassment—or likely both—highlighted the finely crafted planes of his cheekbones, and she thought with a motherly sense of satisfaction that he was a very handsome man. All three of her boys were good-looking, of course, but where Lance was rakish and Jake dangerous, there was an air of romanticism about Tyler. "Come on in the kitchen," she said, taking the opening move. "I've got some dishes to wash right quick."

"Mother."

The word was autocratic. She raised her brows. "Yes?"

"What were you thinking?"

"About what?"

His eyes narrowed. "Don't play that game with me. I watched you set up Jake, and watched him take that fall, and you may have been right to do it, because I see my brother is a much happier man." His mouth hardened. "But don't you dare try matchmaking me again, do you understand?"

Louise sobered at the genuine anger in his voice. "Tyler, I wasn't trying to matchmake you, just trying to help you see that your world doesn't have to be so isolated."

He looked down, and she had a sense of a struggle coming from him, as hot and wild as she could have hoped for, but she also sensed that she might have been wrong this time. His jaw went hard after a moment, and his eyes were hard crystal points when he raised his gaze. "Mama, she's a nice girl, but that's a heart that could be shattered into a million pieces. Is that what you want?"

Louise thought of the exuberant young woman who had brought so much zest into her life in the past few months. "No, son," she said quietly, and sank down into a chair. "That isn't what I want at all."

"Then stay out of it." His control wavered, and Louise saw a bright, hot pain flash in his eyes before he cloaked himself again in stoicism. "Just mind your own business."

"I'm sorry, Tyler," she said sincerely.

He sighed, then relented and kissed her head. "I know. I'll see you Monday, I guess."

Before he could go, however, Louise had to ask. "Is she okay?"

He looked away, and on the flesh of his neck, Louise

saw what his collar had hidden until now, the dark bruising made only in passion. "I don't honestly know," he said in a soft voice.

Pretending she had seen nothing, Louise nodded. "She's a lot stronger than she looks, kiddo. Trust me."

She watched as he made his way back to his truck, feeling a curious mixture of hope and worry at the uncommon disturbance surrounding her son. He'd genuinely loved his wife, and if Louise had always thought Kara a bit too shallow and controlling to be a good wife to Tyler, it had only been her own opinion and hadn't changed the way he'd felt about her. His grief had been acute and deep, and Louise had always suspected that it was only for Curtis that Tyler hadn't given up and followed the woman to the grave.

Thank God.

But his loneliness had begun to eat at her the past year. He likely didn't even know it showed, the way he watched his brothers with their wives, the way he sat off by himself at gatherings. She thought of him, all alone at night, so far from female companionship, and felt sad for him.

Anna had never admitted her crush on Tyler, but Louise wasn't blind. The girl's eyes shone like diamonds when her son appeared. And Louise had not missed the restlessness Ty showed when Anna was around. He couldn't sit still. He paced and prowled and growled like some cornered forest creature, and Louise had thought it was a very good thing. He was attracted to the vibrance of the exuberant Anna.

Biting her lip, Louise wondered if she'd been wrong. Anna would pay the price for this matchmaking attempt, not Louise. Louise had only wanted to give Tyler a chance, to let him find out he was still really alive, but she hadn't stopped to imagine what the consequences of failing would be.

For Anna. Louise had not thought enough about poor Anna.

Chapter 9

Winter in the mountains was long, and as much as she enjoyed it, by the end of January, Anna was beginning to weary of it. They would not see real spring until almost May, and the thought depressed her. Worse than the snows and the long, gloomy nights were the falsely bright January days that brought skiers to town in droves, crowding restaurants and the streets and even the grocery store, where Anna had to wait in line for what seemed like hours even when she ran in for a gallon of milk.

She supposed it was self-defense that made her so sleepy. Like a bear, she would just hibernate the rest of the season. For a week now, she'd been slow to awaken, lost in a thick dream world where flowers bobbed on the high slopes and the skiers had mercifully departed until next season.

One morning she overslept, never even stirring when the alarm went off. Only heaven knew how long she would have drifted in that sunny, narcotically spring-scented world if the phone had not awakened her.

"Anna?" It was Louise, and for a long, long minute, Anna couldn't seem to drag herself close enough to the real world to even speak. She nodded, blinking, then realized Louise couldn't see her.

"Honey, did I wake you up? Do you know what time it is?"

She looked at the clock. As if splashed with water, she sat straight up, remembering that it was Saturday, and in exactly one hour and forty-five minutes a special living-history presentation would begin at the museum. Anna had about twenty stops to make between now and then.

"I'm up," she said. "I'm sorry, I overslept. I'll be by in twenty minutes for the baked goods. Are they ready?"

"Do you want me to have someone else come fetch them? Or I can take them down in about an hour, if that would be easier. The last bit of peanut brittle is almost done, but I can't leave it."

Anna tossed her hair out of her eyes. "No," she said. "I'll just jump in the shower and be there in a minute."

"Are you all right?"

Anna laughed bemusedly. "I feel great, except I sleep like a hibernating bear."

"You'll feel better when spring comes." Louise paused. "You aren't going to run off on me like all the rest of them, are you? You will get used to the winter here in time."

Anna smiled. "I have no intention of going anywhere, Louise. I signed a contract for three years, and I won't leave you. I'll get used to it—or at least learn to live with it."

"You will. We all get the blues this time of year. Trust me, if an old Texan girl could get used to it, it'll be a piece of cake for a New Yorker."

"I will, Louise. Don't worry. I'll be there in fifteen minutes."

She raced through her shower, and left her hair to do

its wild curl bit on her shoulders, without bothering with a barrette. She didn't have to be dressed professionally, since she would change into a costume when she arrived at the museum, and it was a good thing, since nothing fit. Her appetite had also increased—as if she really were going into hibernation, she was ravenous all day long. She hadn't checked the actual gain on a scale, but by the fit of her clothes, she'd put on about ten pounds in a couple of months. At this rate, she'd be as *big* as a bear by spring. She scowled and resolved to pay attention to what she put in her mouth from now on.

Naturally, because she was running so late this morning, the one bra that was still relatively comfortable broke a strap when she put it on, and she had to squeeze herself into another one that she hated, not only for the strangling fit, but also for a weird thread problem that always irritated her skin. Her good jeans were in the laundry, and she had to toss through the drawers looking for another pair that would still button.

At least her red sweater was clean, and it loaned her enough color that she could get away without makeup, which saved another ten minutes. Scrambling through the cupboards, she found half a sleeve of pecan sandies and two apples. The fridge was even worse—a chunk of cheese and a bottle of lemonade.

She'd start paying attention to her diet tomorrow, she thought, and grabbed everything and tossed it all into a canvas bag. Taking the list of errands from the bulletin board on the wall, she hit the Jeep at a run, her boots squeaking on the frozen snow in her yard.

In spite of the irritating need to rush, once she got outside, her spirits soared. It was a crisp, cold day, the sky blazing with bright morning sunlight that made of the mountains an elegant blue-and-white tapestry strung across the horizon.

She ate as she drove, gobbling most of the cookies and

all the cheese and the lemonade between trips to the bank, the cleaners and the house of an elderly docent who had made three costumes for the volunteers. She ate one of the apples on the way up the hill to Louise's palatial home.

As she parked, she caught sight of Tyler's blue pickup, and her heart sank. She'd managed very nicely to avoid him over the past couple of months, but in a town this small, and especially considering that he was the son of a good friend of hers, there was no avoiding him forever. She'd known that, but it still made her feel oddly queasy to think of actually seeing him again.

Steeling herself, she got out of the Jeep. Curtis, blond and getting lanky, appeared on the front porch. "Miss Anna!" he cried, and tumbled down the steps to fling himself into her arms.

His happiness touched her, and Anna knelt to his level to grab him and give him a big hug. "Good morning, Curtis! Did you come to town for the living history?"

"Yep. I got a raccoon hat and everything."

She chuckled. "Well, if you come by where I'm working, I'll let you churn butter. You want?"

"Sure!"

Out of the corner of her eye, Anna saw Tyler come out of the house. Instantly, her stomach tightened, and her heart flipped. He looked so good, straight and tall and beautiful in the morning light, his mage's eyes so clear and deep and unreadable. For the most fleeting of seconds, she thought she glimpsed the same upset and hunger in his eyes that she felt, but then her stomach roiled violently.

Urgently.

"Excuse me," she said, almost dropping Curtis. She raced by Tyler and into the house, and barely made it to the bathroom before losing the entire contents of her stomach in a quick, violent rush.

"Jeez, girl," she said to herself. "Could you be any more dramatic?" She bent over the sink to rinse her mouth and face, touching her forehead to see if she might have picked up a flu bug or something. Nothing but cool flesh. And the truth was, her stomach felt fine now. Too much junk food.

She straightened, using her wet hands to tame a few wild black curls back into place. And for the first time in days, she really *saw* herself. The red sweater made her skin practically glow, even without makeup, and her eyes were as clear and bright as a child's. All that sleep had made her look about five years younger than she was and the extra weight didn't disagree with her.

In fact—she yanked at the neckline of the simple scoop neck of the sweater, scowling at the surprising amount of curvy flesh spilling over the neckline—she looked amazingly voluptuous. She scowled, trying to cover the tops of her breasts decently. She was going to look like the town prostitute in her costume, with its square neckline.

It must be the wretched, uncomfortable bra that had rearranged her curves like this, because heaven knew she'd never, ever had cleavage. Not in all her life—

Knowledge fell on her.

"Oh, my God," she breathed, staring at her vivid coloring, the lushness of breasts, the red of her lips. With a hand that suddenly trembled, she touched her breasts, then her belly, thinking back.

There was a joke in her family that the women never grew real breasts until they had a baby who needed them. They were all skinny and rather slimly built until they had children. Anna had seen her sisters go from girls to voluptuous women, one after the other.

And more than that, they had all been dazzling. Her father joked that he'd made Anna's mother pregnant so often because she was so extraordinarily beautiful when she carried a child. One of Anna's cousins, pregnant at sixteen out of wedlock, had been able to hide everything about her condition except that extraordinary Madonna glow.

"Oh, my God," she said again. It was impossible, but it was a fact.

"Anna!" Tyler knocked on the door, hard. "Are you all right?"

She closed her eyes and took a breath, then yanked open the door. "I'm fine," she said, tossing her hair from her face to look up at him. "Just pregnant."

Tyler stared down at her, fighting waves of furious desire. When she stepped out of her truck wearing that red sweater, her black hair loose and tumbling around her face, he'd been assailed by a vision of storming across the yard, and taking her there on the hood of the car, right there, right now. It appalled him. He didn't feel like this about women.

Not even Kara.

He hated her for it. Hated the surge of bone-deep yearning he felt now, looking at her up close, close to that devourable mouth, the sparkling black eyes, the smell of her hair and her flesh that made him remember all kinds of things he was trying to forget. He stared down at her blankly, until the words finally penetrated. "What?"

She pushed by him. "You heard me. I think maybe that doctor of yours didn't do such a great job."

"What?" He grabbed her arm, having trouble working his mind around to what those words meant. "You're pregnant?"

She sighed. "I'm as surprised as you are. I haven't had a test, but I can tell you it's for sure."

"Wait. You mean it's *mine?*"

"Tyler, I'm late. I have to go." She pulled away. "We'll talk later."

"Damn it, Anna, talk to me. This is impossible."

"Not impossible. It happens, you know." She backed away. "I'm sorry, I have to go right now."

She rushed out, leaving Tyler staring after her in stunned bewilderment.

His mother rushed past him. "Anna, don't forget the brittle!" she cried, carrying the neatly wrapped plate. She gave it to Anna, who took it and bolted.

Louise came back through the hallway, wiping her hands on her apron. He could tell by her expression that she'd heard the whole exchange, but she didn't say a word, only looked at him.

"Is that possible?" he finally asked.

"That she's pregnant?"

"No, that it's mine." He couldn't work his mind around the revelation. "I had a vasectomy. I thought—"

Louise narrowed her eyes. The cornflower-blue irises glinted dangerously. "If you're telling me you slept with her and she's pregnant and you're not sure if it's yours, then you'd better get yourself to a doctor and have them run one of those tests to check your sperm count. Because if you didn't do it, it's an immaculate conception, and while I think she's a fine woman, I don't think she's quite ready for sainthood."

Tyler flushed, in anger and confusion and embarrassment. A man didn't talk about things like this with his mother, for Pete's sake. "I didn't mean I doubted her. I just didn't know that it could happen."

"You had a vasectomy, son?"

He nodded.

"When Kara got pregnant, I suppose." She sighed and put her hand on his arm. "I'm sorry. I wish you'd told me. It would have made things make a lot more sense."

"What things, Mama?" He turned away. "Kara's desperation to have Curtis, maybe?"

"Your guilt," she said simply. "Come on in here and

sit down. Let's have a cup of tea and talk for just a minute.''

"No." The word came out harshly. He took a breath. "It's not you. I just need to think about this." He shook his head. "Do you see what happens when you butt in where you don't belong, Mama? Will you please stay out of other people's lives?''

That hurt her. Tyler saw the shine of tears in her eyes before she turned away, lifting her chin. "I was wrong," she said. "I'm sorry." She looked at him. "If there's anything I can do to help put things right, just say the word.''

"Ah, damn." The wounded expression in her eyes made him bend down and hug her close. "What am I going to do?''

She squeezed him tight and pulled back to press a kiss to his cheek. "You'll work it out, son. I have faith in you.''

"Can Curtis go with you to the museum for a little while? I need to do a couple of things. I can pick him up in a hour, two at the most.''

"Sure. You know where the booth is. I'll be there all afternoon.''

"Thanks.''

From a corner of the dining room where they stood, Curtis piped up, "Miss Anna's going to have a baby?''

Tyler looked at his son blankly. He hadn't realized the boy had been anywhere around, and even if he'd realized it, he wouldn't have expected Curtis to know what *pregnant* meant. "How do you know what that means, kiddo?''

"Cody's kitty got pregnant and she had babies.''

Of course. The kittens had been the center of Cody's life for weeks now. "Well, Miss Anna isn't going to have kittens.''

Curtis rolled his eyes. "I *know*. She hath to have a real baby. Like Auntie Ramona.''

"What?" Tyler looked to his mother for confirmation.

"I was going to tell you. She just confirmed it. She's due in September."

A curious pluck of sorrow struck Tyler's chest, plaintive and sad. And as if he felt it, too, Curtis said wistfully, "I wish Miss Anna was my mommy."

A hundred responses rose to Tyler's lips, but he didn't dare utter a single one of them. "Well, she's not, so you'll have to make do with Grandma." Ruffling his son's hair, he said, "Be good. I'll see you in a little while."

He went straight to the clinic. Before anything else could be decided, he had to know the physical facts.

So early on a festival day, there was no one in the clinic, and Tyler found Ramona filling out forms at the front desk. Her abundant hair was swept into a loose knot on top of her head, and as she glanced up, her spectacles slipped down on her nose. "Hi, Tyler!" she said with a smile. "How are you?"

"I'm not sure," he said honestly. "But I hear congratulations are in order."

An expression of almost blissful happiness crossed her face, an expression so ripe it made Tyler want to sit down and weep. "Yes. I've had my tests, so we know it's going to be a boy. Jake is over the moon."

Tyler hugged her, and gave her tummy a little pat. "I guess you're going to name him for me, huh?"

She chuckled. "Lance said the exact same thing." She took off her glasses. "I have a feeling this isn't a social call, however. Is there something wrong?"

"Yeah." He frowned. "No. I mean, I don't know."

With the gentle touch that made her so beloved by her patients, Ramona gently guided him to a chair. "Tell me about it."

He hated this stuff. It embarrassed him. He hated going to the doctor, hated having to discuss anything with people who poked and prodded. He especially hated discussing something so intensely private. "I had a vasectomy when Kara was pregnant."

"I remember," she said, smiling. She'd made the referral to a doctor in Denver.

"Can they come undone?"

Ramona said nothing for a moment, and Tyler saw that he'd managed to surprise her. Questions rose in the dark brown eyes, but she said mildly, "Yes, unfortunately, it does happen. Do you have reason to believe that has happened to you?"

He laced his fingers together. "Yeah."

"Only one way to find out. I need a sample."

He blushed to his toes. "Oh, God."

Lightly, Ramona laughed, and put a container into his hand. "I'm a doctor, Tyler. I won't tell." She rubbed his shoulder for a minute. "You know the drill. The sooner you get it done, the sooner we'll know."

Mortified, he simply sat there, heat radiating in red waves up his face and over his ears. Ramona pushed him gently. "If you're a good patient, I'll give you a lollipop."

He sighed, a reluctant smile on his mouth. "Do you have any chocolate ones?"

She plucked a round brown sucker from the dish on the desk and held it up.

"Okay." Tyler rolled his eyes and went into the examining room and closed the door.

Anna managed to make it through the day without having a panic attack. On the way home, she stopped at the grocery store and bought a home pregnancy test. It told her what she already knew. She was pregnant.

Her apartment took up the second floor of an historic Victorian house, part of the employment package offered the curator of the museum, since housing was at such a premium in the valley. Her rent was far below market rate, and she loved the charming rooms, with their old-fashioned wallpaper, the claw-footed bathtub, even the quaint, small kitchen. Most of all, she loved the long windows overlooking the splendor of the valley on one side, a view of treetops on another, the mountains on the other.

Tonight, she stood in the living room, leaning against the wall to look at the mountains. Where Tyler lived in the woodcutter's cottage, where enchantment had stolen over them and left her with a child.

It would make a nice fairy tale, but the truth was, Anna was frightened. Her mind whirled with a dozen different considerations—how she would be able to provide for the baby, how it would change her career aspirations, how Tyler was going to react and how much he would want to participate in the child's life.

A part of her felt exuberant and excited and dizzy with happiness. Sipping her tea, she smiled and put her hand on her still-flat belly, imagining a child with his blood, with that noble beauty on its face. And she loved children; she'd always wanted some of her own. It wasn't as if she were some young, naive girl with no options. She was well educated and established in her career, and there was no reason she could not simply raise the baby by herself, as millions of other single women had done. She trusted her ability to be a good parent. She'd had very good training, after all.

And that was the biggest problem of all. She felt tonight an unexpected need to run home to the bosom of her family. She ached to cry on her mother's shoulder, and have her grandmother cook something sinful and cluck over the ways of the modern world. She wanted her sisters to be exclaiming over the blessed event and offering herbal potions that kept their morning sickness at bay, and give her tips on everything from drugs to breast-feeding. She didn't know how she could bear to go through this alone.

But she also could not bear the thought of leaving Colorado. Not after so long a time trying to get here, not after all her dreams and scheming had finally paid off. The idea of leaving now gave her a physical pain, as if some part of her body had become rooted.

The phone rang, and Anna answered it without much energy. To her great relief, it was her sister Mary Frances, calling to chat and complain and gossip. Jack had been caught with another woman, and his wife was divorcing him; Teresa's teenagers were driving her crazy; Catherine was going to have another baby. "You'd think she had enough, already!" Mary Frances exclaimed with a snort.

Anna smiled. Mary Frances had always prized her attractiveness above all things, and had stopped with one daughter, who was as prissy and pretty as her mother. "She loves them. She's a good mother." A pang arrowed through her. If she went home, she could share her pregnancy with her sister. "When is she due?"

"Thanksgiving. You could come home for a visit then, maybe."

"That might be a good time, actually. Or Christmas." Little did they know what she'd be bringing with her. The thought gave her a chuckle, which she swallowed.

"Jack is in so much trouble, he's threatening to move out there with you."

"That would be nice." One or another of them was always threatening to come to Colorado. None of them had yet. If it was Jack, at least he'd keep her secrets.

Mary Frances talked a little longer, then hurried off the phone to greet her husband, just home from work. Anna sat beside the telephone, feeling blue and lonely. She desperately wanted someone to talk to, but the only person in town that she would feel comfortable spilling her guts to was, unfortunately, the mother of the man who had made her pregnant. Awkward, to say the least.

Her stomach growled and, with a chuckle, Anna headed for the kitchen. At least she knew why she was so hungry all the time lately. "Come on, kid," she said aloud. "Let's go get something to eat. I'm thinking a pastrami sandwich."

Louise cooked when she was upset. By the time Alonzo came home from work that night, there were piles of fried chicken, a huge vat of potato salad, enough brownies for an army, and her special green beans with bacon.

Alonzo took off his hat, hung it on a hook and sat down at the table. "Do you wish to tell me what tragedy made all this food appear?"

Until that moment, Louise had managed to remain calm, but the simple sound of the man she was falling in love with unraveled her calm. She put her hands on the counter, bowed her head and burst into tears. "I've made such a mess of things."

Gently he stood up and rubbed a hand on her back. It was an awkward, but welcome, gesture of comfort. "Tell me."

Haltingly, she spilled the small duplicity she had practiced when she sent Anna to the mountain, knowing the storm would likely trap her there. "Now she's pregnant, Tyler's furious, and poor Anna is going to pay the price. In other words, I was just being my usual busybody self, and may have ruined three lives in the bargain."

"I told you this would happen," he said, shaking his head. "You can't do this."

"Thank you," Louise said with a scowl. "That's very comforting."

"Ah." His eyes narrowed. "Now you can't fix it, and you want somebody to tell you it is okay. I'm not gonna do it, Louise. You have to learn a lesson now. Now you have to do what you can to make it right."

"What can I do? The die has been cast."

He took his hat from the hook. "Stop cooking and start

thinking,'' he said. ''I am going to my house now. This makes me mad at you, and I don't want to fight.''

Stunned, Louise watched him go. Then she clamped her mouth shut. Fine. He was just like all the rest. He could just eat in his own house forever, for all she cared.

Chapter 10

Even after the sandwich, Anna felt guilty and sad and alone. Finally, she put on a skirt and a warm coat and walked to the small Catholic church downtown. It was a satisfyingly old place, built in the Spanish mission style, and she loved it. The congregation was small, but devout, and had welcomed her warmly upon her arrival.

The doors were always open, unlike those of many of the churches in cities now, and Anna let herself in quietly. The floors were clay tiles, and could not hide her footsteps, and although there was only one other person in the small nave, she did not want to disturb anyone. She slipped into a pew near the middle and knelt.

Somehow it helped just being here, smelling the incense and candle wax and the church smell that she could never quite identify—mothballs and dust and cleaning products. She had felt a particular love for this church from the beginning, with its Spanish art and the stylized santos and the brightly embroidered altar cloths.

Quietly she bent her head and just let the sense of peace

invade her. The saints had answered her prayers before. Tonight she would only ask guidance. The courage to do the right things for her child, and the wisdom to make good decisions.

She heard the sound of footsteps, but did not look up until a voice said softly, "*Señorita,* may I sit with you a minute?"

Anna recognized Alonzo's voice. "Yes," she said, "of course."

The Mexican adobe maker slid in beside her. "We all come to the church when we are sad, no?" he said, folding his hands in his lap. "Tonight, I was very angry and spoke harshly and wounded a woman I love very much, even though she cannot seem to accept me."

Anna smiled, knowing he meant Louise. "All in good time."

"You know why I'm mad at her? Because she won't mind her own business, and now somebody is going to be hurt, no?"

Ashamed that he knew her secret, Anna lowered her eyes. Suddenly, the mortification of finding herself in such a situation flooded through her, and she felt tears spring unbidden to her eyes. "I shouldn't have done it. I knew better. It was my own fault."

Alonzo took her hand. "Ah, *hija,* there is no shame in loving, eh? And now this new life will come in the world, and maybe make you happy."

His gnarled brown hand was strong around hers, and she clutched it back, nodding, but unable to stop the tears. "I keep thinking of my family. If my grandmother knew, she would be so angry with me."

"They're far away, no?"

"New York."

"Are you going home?"

Anna lifted her head, the answer plain. "I really don't want to. I love this place. I've worked so hard to come here, to live in Colorado, and it would be crushing to have to admit I couldn't do it after all.''

His fingers squeezed hers. "Tell you what. My children, they are far away, too. Grown up, and they no need some old man tellin' them nothing.'' The warm brown eyes twinkled. ''You need anythin', you come to Alonzo, okay?''

New tears welled in her throat, but she nodded.

He winked. "Tell you something else,'' he said. "Mad as I am at that woman, she don't have no daughters, and she feels real bad. We'll take care of you, okay?''

Impulsively, Anna kissed his cheek. "Thank you.''

"Now let me walk you home. It's not far, no? And a mama needs her sleep.''

For several days, Tyler felt frozen. He went through the motions of his days without thinking, as if someone had hit a pause button in his brain. He'd surface suddenly to find himself doing something automatically and wonder how he'd gotten there.

The results of the humiliating test were positive: His vasectomy had indeed failed or grown back or whatever it was they did. It gave him a deeply unsettled sense of lost chances. If Kara had not known of his vasectomy, would she have been less likely to ignore the developing problems in her pregnancy with Curtis? Maybe they would have had another chance, maybe things would have turned out differently if—

But if anything was different, Tyler would not now have Curtis. Untenable.

Three days after the shocking revelation, Tyler crept into Curtis's room late at night, and settled quietly by the wall, watching the child sleep in the soft orange glow of the stove. Curtis slept in his nest of thick quilts, only his blond head and the top half of his face showing.

Even Tyler could acknowledge how much the child resembled him—although Lance repeatedly commented on how much Cody acted like Tyler as a child. Both boys were Forrests through and through. Even when Tyler looked hard, he couldn't find a trace of Kara, except in the boy's tidy nature. He liked things to have a place, and all those things to be in those places, just as Kara had.

As he watched, Curtis stirred and turned to his back, flinging one small arm out of the covers, clutching his stuffed bear close to his chest, and Tyler remembered what he'd said.

I wish Miss Anna was my mommy.

Tyler had seen the way Anna interacted with children. She was natural and easy and calm with them, but she wasn't afraid of discipline, either. More than once, he'd chanced upon her cuddled up in some corner with Curtis on her lap, telling some story in her accented voice. And Curtis hung on her every word, his big blue eyes shining, his face showing his besotted adoration of her. Tyler remembered the way Curtis had hurled himself off the porch at Louise's house, right into Anna's arms. Without missing a beat, she'd knelt to catch him.

Tyler rubbed his face. Curtis had never had a mother, so Tyler had assumed he didn't miss it. It made him feel a little jealous that he hadn't been enough, that no matter what, Curtis still wanted a mother. Like other boys had.

Quietly, Tyler moved to the bed and pressed a kiss to his son's clear, untroubled forehead. Curtis smelled of soap and milk and the baby lotion Tyler still rubbed on the skin that was so sensitive to the dry climate, and the smell went right to his gut. Rocking back on his heels, he let his gaze touch the fan of lashes on the round cheeks, the rosy little mouth, the impossibly fine blond hair.

Waves of love washed through him. It was so easy to love his son. So uncomplicated and straightforward and rewarding. Nothing in his experience had ever come close to equaling it.

With a pang, he thought of the baby Anna carried, a baby he might not ever know, or hold, or have a chance to love. He wondered how the combination of genes between them would work—Tyler was so fair, Anna so dark. Likely it would be dark, like Anna. With her rosy cheeks. He thought of it, a daughter with her apple cheeks and sunny nature, a sister for Curtis.

And into his unguarded mind crept a memory of Anna herself, lying in this very bed, his too-big shirt slipping off her shoulder, her glossy hair spilling around her face.

A fist twisted his gut. He had betrayed himself, and Kara's memory, and Anna, by allowing his lust to overtake him that weekend. There were reasons a man didn't indulge in such casual affairs—because there was nothing casual about that kind of joining. At least not for him.

And there were consequences. Consequences that mainly fell upon Anna, and that made him feel sick.

He had to stop avoiding the situation and at least let her know he acknowledged responsibility. He would see to it that she was well cared for, that her child wanted for nothing.

It wasn't enough, but it was all he could do. Maybe he could talk her into at least staying in Colorado, so that he would be able to see the baby sometimes.

The next day he went to see Anna at the museum. He still had no idea what he was going to say. It just seemed that the only honorable thing to do was just go talk to her. Acknowledge his part in her dilemma.

Their dilemma.

It was a quiet morning. A volunteer docent with a string of pearls around her neck and a forthright manner waved him toward the back of the kitchen of the old house. "Just go on back, honey. She's doing some paperwork."

His feet made no sound on the elegant runner down the hallway, and Tyler was able to steady himself for a moment outside her open door. He paused, taking in a breath, and stepped forward one more step until he could see the office, and Anna, beyond the open door.

It was a small room and, unlike the rest of the museum, a little shabby. Once it had likely been a servant's dining room, or perhaps a storage room, for the plaster walls were unadorned and the floor was ordinary pine planks. With his carpenter's eye, he noticed that the sashes and window frames were plain.

But Anna had not left it so. He almost smiled at the gypsy splash she'd made in the room. A gossamer lavender scarf was draped over the shade of an ancient, ugly floor lamp. A giant travel poster of the Rockies at sunset covered one wall, and pillows in dazzling combinations of red, purple, green and blue covered the aging horsehair sofa, along with a silk shawl, complete with fringes. The bookshelves were crammed full, and on the only remaining wall were dozens of photos. Probably her family, he decided. A handsome, swarthy lot, with striking eyes and lovely hair.

Anna had not yet seen him. She sat behind her desk, scribbling, her cheek resting on her hand. She scowled, crossed something out, consulted a calendar and wrote again. Her black curls were swept into a loose knot at the back of her head, but the riotous mass would not be confined so easily, and curls sprung out at her neck, forehead and temple, giving her an appealingly feminine look.

Although he tried not to do it, he found his gaze on her red, red mouth, that lush and sensual mouth that had given and taken so much pleasure, and felt the predictable stirring in his loins, a heat that spread through his groin and thighs, up to his chest, before he forced himself to glance away, think of other things.

Like the baby she was carrying.

He stepped into the doorway and knocked on the threshold. "Anna, can I talk to you a minute?"

She started visibly, dropping her pencil with a soft
"Oh!" Her startled gaze flew up to meet his, and for one
long, breathless second, Tyler swayed dizzily in the luminous depths of those black eyes. "Tyler," she said.
"You scared me. Come in."

He took a step, but paused. There was not a single clear
space for him to sit. The chairs and long couch were piled
with papers, and Anna jumped up, hurrying around to
move them. "Sorry. I'm a slob, I'm afraid. Just let me
take these, um, papers and things and—" she looked
around for a place to put them "—you can have that chair.
Go ahead," she said, a little breathlessly, when he didn't
move. "Sit down."

He stood there, noticing the soft blush painting her
cheeks, noticing the trembling of her hands and the way
she was trying to pretend it was all perfectly normal, and
something in his heart twisted hard. He sat in the chair
she'd vacated and laced his fingers together, waiting while
she dumped the papers on the floor and scurried back behind the desk. "Anna, I just came to—" What? He
frowned. "I just thought we should at least talk."

"Oh, Tyler." Her voice was pained. "I really don't
want to do this. You don't owe me anything. It just is. It's
just one of those things." She took a breath. "I shouldn't
have been there. I shouldn't have said yes. I shouldn't
have... I should have... I don't know. It's just not your
problem, okay? I can handle it. I'm not a teenager. I'm a
full-grown woman with plenty of support and a good education and lots of experience with children."

When she paused for another breath, he said quietly,
"Anna."

She looked at him, wary and too vulnerable, and Tyler
knew there was only one thing he could say to make this
right. It might be different if she were another sort of
woman, but she was a protected Catholic girl, a virgin until

that weekend, and he suspected the smoke screen of words only hid her very real fear and embarrassment.

"Anna," he said, "will you let me take care of you and the baby? It isn't your fault, or at least not yours alone. I will never be able to sleep nights, thinking of you trying to handle all of this by yourself."

She leaned forward. "Tyler, I don't want to cause you trouble, either. I really will be okay."

He met her gaze. "Anna," he said roughly, "will you marry me?"

"What?"

"You heard me." He found himself holding his breath, unsure of what he wanted her to say, how he wanted her to respond. Of course, she would refuse, but at least his conscience would be assuaged, and they could go on to the next step. Whatever it was.

She inclined her head, and he saw light and dark racing through her liquid eyes. She took a breath. "Yes."

A twist of cold and hot spun through him. "What?"

"Was it a false offer?" Furious heat raced into her face, and Tyler hated himself three times as much as he had when he came to the museum, because in some ways maybe it had been a false offer.

"No," he heard himself say. "I meant it. Curtis is the most important thing in my life, and I can't stand the idea of you taking my child away somewhere, where I'll never see it. I can't stand to think of you alone."

"And I," she said calmly, "am old-fashioned, and I'm ashamed to be single and pregnant. My father, if he knew, would kill me."

Tyler stared at her, his head roaring. Now what? "I think it should be done soon."

"Yes," she agreed. "Um…when is good for you?"

"It's not a business meeting, Anna."

"That's what it feels like. And in a way it is. Let's at least be honest." She squared her shoulders. "We don't know each other well enough to pretend it's anything but a business arrangement. At least now.''

He didn't feel businesslike. He felt hot and cold and confused, and because she'd asked for honesty, he said, "I didn't know I was going to ask you when I came in here. I don't know what the best thing is." He looked at her helplessly. "I don't know anything about this stuff. Do you?"

For the first time, she smiled. "Yes. We need a blood test, and a judge, since no priest is going to marry us this fast. Not even Father Garcia." She pulled out a piece of paper and scrawled "Wedding Details" over the top of it, then began to make a list. "You have to tell your family, and figure out all of that."

His family. Tyler's stomach fell to his feet. "I'll take care of my family. Do you want to call yours? Do we need to leave a little time for them to get here?"

"No!" Her answer was almost insultingly vehement. "I'm sorry to sound like that, but you just don't know the hassles they would bring." She rubbed her forehead. "I'll tell them when it's over and done with. They'll scream that it's not Catholic, and that you aren't Italian, and that their baby is thousands of miles away." She shook her head. "Trust me. This is easier."

"Will it bother you, not having a Catholic wedding?"

Anna fingered the end of her pencil without looking at him. "A little, I guess. I was raised to imagine that big white wedding, the mass and the big party and all of that." She lifted a shoulder. "But we really don't have time to wait. It would take six months."

"Oh." He hurt a little for her, thinking of what she would be giving up. "Later, then, we'll have a Catholic ceremony." He offered a small grin. "With a big white wedding dress, even, if you want."

She smiled. "It's okay." She frowned in sudden alarm.

''It does matter to me, Tyler, that the baby is baptized, and I want to take him to church.''

''I would never interfere with that.'' The thought of her taking the baby to church made him feel right about things, somehow, and made him realize he'd neglected Curtis's religious education entirely. Quietly, he said, ''Curtis will want to go, too, I'm sure.''

''How is he going to feel about this, Tyler? Have you thought of that?''

He met her gaze, and his throat felt suddenly tight. ''Curtis found out you were having a baby,'' he said quietly, ''and he said, 'I wish Miss Anna was my mommy.' That's a direct quote.''

Tears shone in Anna's eyes. ''Oh,'' she said, putting her hand over her mouth. ''I think that's the killer, Tyler. I'm sorry.''

''What do you mean?''

She stood up, and moved to the windowsill and plucked a huge wad of tissue from a box, her face turned away. ''I'm really emotional, and this has been a shock, and unless you want me blubbering all over you, you'd better go.''

Tyler hesitated. Maybe she would like it if he held her for a minute. But maybe she wanted to just be alone for a while. He stood up awkwardly. ''Can I call you this afternoon?''

She nodded, her face still turned away. ''Yes.''

''Maybe we can get things together for this weekend.''

''Okay.''

''I'll just go, then.'' He still felt torn, watching her try to pull herself together. ''Find out about blood tests, tell everybody.''

A tiny sound escaped her, and Tyler stared a moment longer, wishing he knew how to reach out. ''Anna. Are you okay? Are you sure you want to do this?''

''Yes, Tyler.'' She lifted her head, although she kept

her face toward the window. "I'm very sure. I just want you to go now, okay? Call me this afternoon."

Awkwardly, he reached out and patted her shoulder. "Okay," he said, and fled.

As soon as he left, Anna let herself collapse in a heap of pillows and really cry. They were tears of relief and sorrow and anxiety, tears of confusion—and even tears of happiness.

Whatever she expected when she looked up to see Tyler standing in her doorway, it had not been a proposal of marriage. And if it had come from any other man in the world, she would have refused without a second thought.

But she and Tyler were alike in one important way— they both had very old-fashioned values. In the old traditions, when a baby was made, the parents married in order to give it a home. And although it sometimes did not work as well as one would hope, sometimes it worked just fine. Marriages did not have to be founded on wild, passionate love. Mutual respect and similar values sometimes served as a much more stable base.

She had agreed to his proposal instinctively, but now that her emotional storm had passed, she knew it was the right thing to do. Her panic the past few days had risen to almost terrifying levels, and her options had seemed more and more limited. His offer was a lifeline.

And she had genuine faith it would be all right. Oh, not that they would ever fall madly in love, or that they would ever have the kind of marriage she had once dreamed of— a marriage like that of her parents, for example—but she knew she could trust Tyler Forrest to take care of her and the baby, that he was as solid and steady a man as God had ever made. He would also love the child they had made together.

The unexpected sweetness of being able to be a mother to Curtis made up for a lot. His need of a mother had plucked at her from the beginning, and to be able to grant his most passionate wish was worth almost anything.

Drying her eyes, Anna wondered why she still felt so sad. In a way, all her problems were solved. She would be able to remain in Colorado. She would not shame her family by returning to New York as an unwed mother. She would have a husband who was as reliable as the rising of the sun.

A man who did not love her. Who would never love her.

That was the only fly in the ointment, but it was a big, hairy horsefly. She was more than half in love with him now. It was hard to imagine how she would be able to keep herself aloof and apart from that emotion if she lived with him day in and day out. Or, more to the point, night in and night out.

A ripple of longing pulsed down her spine, and she shuddered.

Could she bear to marry a man she loved a little, and would no doubt love a lot someday, knowing he would never recover from the loss of his first wife? She was sensible enough to realize that a lot of what they were about to do—get married, go through a pregnancy and have a baby—would rouse painful ghosts for Tyler. Ghosts that might make him push her away, might make it impossible for him to be anything more than a figurehead of a husband.

If it came to that, could she bear it?

Anna honestly didn't know. The one comfort was that they would marry by civil ceremony. It might be her only way out, if it came to that. If she wed him in the church, it would have been impossible to break the vows.

With a sigh, she stood up and went back to her list. If they were going to marry this weekend, there was a lot that needed to be done. She could be practical when she had to be.

Chapter 11

They met to have blood tests and do the paperwork at the courthouse, and rather awkwardly got it all done. The woman behind the counter beamed at them, and chattered, and Anna felt extremely uncomfortable. When they were outside on the steps, her panic rose in her chest again, and she stopped dead. "Tyler, this is weird. I mean, it feels so strange. I don't know how to act or anything."

He said nothing for a minute. It was a cool, overcast day. By the look of the clouds, they would have snow by evening, and Anna shivered against the wind. She buried her chin in the collar of her coat, feeling as if nothing were real, that somehow she had stumbled into someone else's life.

Anna's grandmother had been a great believer in fate. Maybe Anna's stubborn insistence on coming to Colorado had somehow twisted her fate so that she really was living someone else's life. Maybe she was supposed to be back in Queens with some guy who—

Tyler took her hand. "Do you trust me, Anna?"

She frowned. "I don't know what you mean."

"Just what I said." His thumb moved over her knuckles, and somehow the contact was reassuring, soothing. "Do you trust me to do what I say I will?"

"Yes," she said simply.

"Good." His pale gray eyes never twinkled, but there was a softness in them now that Anna had not seen before. He lifted her hand to his lips and planted a chivalrous kiss on her wrist. "This is not the way weddings usually happen, but I want you to know that I will be a faithful, honorable husband to you. I'll do what I can to make you happy."

A lump rose in her throat. "I know."

"What I want you to do is this—go home and try to figure out how few of your things you can live with." His smile was rueful. "You'll have to either keep the apartment for a while or find storage for most of it until we have a chance to add a couple of rooms on to the cabin."

"But there's so much to be done!"

"Let me take care of everything else, okay? Let me do this."

Looking up into his beautiful face, with his hand clasped around hers so gently, Anna felt a swell of almost painful longing rise through her chest. "Okay," she said. "But if you need me, call me."

"I will." Sweetly, he touched her face. "I will see you again Saturday morning, then. Ten o'clock. My mother is going to come get you for the wedding, and we'll go to her house afterward."

She clutched his hand tightly. "Oh, Tyler, are you sure this is what you want to do?"

He sobered. "Yes."

Anna watched him walk away, so straight and noble, a strange feeling in the pit of her stomach. What was she doing? It seemed odd that they did not kiss.

Or maybe it wasn't odd. They seemed to be doing things

backward—sex, then marriage, then maybe someday love. Maybe.

Feeling panic welling, she took a long, slow, deep breath. The facts were still the facts. She could not face her family as an unwed mother, and she genuinely liked Tyler Forrest. If that was all it was, heaven knew she could do worse for a husband.

At any rate, her problems were solved for the moment, and she would just try not to borrow any trouble.

Tyler had not enjoyed himself so much in years as he did over the next three days. He told no one of his plans except Curtis, who gleefully accompanied him on all his errands. They drove to Denver on Thursday and spent the whole day shopping and planning, taking frequent breaks for snacks. Curtis actually ended up being an imaginative helper, suggesting a couple of things Tyler would never have thought of.

Anna was right, he thought, ruffling his son's hair after a particularly terrific addition. Curtis had the archetypes down pat.

Most of the shopping was for the wedding and the reception itself, but Tyler also went to a kitchen shop and a bath shop and a hardware store to find things he hoped might make Anna's transition to mountain living more comfortable. He worried about how she'd feel living at the cabin, with its electrical and plumbing limitations. If she got sick of it, she could always go down the mountain to Louise's house when she needed to. Hell, he'd done it himself.

For the first time in his life, he also actually enjoyed the feeling of spending money. Like his brothers, he'd inherited a staggering sum of money at his father's death, and he'd touched none of it. He didn't need to. His life-style was simple enough that it didn't require much cash outlay, and he earned a good living with the specialized carpentry he did.

In fact, as he pulled out cash for yet another purchase, he found himself grinning. Why hadn't he done this before?

The answer rippled through him. Kara. She had been almost religious about embracing an antimaterialistic lifestyle, a rebellion against her parents. He'd understood and respected her need for it, trusting that she'd eventually outgrow the need to eschew all material comforts. And he did mean all. She'd boiled coffee on the stove, and worn no makeup, and made shampoo from yucca root. They'd lived together most of his adult life, and Tyler had just fallen into the habit of doing without.

A twinge of guilt touched him. He hadn't even thought of Kara since this all started.

As if waiting in the wings for just such a moment, the demons howled out of the dark corners of his mind, making a mockery of his actions today. And a rush of searing guilt burned into his belly. The dark stain spread like malevolent weeds through his chest, into his throat—

"Oh, Daddy!" Curtis whispered, tugging his hand. "Look!"

He pointed to a scarf draped over a mannequin's dark head, a gossamer scarf with an embroidered gold edge, and tiny gold moons and stars scattered over it.

Curtis's happiness acted as a retardant on Tyler's spreading guilt. There were a living child and a living woman and another baby on the way to think about. His demons could wait. "You're right, kiddo," he said, and turned to the clerk. "Can we get that scarf, too?"

"Certainly, sir." She smiled flirtatiously. "She must be a very special woman."

Curtis answered. "Oh, she is. She's going to be my mommy." He looked at his dad for confirmation. "Isn't she?"

Tyler felt an unexpected rush of emotion. Curtis had no conflicts whatsoever about all of it, and the clear, full-throated joy of the child was worth a lot. "She sure is."

The clerk smiled. "Congratulations."

In the end, Tyler had to recruit his mother's help. But things were finally arranged, and he went home to clean the cabin and make the final arrangements for the wedding night.

Then he had to sit down and wait.

Friday night, Anna could not sleep. She was busy enough trying to make arrangements for her things that she didn't have time to worry for most of the week, but by Friday night there was nothing left to do.

She could not sleep. Three times she picked up the phone to call someone in her family, to at least tell *someone* what was about to happen, and three times she put her hand back in the pocket of her robe. She ached to share the news, to ask advice, to just hear a familiar voice in this strange wilderness her life had become. She was scared to death that she was making the most enormous mistake of her life.

It was too much, too fast. Three months ago, she'd been exactly where she wanted to be, finally curator of her own museum, finally a resident of Colorado, finally free of the vinelike clutches of her family.

Now all she wanted to do was run to them for protection, for validation or sympathy or maybe words of wisdom. But the very act of running so far from them prevented her from doing it. She didn't want them to know how miserably she had failed in her quest for independence. She didn't want them to cluck among themselves and talk about how much trouble she'd gotten herself in without all of them to intervene and keep her safe.

Anna the romantic, they'd say. See what happens?

Pacing her apartment—for the last time, she realized—

she scowled. They thought her frivolous and harebrained because she loved history and books and fairy tales. They thought she couldn't handle things on her own.

In a few months, when she could tell a little more clearly how things would go between her and Tyler, she would break the news of the baby and the husband.

In the meantime, she would just have to pray no one actually did decide to visit. What a mess that would be!

With a start, she noticed that the clock read 2:01. She had to get at least a little sleep—she didn't want to look like a vampire bride. Warm milk was an old standby. Maybe it would work. She padded into the kitchen and put the milk on the stove to heat. Standing there alone, she realized what part of her trouble was.

She shouldn't be alone the night before her wedding. Her sisters and cousins should be here, and all of them should still be awake, talking and eating too much, and sharing tales of other weddings, other marriages. Her mother should be here tomorrow, clucking over her hair and worrying about the guest list and looking splendid in the peacock-blue silk mother-of-the-bride dress upon which she had spent a small fortune, justifying it because she had so many daughters. The thought brought a teary smile.

Most of all, Anna wished for her grandma Maria, the one with whom she had sat for endless hours, listening to her stories. Of all the people in the world, Grandma Maria would understand the things Anna felt tonight—scared and excited and breathless with wondering what tomorrow would bring, if her husband would ever be more than a good provider and a good father. If he would ever learn to love his wife.

Stirring the milk, Anna wished she could see the future, just as her grandmother must have wished sixty years before. She had met her husband only once, for she'd come all the way from Sicily to be his wife, the match arranged by the families when such things were still popular. In Anna's office was a sepia photograph of Maria and her dashingly handsome husband, Salvatore. They both looked frightened and grim in the pictures, two very young strangers who had no idea what the night would bring. If they would even like each other. If they would find the same things funny, or have compatible spirits in any way.

But Anna remembered the way things had been between her grandparents. To his last day on earth, Salvatore had brought his wife a flower—usually snipped from his own garden—every single day.

And when he passed away, Maria had missed him desperately. She wanted to talk about him all the time, tell stories of him, somehow mark the time he'd been on earth and the contribution he'd made to the world. Anna had listened for many hours on many cold afternoons. The two young strangers had not only come to know each other, they'd found a rare bliss.

The world was different now, but Anna and Tyler were as old-fashioned in their way as Maria and Salvatore had been. He would be faithful, which mattered desperately to Anna. He would provide for them. And Anna could be a mother to a boy who wanted a mother more than anything in the world.

With a sense of regret, she realized she should have let her family know she was going to get married. The die was cast now, however, and she would just wait. Maybe it would be impossible to make this work. Maybe she would want more than Tyler could give. Maybe it would be impossible to compete with Kara's ghost.

But maybe, just maybe, it would work out as well as her grandmother's marriage, and if Tyler would agree to take classes with her, they could have another ceremony, a Catholic church wedding, after the baby was born. And all her family could come then to celebrate with her.

Feeling more optimistic, Anna drank her warm milk and

went to bed. And at last she slept, to dream of her grandfather dancing with her grandmother at a wedding.

It was the doorbell that awakened her. Anna, confused after the late night, couldn't quite get her bearings at first. Sun streamed in the windows, bright and buttery, and she groggily looked at the clock. Eight o'clock.

The doorbell rang again, insistently.

She suddenly remembered. She was getting married in two hours! And she'd overslept, and that was probably Louise right now. "Just a minute!" she called, and tossed through the covers to find her robe.

The sound of the doorbell ringing a third time sent her heart skittering into a panic. What if it was Tyler, come to tell her he'd changed his mind? With trembling hands, she opened the door to a young man in a delivery uniform. "Good morning," he said.

Anna looked at him blankly for a moment, then thought it must be something from Louise, and thanked him. Taking the package into her sunny, bare living room, she untied the big, plain box and found three more packages inside. On top was a small, narrow box with a label that said Open last.

It wasn't Louise's handwriting. Anna knew that from the museum. She put it aside as per instruction, and reached for the second, a rather large one marked #1. It was a simple white box, quite heavy. Anna put it on the table and lifted the lid.

And for a moment, she could not move. Through the tissue paper, she could see a swath of deepest wine colored velvet. A simple card sat on top, half hidden in the folds of tissue paper. When she was able to move, Anna took it out.

In a bold, slanted hand it read:

I thought you should at least have a dress fit for a princess. Curtis and I thought you would like this.
Tyler

Taking a deep breath, Anna carefully turned back the tissue paper to see the dress within. Made of velvet that was softer than down, it had a square neckline, with laces made of gold across the bodice. Stunned, Anna stared at it for a long moment before she finally drew it out of the box. It fell in long, elegant pools to the table, the hem and neckline edged with gold-and-white embroidery. Below the dress was a white silk underdress with long, full sleeves and a gathered neck.

For a moment, tears made her view blurry, and she put the velvet and silk aside so that she wouldn't get water spots on them, letting the fabric fall over the back of the couch in lush, gorgeous folds.

The other two boxes contained a gossamer scarf with scatterings of shiny gold and silver moons and stars on it, and a pair of velvet slippers the exact shade of the gown. Stunned, Anna wondered where Tyler had found such a thing. It really was a gown fit for a princess.

Once again, the doorbell rang, and Anna jolted back to the moment. Considerably more optimistic, she flung open the door, and this time it was Louise, who took one look at Anna and gasped. "Child, you don't have much time! Go get in the shower right now!"

"I am, Louise, I am. Just come look at this."

"I saw it." Her smile was a little sad as she walked toward the couch. "He has a kind heart. I'll give him that."

Anna frowned. "Is there something wrong, Louise?"

Louise lifted her head. The usual gleam in her cornflower eyes was subdued. "You're going to have to be real patient with him, Anna. It's just now hitting him."

Fresh dread filled her gut. "Is he— Does he want to—" She stopped and forced herself to take a breath. "Does he want to forget it?"

"Nothing like that. Just be patient with him, sweetie, okay?" She flicked her hand. "Go in there and get your shower. I'll fix you a little breakfast."

"Oh, please, no. I couldn't eat anything."

"Don't be silly. You can't be fainting dead away during the ceremony."

"I won't. It isn't like it's going to last a long time."

"All the same, I'm not letting you leave this house until I see a little food go down that throat. How about some scrambled eggs and toast? Nice and simple and easy going down."

Anna gave up. "Fine. I'll be out in a flash."

At that very moment, Tyler was pacing the living room of his mother's house. Both of his brothers were with him. Their wives had taken Cody and Curtis over to the courthouse to wait for Anna and Louise.

"Are you about ready to go?" Lance asked. "It's nine-thirty."

Tyler looked at him bleakly. "What the hell am I doing?"

Neither of them answered, but Tyler had not expected them to. He turned toward the view of the valley visible through the wide front window. "I don't even know this woman."

"Tyler, if you've got cold feet, maybe it would be better to just call it all off now," Jake said. "Before anyone is hurt badly."

"Too late for that, bro," Tyler said. "Anna is carrying a child she'll have to bear on her own if I don't give her my name."

"Hell, Tyler, we're in the twentieth century—" Lance began.

Jake broke in. "He's right, Lance. Somebody already has been hurt."

Keeping his back to them, Tyler said quietly, "Neither

one of you has any idea how lonely I've been, watching you fall in love, get married, find the life I was supposed to have. And there came Anna out of the snow, like something from a fairy tale, all full of laughter and noise." He paused. "She had purple glitter nail polish on her toenails," he added irrelevantly.

"We all know how hard it's been for you, Ty." Lance approached and clapped a hand to his shoulder. "The trouble is, you shouldn't just leap into something so big because you're lonely, or you feel a sense of obligation. I like Anna, and she might be hurt a little by the stigma or whatever of having that baby without benefit of marriage, but if you marry her and then can't live with yourself afterwards, you'll break her heart into a million pieces."

"We understand each other," he said.

"You think you do."

"Lance," Jake said, firmly. "Why don't you go on down? I'll drive Tyler."

For a moment, Lance did not move. Then, abruptly, he nodded. "I'll see you there." He left, and Tyler watched him drive away with a sense of impending doom.

Jake said nothing for a long time. Finally, he said, "He was just trying to help. He's worried about Anna—but I'm a lot more worried about you, little brother."

Tyler turned, waiting.

"I've got a feeling," Jake said, "that it's Kara in your heart today."

Oddly, it wasn't true. "No," he said honestly. "I just…I just want to do the right thing, but I don't feel anything today. I don't know how…" He felt heat in his ears and looked away. "I don't know how I can make love to a woman I don't feel anything for. I know you guys think it's hilarious, but that's just not the way I operate."

Jake lifted his eyebrows. "Looks to me like you managed all right when she was snowed in up there."

"That was different."

"I'd say maybe you're worrying too much."

Tyler closed his eyes and sighed. "Yeah." He felt winded, his head empty of all thought, all ability to reason. "I guess we oughta just get over there."

Jake stood. "Last chance, Ty."

Tyler squared his shoulders. "Let's go."

Chapter 12

By the time they got to the courthouse, a blustery wind had blown in, and Anna was glad for the warmth of the velvet dress.

Still, her hands were shaking, making the small bouquet of roses and baby's breath quiver, and her head was filled with white noise that carried with it a blanketing, muffling protection. Louise led her into a small, ornate chamber where a judge in formal robes waited, along with Ramona and Tamara—who would, in an hour, be her sister-in-laws. Anna looked at them, and somehow the knowledge of what she was about to do hit her again with a wave of panic.

Ramona, her long brown hair swept into a knot, seemed to sense Anna's sudden misgivings. She smiled and moved toward Anna with a reassuring smile in her warm brown eyes. "You look terrified," she whispered.

Anna grasped Ramona's hand tightly. "This is very weird."

Ramona laughed softly, putting her arm around Anna's

shoulder. Quietly, her head close to Anna's ear, she said, "I've seen how you look at him. Things will work out."

Anna nearly wept. Oh, it was too awful! They all knew she was besotted with Tyler. They all saw it in her face. They'd seen her sighing after him at family gatherings, which had led to Louise's matchmaking attempt, which had led to their getting snowed in, which had led to her making love to Tyler, which had led to her getting pregnant, which had led to this.

Fiercely she gripped Ramona's arm. "I think I'm going to faint."

"Come on." To the others she said, "We'll be right back. The bride is woozy."

Firmly, Ramona led Anna out a side door, into the cold day, where snow had begun to fall. "Breathe deeply," she said. "I think you're hyperventilating."

Anna nodded, and forced herself to take in a deep breath of cold, dry air. She tasted pine and snow, and thought of the fire at Tyler's house, and the way his arms had felt around her, and how beautiful he had been, sleeping by the fire.

Exhaling slowly, she felt herself steady. "For days," she said, "I've been trying to pretend this doesn't matter to me." Tears rose in her eyes. "That it will be all right if things don't go well, and I can never win his love, but the truth is, Ramona, I fell in love with him the moment I saw him, and learning who he really is only made it go deeper. I don't know whether to be happy or terrified."

And just as one of Anna's sisters would have done, Ramona immediately pulled Anna into her arms and hugged her tight, stroking her hair. "Oh, sweetie. He's the loneliest man I've ever known. He needs someone to love him that way." She stroked Anna's hair softly. "Can I give you a little advice?"

"Please."

"Don't make it too easy for him."

Anna raised her head, finding that she could smile a little. "You mean don't accept a date for Saturday if he calls after Wednesday?"

"More or less."

From the other side of the building came voices, and Anna glanced over her shoulder. "Showtime," she said, and turned back. "Thank you, Ramona."

The kind brown eyes twinkled. "Anytime, sweetie."

So it was with rock-steady calm that Anna entered the chamber where she was to say her vows. A hush fell on the room as she entered. Alonzo, dressed in a dark blue suit, his black hair slicked away from his face, held out his arm, and Anna took it, lifting her head.

At last she looked at Tyler, who waited near the judge, and the rest of the room faded away.

He had cut his hair. It no longer gleamed down his back in a silver-gilt ponytail. It couldn't be called short, either, but it had been beautifully barbered into a neat, almost shoulder-length cut that framed his extraordinary face. Against the blue velvet tunic he wore, it was bright as morning, and his unearthly eyes glowed.

Never—never—had he looked as much the prince as he did in this moment. The haircut seemed somehow symbolic to her, and Anna was glad he had done it, had made the effort to make a clean break, as if the warrior prince had come in from the killing fields and donned the dress of a civilized man to please the court.

If only he did not look so dutiful.

Anna kept her head high as she took her place beside him, taking his arm silently as they turned toward the judge. Beneath her fingers, the crisp muslin of his sleeve crumpled and grew soft, and at last Anna could feel the strength and heat at the crook of his arm. She looked at him, and found him looking down at her with a strange, boiling light in his eyes, and for a moment they were lost, simply staring at each other, until the judge cleared his throat a second time and asked again, "Are you ready to begin?"

It was not meant to be real, she suddenly realized. It was dress-up. Tyler had hedged with the costumes, much the way she had hedged by thinking of a Catholic wedding. But as she stood there in velvet he had chosen with all kindness, she realized it was real. Somehow, his gesture had backfired.

By some miracle, Anna had been transformed into a princess. As she said her vows, she remembered that she had sent out a wish to find some magic to draw him to her, and she had done so with the full knowledge that the price of magic was sometimes high.

But she had been willing to pay then, and she was willing still. "I, Anna Passanante, take thee, Tyler Forrest, to be my lawfully wedded husband," she said. Her voice rang in the room, full and strong. "For richer or poorer, in sickness and in health—" and now she paused and said each word clearly, firmly "—as long as we both shall live."

No one else could have seen the faint sheen of sweat on his brow, or could have noticed how his hands trembled when he slid a simple gold band on her finger.

His voice was rough as he spoke his vows, but he held her hands close, and his gaze did not waver. "I, Tyler," he said in a low, rough voice, "take thee, Anna, to be my lawfully wedded wife...."

And he held out his hand, calming suddenly as she put the ring on his finger, noticing as she did so that he had a dozen little nicks and cuts. She would have to see that he put salve on them in the future. His hands were too beautiful to be so neglected.

"You may kiss the bride," the judge said.

They stared at each other. It would be the first kiss since the night in the cabin, months ago. Anna quite suddenly didn't want it to take place here, in the view of so many others. She was relieved when Tyler, as stiff as if he were a puppet, bent and pecked her cheek.

It was over. They were married.

As if some magic had been holding her upright this long, Anna felt suddenly without bones, and before she knew what had happened, she fainted like some Victorian maid, right into Tyler's arms.

Acting instinctively, Tyler managed to catch Anna before she crumpled to the floor. He thought about sweeping her into his arms and carrying her outside for some air, but suddenly found his arms had no strength. He sank to a kneeling position, her upper body against his chest, her head falling backward over his elbow.

Louise bustled over. "Silly child. I told her to eat. You can't go around carrying a baby without getting enough to eat." She chuckled. "Been a long time since I've seen a bride faint dead away."

Protectively Tyler pulled Anna closer to him, putting a hand out to ward off his mother, or anyone else. "I've got her. She'll come around in a minute."

Just as he said that, Anna's lids fluttered, and she started. Tyler tightened his hold just enough to keep her from coming bolt upright. "Hey," he said softly, touching her cheek. "Are you all right?"

"How embarrassing," she whispered. Her rosy cheeks flushed even darker.

Tyler found himself reluctant to let her go. She felt soft in his arms, and a breast nudged his rib cage, and her waist under his hands was a strangely steadying sensation. "Don't be."

Around them gathered his family, and Tyler felt a powerful need to shoo them away, to make them leave him alone with her. Which, naturally, he could not do.

Lance said, "Don't feel bad, Anna. You aren't the first woman to faint in the presence of a Forrest man."

She struggled upright, putting a hand to her head ruefully. Tyler stayed in his crouch. "Take it slow."

Curtis shoved through the forest of legs and halted in front of them. "Daddy," he said severely. "You did it wrong."

Tyler raised his brows. "I did?"

"You're thupposed to kith her on the lipth."

In his arms, Anna tensed instantly. Tyler reached for his son. "Later, kiddo," he said, and helped Anna to her feet. They would take this one step at a time. He couldn't think about later yet.

Anna blinked fuzzily, and he wondered just how much of this was really penetrating. She looked a little shell-shocked. They simply stood there, awkwardly, while the family swarmed around them, kissing cheeks and offering congratulations. Tyler held Curtis's hand so that he could be a part of it all, and the boy beamed happily as his aunts and uncles kissed him. Cody, not to be left out of the commotion, finally came and took Anna's hand on the other side. She smiled at Tyler over that, and a little gust of relief pushed through him.

"Well," Louise said, "the bride is obviously starving, and I've cooked enough for an army. Let's move this party, shall we?"

Tyler kept Anna's hand firmly in the crook of his arm and led her outside. "Carriages with footmen are hard to come by," he said quietly as they stepped outside, gesturing ruefully toward his truck. As per his request, it had been left alone, with no Just Married signs and no cans attached to the muffler. He would have hated the fanfare, and suspected Anna would have, too. "I did take it to the car wash and vacuum."

She smiled, and he saw in it the real Anna, who'd been hiding since this whole thing had come about. "I have a thing about trucks. Carriages are for sissies."

He smiled back, and for the most fleeting of seconds,

they were alone in a world of their own making, separate from the others, who did not understand, who were not part of their joke or their world. It was an oddly pleasant sensation, and gave him strength.

"Curtis," Louise called. "Come on and ride with me."

"No!" he protested, clinging to Tyler's leg. "I want to ride with my mommy and daddy."

Mommy. Tyler had thought he was ready, but the word sliced through his middle like a dagger. A sharp sense of lost chances and lost hopes swept through him, and he bent his head.

"I don't mind," Anna said. "Tyler, do you care?"

He cleared his throat. "Not at all," he said with effort. "You can be the footman, helping the princess with her dress."

Curtis set his mouth. "Helping my mommy with her dreth."

Tyler managed a nod. He felt Anna looking at him, but avoided her gaze. "Let's go."

The reception was interminable. Tyler had known he'd have to let his mother fuss and cook, but had put his foot down about inviting anyone except the family to any part of the wedding, so it was only them.

Even so, it was undeniably awkward. Maybe because of Anna's faint, or because they were all aware of the circumstances of the wedding. Tyler didn't know. He was only aware of the forced smiles and joviality, the false heartiness of his brothers, the almost brittle brightness of his mother's smiles. Tyler wasn't a talker at the best of times—he'd just never really understood the need or the reasoning behind small talk and chitchat—but today every word he'd ever known seemed to have dried in his throat.

Anna, too, was quiet, which made Tyler feel uneasy. He remembered her nervous chattering, her genuine effort to avoid nonstop talking at the cabin, and her inability to do it. He wondered what was going on behind her too-white face, behind those guarded black eyes.

Only the two boys, Curtis and his cousin Cody, seemed unaware of anything off kilter. They zoomed around and tried to sneak sips of champagne and ate like little horses and cheered toasts and wanted to help tear open gifts. Gifts that embarrassed both Anna and Tyler. He could tell she was as uncomfortable as he was with the whole thing.

Finally the meal was consumed, the presents were opened, the toasts were finished, and the group broke up into smaller pieces, leaving Anna and Tyler alone in a comfortable corner, a pile of silver and glass at their feet, ribbons and bows and bits of silvery wedding paper clinging to their velvet.

"Are you okay?" Tyler asked.

She gave him a rueful smile. "As well as can be expected, I guess. Is this weird or what?"

He smiled, glancing over his shoulder to the other room. "Pretty weird," he agreed. "Maybe we should have eloped. It would have been easier."

"And have your mother track us down to the far ends of the earth? No, thank you." She took a breath. "It's almost over."

"Yeah." He plucked a triangle of paper from the skirt of her gown. "I haven't told you, but you look beautiful in that dress. I knew you would."

"Thank you." She smoothed a hand over the plush velvet. "It was very thoughtful, and I haven't thanked you. It's beautiful. I was very touched."

"Curtis helped. We had a good time."

"Is it rented?" she asked. "Do we have to get them back by a certain time?"

"No. It's yours. Maybe you'll have a daughter to give it to someday."

A bright, vulnerable light flared in the blackness of her eyes. "Maybe."

And then they were alone again, amid the chaos that always ensued when his family was together. The world narrowed to her rose-and-white face, to the vulnerable yearning in her expression, to the lushness of that red, red mouth, and Tyler felt his breath catch. "Do you have a wish for one or the other?" he asked.

"Not at all," she said. "But I hope it has your eyes."

"I was just thinking I hope it has yours."

That silent, pulsing communication arced between them, and Tyler reached for her hand. It would be okay, this marriage. Whatever else, he genuinely liked her.

"Daddy," Curtis said, breathless at his side. "Is it time to kith her yet?"

The cocooning field evaporated, and Tyler grabbed his son by the waist. "You sure are a nosy little boy. What is this about kisses?"

Curtis sobered, his blue eyes very wide. "Cody told me that's what his mommy and daddy do. They kith. A lot."

Tyler glanced at Anna over the boy's head. They would have to be careful over the next few weeks to be aware of Curtis's eager eyes, his passionate wish to be part of a family. She nodded.

"Okay, buddy. A kiss you want, a kiss you shall have."

Thankfully, everyone else was in the other room, paying them no attention, because even the thought of kissing Anna brought a thick flush to his skin. The low couch was awkward, and he stood up, holding a hand out to Anna, who rose gracefully. A long black wisp of hair curled on the white flesh of her shoulder, and with some distant part of his mind, he wanted to kiss that place, wanted to feel that wisp against his face as he opened his mouth on her flesh.

So tiny. She was so tiny standing there before him, her eyes raised, her hand clasped lightly in his. Tyler tugged her close and put one arm around her shoulder, the other on her cheek, and suddenly his heart was beating very hard. Suddenly he wanted nothing more than this very thing, to be feeling her small, neat form against his, to caress the silkiness of her skin, to savor the anticipation of tasting—at last—that delectably kissable mouth. He had the odd sense of molecules and atoms magnetically aligning with the force of their meeting, felt a dizzy sense of rightness he did not question.

He bent close, closed his eyes, and kissed her.

At the press of their mouths, something deep within him exploded, a rush of denied yearning and loneliness and sorrow, mixed with the flavors of tea and sugar on her lips, mixed with the purely erotic sensation of her lush, giving lips, the nearly inaudible sound she made as he kissed, and kissed, and then sought entry to the honeyed darkness of her mouth. At the touch of their tongues, at the narcotic slide, he felt a brief, stunning recognition of the fit they made before the pure pleasure of it overtook him and he pressed her close to him, reveling in the press of her breasts against his rib cage, the guilty pleasure of her belly against his member, a member that grew more alert and eager the longer the kiss lasted.

And it lasted, because he could not let her go. Did not want to stop kissing her. Forgot where they were, what they were doing, why he had begun. He only kissed her.

And kissed her.

And kissed her.

Until she faintly pushed against him, and he emerged a little, just enough, from the enchantment to realize that they were no longer alone. That that heated, impassioned moment had attracted an audience. They were pretending not to notice, but he saw them from the corner of his eye, peering around the doorway, one or two, looking away when they saw that they were observed.

Tyler didn't let Anna go. He caught her face in his hands and looked into her liquid eyes for a long time. There was no need of words.

Lance, never one to tiptoe, made a whooping noise. "Three cheers for the bride and groom!"

Anna looked abashed. Telling himself he did it to comfort her, Tyler reached for her hand and clasped it secretly behind the heavy folds of her gown.

The snow picked up all afternoon, and it finally grew troublesome enough that the reception broke up early, much to Anna's relief. The day had been a bit of a strain, and she just wanted to go somewhere quiet, somewhere there weren't a dozen eyes peering at her in concern.

It was only as she donned her coat that she realized she had no idea what she and Tyler were going to do now. Go back to the cabin? She had packed most of her clothing into a small suitcase, but hadn't really given any thought to the fact that this was her *wedding* night, or what that would entail. She'd packed a warm flannel robe, and a nice enough flannel nightgown, thinking of the cabin and the cold night she'd spent there.

And now, because she didn't want Tyler to think she expected anything, she was embarrassed to ask where they were going. She waited near the door, deciding she would find out when they got wherever they were going.

One minute at a time, she'd get through this. Within a few days, they would find their pattern.

Louise snagged her hand. "Don't you dare get away yet, sugar. I have something for you."

"Oh, Louise, you can't. You've done enough already."

"Don't I know it!" She tugged Anna's hand and pulled her into a bedroom. "None of this would have happened if I hadn't been an old busybody, and you have to let me make it up to you."

With a start, Anna realized that the ordinarily bustling, energetic Louise had been quite subdued today. There were lines of strain around her mouth, and her cornflower eyes did not hold their usual twinkle. Impulsively, Anna reached out and stroked her arm. "You've been wonderful. Thank you."

Louise's eyes filled with tears. "You are the sweetest child. If that son of mine gives you any heartache, I'll never forgive myself."

Anna scowled. "I'm perfectly capable of taking care of myself, Louise. Honestly, why does everyone think I'm so delicate?" With a sigh of frustration, she moved away, looking out the window to the falling snow. "I traveled two thousand miles to make a new life for myself, and one of the reasons I did it was because my family was always sure I could never do anything on my own."

She turned back. "I'm a lot stronger than you think."

The troubled expression on Louise's kind face did not ease, but she nodded, and reached for a package. "I got you something special, but I don't want you to open it here. Wait till you get to the lodge."

"The lodge?"

"Didn't anyone tell you? Lance wanted to do something special, and he set up a night in the celebrity suite at the Alpine Lodge for you. I'm keeping Curtis."

"Oh." Anna sank onto the bed, holding the big package in her hands. The Alpine was an old, elegant ski lodge that catered to the highest levels of the moneyed crowds that came to Red Creek to ski. The ordinary rooms were the ultimate in mood and style and luxury—Anna couldn't even begin to imagine what the celebrity suite would be like.

And she would spend the night there. Alone with Tyler, who had kissed her with the kind of mind-numbing passion a woman only dreamed of. He wanted her physically, of that she had no doubt.

She also had no doubt that he would expect to make love to her tonight. It was what one did on wedding nights.

The thought of it made her feel weak and hungry. The

thought of Tyler's bare, warm flesh next to hers, his mouth and hands doing all those amazing things…

But she wasn't entirely sure she was ready to have sex with him again. Not yet. It was too intimate, too intense, and she felt too vulnerable as it was. If she let him make love to her tonight, she would never be able to build her defenses, and then, if things didn't work out, she would be devastated.

No, she had to somehow keep him at arm's length for at least a week or two, until she got her sea legs. Or marriage legs, in this case.

The decision made her feel stronger. "Thank you, Louise," she said, and stood up. "I think it's probably time to go. I appreciate all you've done for me."

"Take care, Anna. I do love you like a daughter, you know. Like the daughter I never had."

"I know," she whispered, hugging Louise tight. "I know."

Chapter 13

The Alpine had been built in the early thirties of native stone and split logs, with commanding views of the valley and special shuttles to the ski areas that spread in a hundred-mile circle around Red Creek. Within, the dark-timbered ceilings and sloped roof and carefully chosen but comforting furnishings gave it the feeling of an old-world hunting lodge.

The *king's* hunting lodge, Anna thought as they entered the hushed lobby. It boasted one of the finest restaurants in the country—so exclusive and esteemed that jet-setters had been known to charter a plane in from L.A. or Palm Springs to have dinner. Anna had been there once, when Louise insisted upon giving her a welcome-to-Colorado dinner. The prices had assured she would not return anytime soon.

But she'd thought it beautiful then, and it was no less beautiful now. Standing in the tastefully appointed lobby with Tyler, she breathed deeply, smelling that faint scent of money and taste that was so much a part of such establishments.

Neither she nor Tyler had had much to say on the short drive up here. He checked them in while Anna distracted herself from the upcoming evening by trying to name all the flowers in a huge vase. Foxglove, lupine, delphiniums, cornflowers. A tall blue flower stumped her, but then Tyler and an obsequious bellboy appeared to lead them to their suite.

When the youth had pointed out the features of the room and been tipped generously, then sent away, Anna finally let out her breath. Tyler stood in the middle of the first room, staring around with the same wonder as Anna. He whistled softly. "I don't want to seem like a hick, but I've never seen anything like this."

Anna laughed nervously. "Me either."

Two walls were almost completely made of glass, revealing a darkening view of the valley in breathtaking splendor on one side, a view of thick trees far below them on the other. A balcony beyond sliding glass doors invited the occupants to wander out to gaze upon the astonishment of nature in the Rocky Mountains.

Within, the room was luxuriously appointed, with couches and chairs in sturdy but elegant fabrics, muted to reflect the colors of nature beyond. A table groaned with various food and drink offerings, and a bar sat in one corner. Not simply a small refrigerator, but an entire bar, complete with a small sink. In a silver bucket sat a black bottle of champagne on ice.

Through an open door, Anna saw the bedroom, with a king-size bed and another wall of glass. She looked away from the bed.

"Well," Tyler said, clearing his throat. "We may as well enjoy it." He shrugged out of his coat and moved toward the table. "My brother certainly does know how to indulge."

Anna still carried the box Louise had given her, and she put it down, then took off her coat and hung it up neatly before joining Tyler at the table of food. There were sweets and savories, food carefully prepared and displayed. A silver pot of cheese fondue steamed in the middle of a sea of fruits, breads, crackers and vegetables, and Anna made a small, pleased sound. "I love fondue." She speared a cube of crusty French bread and dipped it, then moaned softly in pleasure when she tasted it. "Oh, that's wonderful. Try it."

"I've never eaten fondue," he said.

"Never? You are truly deprived, Tyler."

He gave her a small smile and followed her lead, dipping bread into the cheese sauce. His eyes widened. "You're right."

Anna had been patently unable to eat anything but the smallest nibbles all day, but the first taste of the fondue made her stomach growl—loudly. Gratefully she sank into a chair and shifted the tray so that it was close. "Don't tell your mother—she'd be crushed if she knew I couldn't eat at all earlier—but I am totally starving, and I think I'll just make a pig of myself, okay?"

"Ditto," he said. "First, though, I have to get rid of this tunic. It's really hot." Comfortably he unlaced it and shrugged out of it. Anna tried not to stare. Below the knee-length tunic, he wore a dashing shirt made of crisp white muslin, with full sleeves, and tight-fitting black jeans. With a quick gesture, he loosened the ties at the throat of the shirt, and it fell open to reveal a wide triangular slice of golden chest scattered with gilded hair.

In response, a thick heat moved low in her belly, and she looked away. "You look like a pirate," she commented lightly.

"Yeah?" He settled on the chair next to her. "A hungry pirate, then. I'm starving."

"How could you live to the age of—" She broke off. "I don't know how old you are, Tyler."

"Thirty-one." He inhaled a slice of cheese from another tray. "How old are you?"

"Twenty-five."

"And what is your middle name?"

"Kristine. You?"

He shook his head good-naturedly. "I'm not telling. My mother gave us seriously strange middle names. Not that Tyler is exactly ordinary."

"I like it."

He met her gaze. "Do you?"

Anna was captured in spite of herself, captured by the persuasive charm of a man who knew what pleased a woman, and who intended to indulge that pleasure as soon as possible. Approval and desire emanated from him like a scent. "I do," she said quietly, then straightened. "But you have to tell me your middle name."

"We can make a deal, if you like. You tell me how much you weigh, and I'll tell you my middle name."

"Not fair. A woman does not reveal that information."

His grin said he knew that.

"Fine, then," Anna said, dragging a slice of apple through the cheese, "I'll just ask Curtis."

"Curtis doesn't know."

"Right. What kid doesn't know his father's whole name?"

"Mine."

"I'll find out somehow." The taste of cheese exploded on her tongue. "That is so amazingly good, I can't believe it. How is it that you've reached the ripe old age of thirty-one without eating fondue?"

He lifted a shoulder. "You have to understand how we lived." His brows drew down. "I'm trying not to mention Kara at all, Anna, but it's hard. I spent a good part of my life with her."

"I don't mind," she said, and meant it. "I don't want to be compared to her, but you shouldn't have to avoid mentioning her name. How did you live?"

"Very simply, I guess. Kara was very serious about a back-to-nature kind of life. We didn't eat any meat or cheese or sugar or even coffee." He looked at the rolled slice of ham in his fingers and grinned. "Obviously, she was more of a purist than I."

"And you had no electricity or running water or heat."

"Nope."

"Do you think she would have eased up after Curtis was born?"

He frowned over the tray and selected a cherry tomato. "I don't know. I don't really think so, to tell you the truth. She was dedicated." He paused. "After she died, it made me feel kind of guilty when I started changing things, but she was always too intense about it—and it's damned hard to raise a kid like that."

"I can imagine." Anna touched her tummy, thinking with suddenness of the baby inside of her, the baby who had brought this moment about.

Tyler caught the gesture and, with a tenderness Anna did not expect, put his hand over hers. "I'm really happy about the baby, Anna. We can do things to the cabin to make it bigger. Maybe add some more solar panels, or even get Lance to contract the electric lines. I won't make you live like a monk."

His hand was warm and broad and strong, and Anna covered it with her other hand. "Things will work out."

He was so close Anna could smell the shampoo in his hair, and the lingering traces of aftershave. "Are you happy, Anna? About the baby, I mean?"

"Yes." There was, for once, no need to embroider.

Suddenly, the awkwardness fell between them, and Tyler straightened, looking over his shoulder. "What did my mother give you?"

"Oh, I'd forgotten. I don't know." Glad to have something to do, she jumped up and sat in a chair a few feet away to open it. Below the festive wrapping was a department store clothing box, and Anna lifted the lid, afraid suddenly of what she would find.

It was a negligee, made of sheerest white silk, with elegant white-on-white embroidery along the edges and on the bodice. Or what there was of the bodice, she thought as she drew it out of the box, blushing furiously. A silk wrapper matched. "She has exquisite taste," Anna said, without looking at him.

"Yes," he said.

Anna heard the rawness in his voice with a ripple of trepidation, and forced herself to look at him. She surprised an expression of bleakness on his face. "Tyler, what's wrong?"

He said nothing for a long moment, staring at the gown as if it were a serpent. "I wish I had more to offer you, Anna," he said quietly. "I wish this was the wedding night you deserved, that you were going to put on that gown for a man who—"

He broke off, but Anna finished the sentence in her mind: a man who really loved her. Hastily, blushing even more furiously, she folded the gown. "It's okay," she said.

"No," he said vehemently.

"If it bothers you that much, we can just annul it tomorrow, you know."

They stared at each other across the small space. "No, we can't," he said.

Anna bowed her head. "No, we can't. Curtis would—"

"Exactly." He laced his fingers together, leaning forward with an earnest expression. "Anna, I'm sorry. I wasn't thinking that I wish I hadn't married you. I was wishing you had someone who—" Color stained his cheekbones, and he swallowed. "I have the social graces of a buffalo, and what I was thinking is how much I wanted to see you in that gown, and how much I want to put my hands on you.'' His eyes darkened. "I was thinking that you deserved a lot more than that.''

It touched her. "It's okay.'' With some relief, she realized this gave her the opening she'd been looking for. "The truth is, Tyler, I've been worried about the sexual end of all this.''

"We seemed to do okay before,'' he said dryly.

Anna took a breath. "It's not the compatibility I'm worried about. I just don't think I'm ready to be so intimate with you yet. It was different before. It was…just…it was different, that's all. But I think we need time to know each other before we do all that again. I mean, if we ever decide we want to, or— Well, I guess we will want to sometime, I guess.'' She heard the way her thoughts were tangling and how she was babbling, and the more she said, the worse it got, but she couldn't seem to stop. "I can't see never ever having sex again, you know, but I wouldn't want you to feel you had some duty, and though maybe we want some more children someday, I just don't—''

"Anna.''

She clamped her mouth closed.

He lifted one eyebrow. "I'm glad to see the old Anna is in there somewhere. I was beginning to get worried.''

She shook her head. "Sorry.''

"I don't mind.'' He stood up and closed the space between them, coming to kneel in front of her. "I won't lie to you, Anna. I'm disappointed. I've been sitting here wondering how long we had to talk before I could decently make love to you.''

"Oh.'' She looked down. "I'm sorry. I didn't think you…''

With one long-fingered hand, he brushed a curl from her face. "What? You didn't think I wanted you? You didn't think I'd mind if we just put it off?''

"I guess. Something like that.''

His nearness sent a rippling through her, a quiet cry of yearning she forced herself to resist. She stared at her hands, clasped tightly in her lap, and willed herself not to notice the way black denim clung to his lean thighs, the way light burnished his golden skin.

He was silent for so long that she was finally forced to look up. To find him looking at her. "Anna, I've only made love to two women in my life." He lifted his hands to her face, tilting it upward. His thumbs moved lightly over her chin, grazed her lips, moved away. "After you left, I dreamed about the way you felt, about how you made me feel, and I was angry. I didn't want to have those thoughts."

His voice was low and raw, and his pale gray eyes bored into her, touching her face, every inch, as if it were a terrain that puzzled him. His mouth was only inches from her own, that talented, giving mouth, and she wanted it. But she forced herself to remain very still.

"I'll respect your wishes," he said finally, "but I'm not exactly thrilled about it."

She sighed in relief, but before it was complete, his mouth closed on hers, gently, and she found the sigh turned into a soft moan. He kissed her with great restraint and, perversely, sensual temptation, as if he knew how she felt the stings of arousal with every brush of his tongue, with every slow sup of his lips.

He ended the kiss, then rested his forehead against hers. "Whew."

Anna closed her eyes, awash suddenly in a swell of fierce love. Where his brow touched hers, it seemed there was a burning link, carrying her thoughts to him, and his to her. She smelled his skin, and pine and wood smoke, and felt his hands on her neck and jaw, and his thighs against hers, and for one long, floating moment, she felt as if this were no accident, as if time and fate had overcome great obstacles to bring them together. As if they had not only just met a few months before, but had known each other always, in the heavens, through all the centuries.

Moving in that airy place, Anna unclenched her hands, and was about to lift them to put them on his body when he shifted away. "So," he said, letting her go. "Do you want to play cards or something?"

Blinking, Anna said, "Uh, sure. Poker?"

He grinned. "You play poker?"

"Yes. Very well, as a matter of fact."

An impish expression crossed his face. "Well, there may be some interesting possibilities in that."

With surprise, Anna realized that prickly Tyler, silent mountain man, could be every bit as charming as his brothers when he chose to be. It made her wonder how much of himself he had hidden—and what had led him to hide it. Responding to his teasing, she grinned. "Yes, there just might be."

"Good, then. I'll find some cards."

"And I'm going to change."

"Into something more comfortable?"

Anna glanced at the wispy silk gown. "Not *that* comfortable."

"It was worth a try."

He actually had a dimple. He'd never smiled wide enough for her to see it before, and a wave of happiness went through her. By some miracle, Tyler was actually happy in this moment. It made her feel humbled and grateful. "I'll be right back."

The bellman had taken their bags into the bedroom, and Anna opened hers to find something more comfortable to put on. The velvet was amazingly heavy, and she felt weary from dragging it around all day. The tunic hooked in the front, and she shucked it with a sigh.

"Hey!" Tyler called. "There's a stereo in this cabinet! Do you want to listen to some music?"

"Sure. Whatever you want."

It came on, something classical Anna didn't recognize. Hanging her tunic up carefully, she bent over the suitcase, looking for the flannel gown and robe she'd brought with her. They weren't there.

Twice, she carefully took everything out of the suitcase, and frowned. She distinctly remembered putting it in the bag, along with her toothbrush, the very last.

Louise.

Anna sighed. The woman just could not help herself. It was pointless to be annoyed. She took out the jeans and her favorite red sweater, and changed into those instead. The button wouldn't close on the jeans, so she left it undone and pulled the sweater down over it. Soon, she supposed, she would have to break down and buy some new things.

Putting her hands over her tummy, she turned sideways to look in the long mirror over the dresser. "How you doing, kid? Feeling okay in there?" She could see no visible difference in her tummy yet, but standing there, she wondered how it would be in a few months, when she got rounder with baby. It gave her a curious sense of excitement to think of it, to think of her child growing in there.

Humming happily, she padded barefoot back into the other room.

Tyler spent the whole evening moderately to extremely aroused, depending on the moment. They settled on the floor to play poker, Anna drinking bottled water while Tyler sipped champagne. In the background played quiet classical music, and snow fell with cocooning quiet beyond the windows, beautiful against the night. They filled a plate with olives and a variety of cheeses and cherry tomatoes, and nibbled as they played for pennies, which they'd called down to the front desk to get. The maid had giggled when she brought the neat, heavy rolls in exchange for a five-dollar bill, and when they closed the door behind her, both Tyler and Anna had laughed. "We can never tell a soul how we passed this evening," Anna said.

"Not a soul."

Now, several hours later, the piles of pennies were almost evenly divided, as they had been all night. She played well, and although he'd expected everything to show on her mobile face, she was remarkably able to school her features in poker. When he commented, she said simply that her brothers had taught her well.

Tyler had sipped his way through several glasses of champagne, and felt agreeably warm and a little expansive from it. He didn't feel like himself tonight—his usual sense of awkwardness was missing. It was easy to talk about little things, and to laugh, and to smile at Anna's jokes. Maybe it was the unaccustomed comfort of the hotel room, or the champagne, or the relief of getting through the day without major incident.

But he suspected it was Anna making him feel this way. It was just easy somehow to be with her.

At least in some ways.

It was not easy to sit across from her and respect her wish to avoid sex. Her red sweater, the same one she'd worn the day she told him she was pregnant, was damned near as sexy as the silk nightgown would have been. The simple lines clung to her curves with a soft texture that begged petting, and the round neckline exposed far more of her breasts than he thought she realized. Her body had changed with pregnancy, and one thing that was different was those white swells of breast over the sweater. Voluptuous curves. Curves he wanted to trace with his tongue.

He wondered if her breasts had grown more sensitive, too. It happened. She'd been very sensitive before, and vocal, as he recalled. The memory, coupled with fresh temptation, sent blood rushing in alert readiness to his loins.

"Dealer takes two," he said, tossing down a three and a six.

They showed their cards. Tyler won with three kings, but Anna was close with three tens. He scraped the pennies toward his pile, then stood up to stretch and pour a little more champagne. "Let's change the stakes to make it more interesting," he said, sitting down again.

"Yeah, we're pretty evenly matched, I'm afraid. What do you suggest?"

He shrugged. "I don't know. Truth or dare?"

"Okay."

She won the first round. "Truth or dare?"

"Truth."

She scowled. "How boring."

Tyler chuckled.

"Let's see." She narrowed her eyes and bit on her lip. "Tell me something you did as a kid that your mother never found out about, and she would have killed you if she knew."

"Well, living with Jake and Lance, you might imagine there were a lot of things like that." He thought for a moment. "One of my favorites was when Lance and I jumped a freight train and rode into Denver, then back."

Her mouth fell open. "She never found out? Weren't you gone a long time?"

"Not really. Most of a day, probably, but that wasn't all that unusual. We were country kids."

Tyler lost the second time, too. He took truth again, but when she asked for his middle name, he shook his head. "Make it a dare."

With a gleam in her eye, Anna said, "Sing me a song."

He laughed. "I'll get you for this," he said, but dutifully sang "Mary Had a Little Lamb."

She lost the next round. Tyler immediately thought of asking for some article of clothing, but she asked for truth. "Now who's wimping out?"

Serenely, she smiled.

How could she be so unrattled? He knew she wanted him, though maybe not the same way he wanted her, which was quickly becoming a mindless, heated, animal thing unlike anything he'd ever experienced, even as a randy teenager waiting for his wedding night with Kara. "Tell me," he said, "about the first time a boy touched your breasts."

Color flooded her cheeks. "Tyler, that's not fair!"

He grinned. "You picked truth."

She took a breath. "Okay, it was Johnny Dinero and we were making out after a school dance and he slipped his hand under my blouse."

"Did you slap him?" He could just see that—moral indignation bristling around her like a halo.

"No," she said, and smiled. The expression was fertile and sensual and devastatingly female. Awareness made of her eyes liquid pools. "I liked it."

Tyler inclined his head. "Touché," he said, and let go of a sigh. "I'm way outclassed."

"You asked for it."

"Is it true?"

She only smiled and held out her hands for the cards. She lost again, a pair of aces to his full house. "The heavens are obviously on my side," he said. "Truth or dare?"

"Truth. I don't trust you with a dare."

Tyler considered carefully. What question would a woman absolutely refuse to answer? "How much do you weigh?"

With a sigh, she rolled her eyes. "Dare."

Tyler laughed. It surprised even him, that delighted sound rolling out of his chest, deep and…jeez, happy. "Give me some article of clothing that you're wearing."

"Oh, all right. I'll tell you how much I weigh."

"Too late. You know the rules. You have to take the dare."

She pursed her lips, considering, then reached behind her, did something, and then reached under her sleeves to pull her bra straps, first one side, then the other, tugging the bra out of the right sleeve. She put it in his hand.

It was not a sexy item of clothing, just a simple white bit of cloth, but it still held the warmth of her body, and Tyler felt a sizzle move from his hand to his groin with electric pain. He looked from the fabric to her, frankly admiring the looseness of unbound breasts below the soft red fabric. "Much better," he said.

Anna thrust the deck at him. "I'm not going to lose anymore, so you may as well prepare yourself."

He grinned. "Yeah? Famous last words." He tossed the bra aside and shuffled the cards thoroughly. "I'm telling you, Lady Luck is with me."

"We'll see."

With a flourish, he dealt the cards, set the deck aside and picked up his hand. It took everything he had not to chuckle, and in fact he forced himself to frown.

With a royal flush.

He glanced at Anna, but could read nothing in her face until she raised her eyes. There he saw the shine of triumph. "I'll hold," she said, her voice low and sexy. "But let's raise the stakes."

"I'm game. How?"

"It's a dare. And no matter how ridiculous or embarrassing, the other person has to do it."

"You sound pretty sure of yourself, missy. You planning to humiliate me in public?"

"You deserve it."

"But what if I win?"

She lifted a shoulder. "I'll take my chances."

Tyler smiled then. "It's a bet, then."

"Are you going to draw?"

"Nope." He spread his cards.

Anna stared blankly at the hand for a moment, and he

recognized the stunned expression. She'd lost. "You are unbelievably lucky," she whispered, and turned over her cards. A straight flush.

"I win," he said, and could not keep the huskiness from his voice.

"Yes."

Anticipation, thick and rich, spilled through him, and he allowed himself the luxury of drawing out the moment, sorting through his choices, allowing her the same giddy anticipation.

And he knew she anticipated. Her breath came more quickly, and her eyes had grown heavy-lidded, and the aura in the room was suddenly tense, hushed, waiting. Tyler let his eyes wander over her mouth and thought of asking for another kiss, then moved his gaze lower, to her neck, then lower still, to the aroused tips of her breasts below the sweater.

And he knew what he would ask. "Come here, Anna," he said. "Let me claim my prize."

Without speaking, she rose up on her knees and moved closer to him. "Even on a double dare, you don't have carte blanche," she said.

"Two things only."

He reached for her, sliding his fingers under the neckline of her sweater at either side. "You don't have to do anything at all. Just sit right there." He moved closer and, slowly, slowly, enjoying every inch of the journey, he slid the soft red fabric down her shoulders, first exposing creamy white shoulders, delicate as the wings of a dove, then the swell of her upper breasts. "This is the first thing," he said.

At last her breasts, white and round and uptilted, were free. Anna made a soft sound, but she did not move, and he worried that he'd upset her. Tyler glanced at her face.

Her eyes were closed, her chin was faintly lifted, and her nostrils were flared. The lush red lips were faintly parted to let her hurried breath through. She was as aroused as he, but struggling not to show it.

The dark rose nipples were aroused, and Tyler sighed as he bent close. "This is the second part," he said, "and then I'll let you go. Just let me—" he moved his mouth very close to the tip of her left breast and flicked his tongue over it "—taste you." Trembling with desire, he opened his mouth and drew her inside his lips.

And he was lost, lost in the soft cry that escaped her, lost in the taste of nubby flesh, lost in the sensual pleasure of giving and receiving pleasure like this. Anna shivered against him, her hands lighting on his shoulders, then in his hair.

Delirious pleasure. Every inch of her. Every sound, every movement. Every—

She gripped his hair tightly. "Tyler, please stop now."

He raised his head, hearing the urgent sound in her voice. There was anguish on her face, and she whispered, "Please."

Tyler released her abruptly, shattered by his own driving sensuality. "I'm sorry," he said gruffly. "I'm going outside for a minute, okay?"

Careful not to look at her, he yanked open the glass door and stepped out into the cold, cold night.

Chapter 14

Anna was shaking all over—bone-deep trembling she could not seem to still, no matter what she did. She was grateful that Tyler had given her a moment to collect herself.

Until that last moment, the teasing between them had seemed harmless. Anna had been drawn into his passion because she was so hungry for him, but it had seemed like a game until the last.

Until that big head lowered close to her breasts, until his beautiful mouth closed upon her, hot and wet, and skillful. She had fallen adrift on the feel of him, on the erotic pleasure he gave so easily, on the wonders of him wanting her at all, much less with the passion she sensed in him tonight.

That passion was part of the hidden Tyler, a passion vast and deep and too long denied, a passion that held a fierceness that frightened her. She remembered the way they had bruised each other with the force of their passion that night at his cabin, and knew she could not hold him off forever. Whatever else there was between them, she suspected the physical link was far more intense than was usual.

But it was that very intensity that terrified her. That passion would engulf her, devour her, snare her heart and soul and mind, until the real Anna was submerged somewhere in a desperate, doomed love for a man who would never love her in return.

Shakily she fixed her clothes and retreated into the luxuriously appointed bathroom. On impulse, she stripped and turned on the shower, very cold, to break this spell. She yelped when she stepped under the spray, but it provided the shock she needed.

Sooner or later, she would have to make love with him. Probably better sooner than later, if she was to blunt the ferocity of his barely contained passion. But even standing under a cold shower, she couldn't imagine how she would do it without losing herself in the bargain.

A bit of remembered sexual lore popped into her head: If a couple put a penny in a jar every time they made love the first year, then took a penny out every time after the first year, they would never use up the pennies in the jar.

Maybe it was just normal chemistry, and would burn itself out. Maybe she didn't have to be so afraid. Maybe she was fighting the wrong fight.

In a sudden decision, she turned off the shower and wrapped herself in one of the enormous bath sheets hanging on the racks. Rubbing her skin hard to make it glow, she hurried into the bedroom and found the silk gown Louise had given her. With anticipation knotting in her belly, she donned the wispy fabric and went to find Tyler.

He still stood on the balcony in the falling snow, staring out into the darkness. Anna stepped over the cards on the floor, and went to the door. "Tyler," she said quietly. "I'm sorry."

Without turning, he said, "I'll live."

She winced. She had really hurt his feelings. "Tyler, why don't you come inside?"

"In a minute."

She gathered her courage, and said, "I have a surprise for you."

He turned, simply swiveled in place, putting his hands behind him on the rail. In the full-sleeved shirt and black jeans, his hair tossed by the wind, snow falling around him, he looked like the ghost of a pirate. An angry pirate.

His pale gaze flickered downward, caressing her form below thin silk, and she saw his jaw harden. "I'm not really in the mood for a virgin sacrifice," he said.

Stung, Anna took a step backward, then stood her ground. "I think *virgin* is the wrong choice of words here."

"*Sacrifice* isn't."

She stared at him, hurt welling up in her chest. Without a word, she turned and walked away, holding up her head so that he would never know how deeply he'd wounded her. Damn him.

Resolutely she climbed into the enormous bed and curled into a fetal position of comfort. Until she lay down, she had no idea how exhausted she was, but the instant she was prone, her body gave a collective gasp of relief, and the long night before, and the long day, and the demands of the pregnancy, caught up with her. In moments, she was sound asleep.

Tyler stayed on the balcony until he was chilled from his bones outward, until he was absolutely certain he could trust himself to respect the distance Anna had asked for. Closing the door behind him, he listened for her in the suite. For all he knew, she might have left.

A move that might be best for both of them. Quietly, he moved through the sitting room and peeked into the bedroom. Until he saw her small, still form, the black hair flung over the pillows, and felt relief course through him, he didn't know how much it mattered that she'd stayed.

On the wide expanse of the enormous bed, she barely took up the space of a postage stamp. Half of him wanted to crawl in next to her, but the other half—the sensible half—told him he would only make things worse if he did.

His head ached vaguely from champagne, and there was a hollow thud of shame in the region of his heart. Turning away from the temptation of Anna, he moved back into the sitting room and, from long habit, bent down to pick up the cards. His winning straight flush was scattered from the force of his need when she had moved toward him at last, and he halted, assailed by a vision of her kneeling before him in her red sweater. With it came heat and need, and a new stab of guilt.

Idly, he picked up the cards and dealt them into a game of solitaire. All his life, he'd held himself to be made of better cloth than his father and brothers, taking quiet pride in his devotion to one woman, when they all seemed to want dozens. After Kara's death, he'd clung to chastity as if it were a life raft, arrogantly secure in his moral superiority.

But both of his brothers had proven their steadfastness when they found the women meant for them. Between them, Jake and Lance had probably had more women than Tyler had ever seen, but all conquests were forgotten when they found The One.

What an arrogant fool he'd been all these years. Because he found Kara when they were young, Tyler had never been tested. He'd found harmony and satisfaction in his wife, and he'd never needed to look beyond his own front door. Afterward, his grief had been so encompassing for so long that even managing to take care of Curtis had taken every scrap of physical and mental and spiritual energy he owned.

What would he have been like if he'd never met Kara?

He wondered if he would have charmed women into having sex with him, as his brothers had, never regretting the liaisons because, as Lance was fond of saying, he gave them something worth remembering. Kara had instinctively understood his teenage lust, and even when she did not allow intercourse until their wedding night, she had known a lot of other tricks to keep him from going insane. By the time he was sixteen, Tyler had had a lot more regular sex than anyone he knew, though he hadn't talked about it. It had been private, personal.

And because he'd explored the world of the senses with one woman, he had developed no inhibitions except the one against sleeping with anyone else. Together, he and Kara had explored the farthest reaches of sensual pleasure.

He frowned at the cards. Poor Anna. She had been a virgin when he took her the first time, and his memory of that night brought with it a roar of noise and heat and steam. Even now, he could hardly believe they had found such furious physical accord, that they had torn into each other the way they had. That night had held the force of a speeding train.

And Tyler had not recovered. He'd taken refuge in his arrogant, morally correct world and gone into a state of deep denial about his hunger for her. A hunger he had been able to deny neatly until he kissed her this afternoon. And then he'd turned into a caricature of a lustful man, unable to think about anything but having her, unable to do anything without trying to meet his own selfish need of her.

But even now, he ached. Even now, all he wanted was to lie down next to her, flesh to flesh, and tumble into the narcotic world of sensual pleasure. The way he felt in this moment, he'd abandon himself to erotic addiction to Anna's body for the rest of his natural life.

Covering his face, he groaned softly. The trouble was, he didn't want a trembling, frightened Anna. He wanted

her whole, and giving herself freely. Sex, married or un-
married, was not the sin. Coercion was. If he coerced her,
he really would be no better than his father.

In the meantime, they would have to sleep together in
the presence of Curtis, especially since there was only one
bed in the cabin. Curtis would not understand if one of
them slept on the couch, and anyway, that would get old
real fast.

Tyler rose and turned off the lights. A truly moral man
would be able to sleep beside a woman he desired and
leave her alone. That would be his test.

Before he undressed, he turned off the bedside lamp.
Through the windows came the soft grayness of a snowstorm at night. It gave the room a silvery, almost enchanted
glow, and for a moment, Tyler admired it, feeling himself
calm and center on the quiet of the falling snow. Nature
had a way of putting everything into perspective.

He stripped to his boxers and climbed gently into the
bed. Although he stayed as far as he could on his own side
of the bed, it was impossible to completely ignore the
warmth of her body on the other side. Impossible not to
hear the even, steady whisper of her breath. Tyler resolutely closed his eyes, and when his mind was tempted to
stray toward the delectable bit of woman nearby, he imagined the snowy sky, silent and peaceful.

Anna was awakened by the insistent press of light
against her eyelids. Twice she tried to burrow back into
the pillows, but no matter which way she turned, the light
was bright and inescapable. Finally, she shifted and opened
her eyes to a room bathed in the brilliance of bright morning sunlight sparkling against undisturbed snow. She
blinked against it without moving, waiting for her brain to
follow her into this world.

She stretched below the covers, and her foot encountered flesh. She turned over more completely. Tyler lay

sprawled on his stomach, the covers tangled in a knot around his waist. The light had evidently not bothered him in the slightest, for he slept on obliviously.

Anna plumped her pillow a little and took the moment to observe him privately. The thick blond hair was scattered over his face and the pillow, and his jaw was bristly with unshaven beard. Even in sleep, he did not lose that guarded look, that wariness that surrounded him like a cloak, and it made Anna sad. Everyone should have the freedom of putting down his burdens while he slept.

She ached to touch him, to slide her palm down the smooth, supple length of his back, over the firm, well-formed shape of his backside. Where her toes had encountered his furred calf, she let them stay, since it had not disturbed him.

In this moment, he did not look like a prince. Only a man who had suffered too much, first at the hands of his father, then from the loss of his beloved wife. A man who lived too much alone, too far away from those who could have helped heal his wounds.

But somehow, Anna carried his child in her body. By magic or fate or the saints, she had been given the task of reaching out to him, of trying to shatter the walls he'd erected to protect himself—or, failing that, at least going behind the walls herself to keep him company.

It had been selfish of her to hold him at arm's length last night. She wanted him at least as much as he wanted her. It meant risking her heart, but she suspected that heart was already lost, and in the meantime, she might give them both joy to remember.

Hesitantly, she reached for him, and gave in to her wish to touch his warm, strong back. He stirred the smallest bit, and Anna scooted closer so that she could reach him better. She trailed her hand down his back, then, more daringly, over his hips and the lovely firmness of backside. It aroused her oddly, and she grew bolder still, brushing her hands down under the covers, over the backs of his thighs. He made a soft noise and shifted onto his side, but did not awaken.

Anna smiled to herself, and stilled until he fell deeply asleep again, taking pleasure in simply gazing at his face, at the crease on one cheek and the scatters of hair over his forehead. When she was sure he was fast asleep again, she ran her fingers down his chest, through the silky hair between his nipples, down his flat stomach, and wickedly lower, to the heavy flesh nestled between his thighs. It responded with a delightful little leap and, with a few more light, teasing brushes, grew solid and thrust against the light cotton shorts.

His hand closed around her wrist. "Anna, no."

She looked at him. "I'm ready, Tyler. I was selfish last night. I want to make love to you."

He closed his eyes, but did not release her hand. "I can't, Anna." He swallowed. "I was dreaming of—"

"Don't say it." She pulled out of his grip. Humiliated and burning with shame, she struggled with the covers. "I understand."

Before she could bolt, he snagged her around the waist, hauling her close to his body in a cradling hold. Anna covered her face with her hands. "Let me go," she whispered, holding herself rigid.

He stroked her hair. "I don't want to be thinking about another woman when I make love to you, Anna."

She swallowed, struggling to keep her voice even. "I already told you, I understand." She pulled against him, but he held her firm, his arms around her, his chest against her back.

"Anna," he said quietly, and kissed her shoulder. "Let's take it easy on each other for a while. Let's just find out where we are, before we try to patch the gaps with sex."

She turned to look at him. Gently, he touched her face.

"The only struggles we're having are about sex. It seems to me that maybe we're just not ready for that."

Anna realized it was true. The only awkwardness that existed between them came about because of sex— whether to indulge or not, when and how, and who was ready and who was not. She nodded.

His hand rested easily against her face, and now he touched her cheekbone with his thumb, smiling gently. "I think you know it has nothing to do with how much I want you." He cast a regretful glance downward, over her body. "Because God knows, I do. But we're going to hurt each if we keep this up."

She lifted a hand and brushed his hair back from his forehead. "You're right. We'll just take it one day at a time." She smiled. "And aren't you glad yesterday is over?"

He grinned. "Yeah. What do you say we get dressed and go have a ridiculously expensive brunch on my brother, then get Curtis and go home."

A weight dropped from her. "Great idea."

Chapter 15

Winter waned in the valley over the next few weeks, and Anna didn't know if it was the promise of spring in the air, or the simple agreement she'd made with Tyler that Sunday morning at the hotel, but things were surprisingly smooth and peaceful. Anna settled in with no fuss at the cabin, and a routine quickly developed between her and Tyler and Curtis. She learned to cook on the potbellied stove after a few disasters that benefited only the dog, Charley. She got used to the drive up and down the mountain very quickly, too, and learned to make lists so that she wouldn't forget anything important on a trip to town.

Tyler had a major renovation job to do, for an old house purchased by a wealthy Denverite, and Anna gladly condensed her workweek to spend more time with Curtis while Tyler worked.

Nights were the most difficult. Tyler worked on finishing the loft so that they could move the bed upstairs, but until it was done, there was nowhere for them to sleep except together in the same bed. Tyler never made a move toward her, and never seemed to have the trouble Anna did falling asleep. She coped.

In general, it was like living with a good friend, or a brother. Their relationship was utterly chaste, without a single external hint of the things boiling beneath the surface, but Anna found she enjoyed being with him tremendously. He had a quick, bawdy sense of humor, and a frank way of speaking that she found refreshing. In the evenings, they played games with Curtis, or read, or talked. They didn't play cards.

Meanwhile, the baby within Anna grew astonishingly fast. It amazed her how well she felt as the baby grew. Her initial exam had indicated nothing at all awry, as she'd known it would. As she passed from the first trimester to the second, she stopped needing so much sleep, as well, although her appetite slowed down not at all.

And the phenomenon she'd observed in her sisters was true for Anna, as well. She had never in her life been the sort of woman to cause a stir when she went out, but now men stopped in the streets to look after her. She got honked at by boys way too young for her. Clerks and baggers at the grocery store flirted outrageously.

Anna was fairly sure she could get used to it.

One Sunday afternoon, as Anna cooked a big pot of her grandmother's spaghetti for supper, she felt the baby kick. It was a tiny, fluttering sensation, but she cried out in surprise. Tyler dropped the wood he was whittling and rushed over. "What is it?" he demanded.

Anna smiled and reached for his hand. "I felt the baby," she said, awed, and put his palm over the place. "There!"

He pressed his hand close, looking first at her tummy, then at Anna. "I felt it."

And for the first time since the wedding, they fell adrift in the magic of their own special world, a world no one but the two of them could enter. Anna saw a silvery shine light his pale eyes, a glow of wonder and true joy, and a swell of painful love swept through her.

Curtis ran into the room. "What? My brother?"

Anna laughed. "It might be a sister, you know."

"I wanna feel, too."

"Sure you do." She reached for the little hand. "You have to be very still, and wait for a minute."

"I don't feel nothin'."

Beside her, Tyler chuckled. "Hang on, kiddo. Just wait."

Suddenly, Anna felt the flutter come again, and Curtis's mouth dropped open. "There's really a baby in there!" He put both hands on her tummy, his eyes wide as saucers. "I feel him!"

Anna laughed, and next to her, Tyler laughed softly, too, one hand falling on her shoulder in silent adult communication. "Can you tell if it's a brother or sister yet?"

Seriously, Curtis frowned. "Nope." He backed off and wiped his hands on his legs. "Doesn't that hurt?"

"No, not even a little bit."

"Okay."

"Go wash up, kiddo," Tyler said, his hand still on her shoulder. "We're going to eat."

As he bustled off, Anna put her hand on her belly again, still charmed by the wonder. Very softly, Tyler pressed a kiss to her temple and let her go. "I'll set the table."

Anna hurriedly bent her head to hide the swell of tears the tender gesture gave her, and only nodded.

"I'm ready, Daddy!" Curtis called.

Tyler put aside the stair spoke he was carving. "Coming!"

Since Anna had come, she had largely taken over the duty of putting Curtis to bed, a job Tyler hadn't minded relinquishing. But he was always there to tuck his son in, too, and it had become a treasured time for all of them.

Anna had instituted prayers, which she heard very solemnly, kneeling at his bedside while Tyler checked the stove. Then Anna and Tyler each gave Curtis a hug and kiss, and he loved to say, "Night, Mommy. Night, Daddy."

It had been difficult at first, but Tyler had found it impossible to resist the unrivaled pleasure Curtis took in having a mother to call his own. Tyler knew Kara's place in her son's life would become clear to the boy as he grew, and for now, having a flesh-and-blood woman to love made him deeply happy.

Anna shot him a warning glance when he entered the cozy, yellow-lit room and, alert, Tyler settled beside Curtis on the bed. "Ready for a kiss, champ?"

Kneeling beside the bed, Anna smoothed the hair from Curtis's face, and Tyler realized he was weeping silently. "Hey, come here." He gathered his son, smelling of baby lotion, into his lap. "What's wrong?"

Curtis lifted his head. "How does the baby get out, Daddy? Cody tol' me hith kitties came out his cat's bottom and there was lots of blood."

Tyler glanced at Anna and raised his eyebrows.

She sat next to them on the bed and put her hand on Curtis's back. "Well, it isn't exactly easy," she said, making it sound like something simple. "But it isn't as bad as it sounds." She bit her lip, and with a glance at Tyler gave him the ball.

Tyler had always been as open with his son as he was able, but this was a little different. "There's a special slide inside a woman, and the baby comes out between her legs."

"Oh." He sounded much relieved. "Will it hurt?"

"A little. But then it's over, and you get a baby, so it's worth it."

Curtis said nothing for a long time, and Tyler waited, sensing this wasn't quite finished. The boy folded and unfolded his fingers, seemingly absorbed in the fit. Finally he said, in a very quiet voice, "Can't you send the baby back?"

"I thought you were happy."

"My first mommy died when I was borned." He burst into tears. "I don't want my new mommy to die, too."

The knife sliced straight through Tyler's gut, and for one moment, he couldn't breathe. Anna touched his wrist, but he couldn't look at her, overwhelmed as he was with a strange sense of dread and grief that took him totally by surprise.

"Curtis," Anna said softly, "come here, honey, and let me hold you. I want to tell you about something."

He went willingly, and Tyler stood up and turned away, trying to regain his breath so that Curtis would not be even more frightened.

"What?" Curtis said. "Are you going to die, too?"

"No," she said clearly, firmly. "You know how many babies my mommy has?"

"Three?"

She chuckled. "Eight. So she had plenty of babies and she's still alive. Sometimes, a woman is sick, and her body doesn't feel good when she has a baby inside of it. Your mommy was sick, but she wanted you so much that she had to have you."

Tyler struggled to listen calmly, to find some rock in the spinning world to cling to, but his vision blurred, sending the stars in the black sky into long slashes of white.

"Is she sad now?" Curtis asked.

Tyler braced an elbow against the windowsill, and bent his head into his hand.

Anna's voice, too, sounded a little unsteady, but she said, "No. I'm sure that she is with you every minute of every day, making sure you're safe, and that you have people who will take care of you."

"She's an angel."

"Right."

"Can she see me right now?"

"Yes." The word was a whisper.

Tyler wiped his face on his sleeve. Emotions clogged his throat, but he urgently felt the need to turn. Anna sat on the bed, her face streaming with tears, the yellow light from the stove catching the edges of her hair so that she looked as if she were an Italian Renaissance painting of the Madonna. In her arms, Curtis was as blond as a cherub. His face wore a sober, wondrous expression, his eyes cast heavenward.

"Thank you, Mommy," Curtis said to the air.

A wash of tears blurred the picture again and, struggling to keep them from spilling over, Tyler did not dare blink. He crossed his arms hard and willed them away. The black of Anna's hair and the gold of the fire and Curtis's hair formed bands of smeared light. Rigidly, Tyler stared, trying to keep his emotions in check.

And for one, fleeting, endless second, it seemed there was a pale shadow moving around Curtis and over Anna and somehow obscuring his view of them. At that moment, Charley whined softly from his post at the foot of the bed, and a strange terror bolted through Tyler. He blinked, and felt tears spill, but there was only Anna and Curtis, heads bent together. Anna murmured something and began to sing softly, rocking back and forth with his son in her arms.

On puppet legs, Tyler forced himself to move across the small space between them. He pressed a kiss to Curtis's crown. "Good night, son," he said.

And fled.

Anna tucked Curtis in and sang a lullaby. "I love you, sweetie," she whispered, pressing a kiss to his forehead.

A gleam lit the bright blue eyes. "I love you more."

"I love you most."

"You're bigger!" he cried, and giggled.

"Night."

Quietly, Anna went into the other room. Tyler sat on the couch, staring at the fire. His long back was rigid, his hands were folded and pressed to his mouth. For a moment, Anna paused, wondering what his thoughts were, and if he'd be willing to share them.

She had worried about this, about the moment when everything sank in. He'd been too calm, which meant his feelings were buried. It wasn't natural for a man who had lost so much to absorb the new marriage and impending birth without at least a little worry or angst or *something*. Especially a man like Tyler, who felt things deeply, and who had been taught by his father that such feelings were unmanly.

Anna thought he'd probably hidden his feelings even from himself, but the conversation with Curtis had dragged everything into the open. His expression had been one of panic.

Taking a breath, she crossed the room to sit down beside him, and put a hand on his back. "Are you all right?"

His head fell forward, as if weighted by dark thoughts. "No."

Instinctively, Anna simply rubbed the long muscles in his back, over and over. "Do you want to talk about it?"

He jumped up, pulling away from her, and put one arm on the mantel. "I don't think I can do this, Anna. I can't stand it. I can't stand to think about it."

A breathless panic dripped from the words. Anna had pegged it right. Still, she wasn't quite sure how to respond. Did he really mean he couldn't face it at all, or was this just the first, brutal realization of the fact that he was going to be facing another pregnancy and birth? She frowned. "Tyler, come sit down, please."

He shook his head, his jaw hard. "Please, it's not you. I just can't breathe."

"Okay. Can you listen?"

"Yeah."

"I mean really listen."

With visible effort, he straightened and looked at her. Anna wanted to weep at the expression she saw there—a combination of panic and sorrow and genuine confusion. "Yeah."

"I'm not sure what's scaring you the most, but I'm guessing you're just now realizing that I have to have the baby sometime."

A curt nod. "It's not rational. I know that. But it doesn't seem to matter. It makes me feel sick to my stomach."

"Given what you've been through, that's not surprising. And we both know there are no guarantees. I wish there were." She gave him a rueful smile. "If you think it's scary from your side, you should be in my shoes."

"Are you afraid?" He asked the question as if the possibility had never occurred to him.

Anna laughed. "Well, of course I am. All new mothers are. It's normal. You hear stories." She rolled her eyes. "When my female relatives got together after one of them had a baby, you would not believe the birth stories they told. I remember I was in a hospital waiting for my sister Catherine's baby to be born, and there was some woman screaming bloody murder at the top of her voice the whole time. I was sure she was dying, but my mother just sat there next to me, reading the newspaper like it was nothing."

Tyler looked green. "What happened to her?"

"She was fine. It was her fourth baby, and he was born in two hours, but she liked screaming. My mother said some women curse, some scream, some just get completely vacant, like they aren't there." She raised an eyebrow. "Were you there when Curtis was born?"

He gave her an ironic smile. "Yeah. But Kara would

never have allowed anyone to think she wasn't the ultimate earth mother. She had no drugs, and had music on headphones, and I was supposed to rub her feet, but I have to tell you, Anna, I didn't like being in there. I know it's old-fashioned, but it doesn't seem like any man has any business in there.''

"I'm so glad you said that." Anna smiled. "I'd much rather you didn't come in. I don't want you looking at me all sweaty and piggy and crazed— I mean, what if I'm one of those women who scream expletives?"

A genuine smile broke the dimness of his expression. "I find that very hard to imagine." The smile turned into a chuckle. "Very hard."

She shrugged. "You never know. I'd just rather you let me do my business with other women. Maybe your mother will come, and Ramona will deliver it. She's about a month ahead of me, so she should be ready by then."

He went suddenly rigid again. "She might not be the one to deliver the baby?"

"Tyler, she's pregnant. If she goes over, she won't be ready to plunge into work that fast."

"Damn. I don't want anyone else to do it."

Anna held out her hand. "Tyler, please sit down. You're giving me a crick in my neck."

He ignored her hand, but perched on the chair across from her, sullenness back.

"If you worry like this all the way through, you will be no earthly help at all when the baby is born."

"I know." He swallowed. "It was just so awful, Anna. Losing her like that. I felt so guilty."

She'd leave that alone for the moment. "Tyler, I'm not Kara."

He had the grace to look ashamed. "I know." His mouth tightened. "But you're so small, Anna. How can it be possible for you to have a baby? Will Ramona do a C-section or something?"

"No." She grinned. "I only look small, Tyler. Where it counts, I have plenty of room." To illustrate, she put her hands on her body. "I'm made for this. Hips, pelvis. The women in my family have babies very easily. Every one of my sisters were walking around in an hour, and fixing meals three days later."

"Really?" Cautious hope shone in his eyes.

Anna smiled. "Really." She stood up and put one hand on either side of her hips. "Look at that spread."

He reached for her, and put his hands on top of hers, very seriously examining the space between their hands. "This is what matters?"

"One of the biggies. I'm also quite healthy, in case you haven't noticed by my appetite. Having babies is very natural for ninety-five percent of us."

He raised his eyes. "I don't think I could face it again, Anna."

A strange pang struck her heart. Did that mean he might be growing to love her? "Everything will be fine, Tyler. Trust me."

He moved his big palm over the low round of her belly. "Is she moving now?"

As if to accommodate him, the baby fluttered against his hand, and Tyler went completely still. Looking down at him, at his shining crown and his strong hand over her stomach, Anna found herself stricken with shattering love. She ached to put her hand against his hair, to touch his face, to kiss his sober, beautiful mouth, but she didn't. She simply let the emotion wash through her, sweet and sad and yearning, and let him greet the baby they had made.

When her throat was not quite so tight, she teasingly said, "Why do you call it a she? Curtis is sure he's having a brother."

"I don't know," he said, looking up at her as he moved his hand around, seeking the faint flutters again. "I think I'd like that, to have a daughter."

"Do you have any ideas about names?"

"Maybe." He let her go, and Anna sat back down on the couch across from him, mainly so that she wouldn't be tempted to simply leap on him, and probably humiliate herself again. If anyone was to make a move, it had to come from Tyler. Anna had tried twice and been rebuffed. "Do you?"

"I haven't thought about it much yet," she said.

"Well, I thought about Ramona, because it's a pretty name, but also because she saved my brother's life." He cleared his throat and looked away. "She was also Kara's doctor. If it wasn't for her, we probably would have lost Curtis, too."

"It is a pretty name. I might go for that, but I'm not willing to commit myself yet. What about boys?"

"That I don't know."

"Maybe something very old and honored, like Michael."

He considered. "That might work. I guess we have time."

"Yes, plenty." Anna folded her hands. "There is something we need to discuss that hasn't come up yet, however. I was waiting for you to bring it up again."

He frowned. "What?"

"We're going to need more room. At least a bedroom. The loft will be too cold for the baby, and I don't like that thought much, anyway."

He nodded. "You're right. That was why I added Curtis's room. But there will be four of us. Maybe I'll talk to Lance and see about getting some plans drawn. You have any ideas about what you'd want?"

So polite. Everything was always so blessedly polite. Anna suddenly couldn't bear it. "No, I'll leave it to you. I think I'm going to take a shower and get some sleep."

Tyler only nodded. "I think I'll read for a while."

* * *

Tyler waited until Anna was sound asleep, then donned his coat and boots and went outside with his dog. It was a cold, crisp night, the sky full of stars. He looked up at them in appreciation. So often, when people came from the city, the thing they could not believe was that there were so many stars they'd never seen. The sky was thick with them, but city lights obscured a lot of them, just as even faint pollution dulled the daytime blue.

With Charley close by, Tyler set out walking. In the deep darkness, he stuck to the road, simply walking in the night, trying to chase away his demons.

For Anna's sake, he'd submerged some of the feelings Curtis's misgivings had roused in him, but the truth was, tonight he missed Kara with a more piercing and painful grief than he'd felt in years. He didn't want to be having a baby with another woman. He didn't want to think about names. He wanted not to be here in this present, but back in the past, where Kara still lived.

Since marrying Anna, he had not allowed himself the maudlin luxury of speaking aloud to his dead wife, but alone now, and under cover of night, he did. "This is so strange," he said. "I hope I haven't made a big mistake. We were together for so long that getting married was natural, and Anna can never take your place." His booted feet crunched against the gravel. "I do like her, though. If it had to be anyone, I'm glad it was Anna. She genuinely loves Curtis, and she's easy to be around."

A cutoff from the main road led into the trees, and Tyler realized where his feet and heart had led him. To Kara's house.

In the bright night, he could see it clearly, a long, rambling single-story house with a deeply peaked roof. The external walls were made of long split logs, the blank windows were framed with golden pine, the door was worked with an alternating diagonal pattern of light gold pine, and grayish aged pine, and the whole was varnished and carved. Approaching it, Tyler was amazed at what beautiful work he'd done. "I really did love this. It turned out exactly right."

Charley wagged his tail.

Kara, inspired by a man in the southern Colorado mountains, had wanted to build a castle from the ground up. Tyler was much more practical, and had convinced her that a modern house, designed with the environment in mind, would be a far better idea.

Together they had scoured back issues of *Mother Earth News*, and *The Farmer's Almanac* and any other back-to-nature publication they could find for the latest in earth-friendly building. Tyler owned nearly five hundred acres up here, and they had scoured every inch of it, as well, to find the perfect home site.

A site, Tyler thought, rounding the house, that was incredibly beautiful. Sitting in a wide meadow protected on the north and west by thick forest, it would weather winter storms and summer heat with equal aplomb. A flat of land to the south would provide some vegetables. There was no danger of erosion, or flooding, or even avalanche.

Below, down a gentle slope dotted with trees and pink granite boulders that glittered with mica, lay Red Creek. Most of the lights were out at this late hour, but Tyler could see a few streetlights, and the red of a traffic light, and even the faint pinpoints of a moving car's headlights. The daytime view made the town look like a quaint Swiss village.

Slowly, he turned and headed to the house itself. From below a rock near the back door, he took a key, then climbed the steps to the wooden deck that was placed to take advantage of winter sunshine and summer shade. It gave him a glow of pride to remember how carefully he'd planned every detail.

Just inside, he paused, waiting for his eyes to adjust to the thicker darkness. The last time he was here, Kara had been with him, just a few days before she went into labor too early.

She had not been feeling well that day. Tyler had worked on the flooring in the kitchen while she sat in a patch of sunlight, her blond hair caught in a knot at the nape of her neck, her makeupless face extraordinarily pale. That afternoon, she had kept her hand over her belly, and by her expression, Tyler had known she was a million miles away. Twice he had asked her if she was all right, if she thought they should drive into town—or maybe even into Denver.

Both times, she had simply shaken her head and looked back into whatever interior landscape so occupied her. At the end of the day, they had walked very slowly back to the cabin, both silent with the strain that had marked their relationship since he told her about his vasectomy. Finally, winded, Kara had stopped at the meadow that surrounded the cabin. "Tyler," she had said, "try to understand that this is the thing I've most wanted in my life."

But even then, sick with worry, he'd been unable to totally forgive her for risking her life. Instead of granting the absolution she was asking, Tyler had simply looked at the house and said, "I think we can move in within a couple of months."

A week later, she'd been gone. And Tyler had never given the absolution. Not even when he held her hand in the hospital, with the knowledge of her impending death hanging over them.

Walking from room to room in the dark house, Tyler felt the old sorrow pounding in his veins like a virus. A virus, he thought, that had no cure. "I'm so sorry, Kara. I wish somehow I could make it up to you." He looked around him, seeing what should have been—the softly woven carpets and the pictures on the walls, and Kara and Curtis reading a bedtime story on furniture he'd made.

Sinking to the floor, he buried his face in his hands,

aching for all that was lost. All that should have been and had been lost to him in foolish, arrogant pride. His heart felt like a black hole, so empty that the emptiness sucked everything else into it.

How could he bear to continue this masquerade?

But how could he halt it?

Impossible. The whole thing was impossible.

Weary at last, Tyler relocked the door and went back to the cabin where his new wife slept. In the darkness, he undressed and, careful not to disturb her, he climbed into bed, somehow grateful for the warmth she provided.

As if she sensed him, Anna turned over and curled against his arm, her hair brushing his shoulder, her soft, round breasts close against his rib cage, her knee just touching his thigh. After two months of sharing a bed with her, he'd thought he'd finally grown used to the discipline he needed to keep his hands to himself, but tonight, her nearness assaulted him anew.

Clenching his fist, he moved slowly away from her, turning his back to the ripeness of her warm, sleepy body. If he loved her, this furious lust would be an appropriate expression of that love. As things stood, his visions were physical, carnal manifestations, and he didn't think it was fair or right to indulge them.

Not when Anna was in love with him, and she would be making love.

Gripping the pillow close to his chest, Tyler hugged the edge of the bed and willed his arousal to subside, and finally, he fell into merciful sleep.

Chapter 16

He dreamed he was back in Kara's house, in the daylight. It was summer, and the windows were thrown open to let in the fresh, cool mountain breezes. Somehow there were rugs in place, and something cooking on the stove, and, bewildered, Tyler called out, "Hello?"

From around the corner came Kara herself. She smiled. "Hi, Tyler."

Confused, he said, "You're dead. How can you be here?"

With a gentle smile, she said, "They let me come back for a day."

Stunned, he stared at her, wonder and joy swelling in his chest. "Can I touch you?" he asked, ashamed that his need showed in such husky wildness in his voice.

"Oh, yes," she whispered.

Tyler reached for her, and somehow, in the way of dreams, they were in a bed in the sunny room that was going to be their bedroom, close together under thick quilts. She curled against him, spoon-position, and he put his hand over her breast, sighing at the texture, that heavy softness, the nudge of an aroused nipple against the heart of his palm. "I can't even tell you how good that feels," he said, and rubbed the tip lightly, hearing a soft groan of pleasure come from her throat.

She wore a simple white gown made of something he thought was silk, and Tyler felt a little confused for a moment. Kara only liked cotton or flannel, disdaining silky things as unnecessary luxury.

But the lure of her sweet flesh swept away his confusion. Eagerly he slid his hands below the fabric. Her thick hair brushed his face, and he groaned at the freshness against his nose. He closed his hands around her naked breasts, the fulsome softness filling his hands exactly, sending an agony of arousal through him. He kissed her neck, suckling hard at the tender place, and she shuddered in approval, turning to him, offering herself.

Tyler opened his eyes slightly, only enough to guide himself to his destination. He bent his face to her breasts, brushing his mouth, then his hungry tongue, over the swells of satiny flesh. He shifted to take his weight on his elbows, and gathered her breasts into both hands so that he could kiss and tease and please her. He felt her hands in his hair, heard her small sounds of pleasure, felt her arch into him, nestling herself against his erection. At last he took one pert nipple all the way into his mouth, and the sensation went through both of them like a thunderbolt, and his low moan mixed with her womanly one, a melding of notes in perfect harmony.

With effort, Tyler tried to rein in his urgent hunger, and moved to the other side, tugging and suckling until she writhed against him in an agony of need that matched his own.

She gripped her hands in his hair almost painfully, and whispered his name.

Tyler shattered awake to find it was no dream. He had

burrowed under the covers and taken away her nightgown, and his mouth was filled with the deliciousness of aroused breast, and his organ was heatedly cradled at the juncture of her thighs.

But it was not Kara. It was Anna. Anna who felt so magnificent, who shivered with yearning, who arched with passion against him. A fierce joy pushed through him at that, a pointed hunger he could not have halted even if he had the will to try. It was not a dream. He had sweet Anna in his arms, her bare breasts against his mouth, her moist heat an irresistible invitation, and he thought in a disconnected way that he should have known it was Anna, because Kara had never responded like this to him, had never shivered or clung to him like this, had never allowed herself to fall apart like this.

In fierce longing, he moved to kiss her neck, to bite her a little and elicit that sobbing cry, and then took her lips with all the force he had denied these long, long weeks, and he felt Anna respond with the same gusto, her teeth against his lip. Her breasts pushed into his bare chest, and he reached below the covers to push away the clothes that stood between them.

"Good morning!" came a voice, then the *thunk* of a small boy's body landing on the foot of the bed. "The sun is shining. Maybe flowers will come up today."

They froze. For an instant, Tyler looked down into Anna's eyes and saw there his own rueful smile. Softly, he kissed her once more. "Later," he whispered.

Wickedly, she touched him as he shifted away. "Please."

With a regretful sigh, he moved away from Anna, feeling her slip the nightgown back upon her shoulders under the covers, as Curtis scooted up to lie down next to his dad. "Will flowerth come up today, Daddy?"

"Not quite yet," he said. "Not much longer."

* * *

Anna had to go to work that morning. As spring neared, she had to try to focus more on work in order to prepare for the annual Spring Festival, which drew tourists—and their money—by the droves into Red Creek. Often the festival brought in more than three-quarters of the funds the museum was able to raise throughout the year.

It was pleasant enough in her office. The optimistic sound of snow melting in drips lifted her spirits, and she hummed quietly as she added figures and typed up tentative plans to present to the Friends of the Museum. Every so often, she remembered the feeling of Tyler around her this morning, the husky, needy sound of his voice, and a shiver of anticipation went through her.

Just after lunch, Louise appeared at the office door. "Anna?"

"Hmmm?" She punched a number into the calculator and scribbled it on a spreadsheet.

"Ah, you have a visitor."

Still Anna had no presentiment that her world was about to turn upside down. "Oh?" She looked up.

And froze. For one long moment, all she could do was stare in dumbfounded shock at the familiar face, unable to place it so far out of context. A woman in her early sixties, with thick salt-and-pepper hair cut into an elegant and flattering style, her face remarkably unlined for her age. The green wool suit had traveled well, of course.

"Mama!"

"Surprise!" the woman cried, holding out her arms as she came into the office. Behind her came others, her father and her little brother Tony and her brother Jack, who gave her a sympathetic look as they trooped in.

Anna gaped at them, unable to act, while her mind raced in a frenzy. The moment she stood up, they would see that she was pregnant. The four-month mound of her belly was not instantly obvious to the rest of the world, but on her small frame, it showed. And her family would notice.

Caught in panic, Anna looked to Louise, who simply smiled at them all, proudly. It occurred to Anna that Louise simply assumed Anna had told them all. It was only natural that she would, of course.

Of course. Except she hadn't. The time had never seemed right. How did you break something like that, for heaven's sake? "Mama, I just thought I'd let you know I'm married and there will be a baby in the fall."

Looking from one of them to the other, Anna realized the moment had arrived.

"Anna, aren't you happy to see us?" Hurt showed in her mother's black eyes. "We thought it would be such a nice surprise."

"It is!" Damn the consequences, she thought, and rounded the desk, hoping the hustle and bustle in the crowded office would help put off the inevitable for at least a few moments. She hugged her mother, smelling the familiar cologne and hairspray. Anna tried to keep her belly apart, but no such luck. Her mother made a soft, shocked noise and pulled back, looking down.

"What's this?"

Her father moved forward, frowning. "You're pregnant, Anna?"

"Well, yes, but—"

"And you didn't tell us?

"Who is the creep?"

"A baby!"

"How long have you known?" her mother asked.

"When were you planning to give us the news?" her father demanded.

"I knew it!" exclaimed her brother.

A bright, loud whistle cut through the exclamations, and they all turned toward Louise in surprise. "Let's take things one step at a time, shall we?" she said, and stuck out her hand. "Hi. I'm Louise Forrest, Anna's mother-in-law. I gather you are Mr. Passanante."

"Mother-in-law?" he echoed, shaking her hand. "Anna, you're—"

"Married," she said, and clasped her hands nervously.

"Thank you, Mary!" her mother breathed, crossing herself dramatically.

"You must be Mrs. Passanante," Louise said agreeably.

"Oh, call me Olive, please. My husband is Salvatore, after his father." She pointed to the others. "That is my son Tony, and Jack, who came with us to run away from his life." She seemed to run out of steam, and looked back to Anna. "Oh, Anna," she said sadly. "I told them they were wrong. That you'd be okay out here. That you were a much more sensible girl than they thought."

Anna opened her mouth, then closed it. This was what she had most dreaded, the disappointment in her mother's eyes. Bleakly, she simply looked at her. "I'm sorry."

Olive shook her head slowly. "And you didn't even tell us! Who made your dress? Who fixed your hair? How could you leave us out like that?"

"I'm sorry," she said again.

Her father touched his wife's shoulder. "I'm very disappointed in you, Anna."

Anna bowed her head, brushing a lock of hair from her cheek, her face burning with shame. "I know."

Jack stepped in. "Time enough for all this later," he said with false cheer, and hugged her. "Boy, kid, you don't mess around, do you?"

Anna clung to him. The brother closest to her in age, he had always had more in common with her than any of the others. Like Anna, he'd longed for more than the horizons he'd been given, but he'd never been able to focus on how to get it, and he moved from one spot of trouble to the next. As Anna hugged him, she breathed in the spicy scent of his aftershave, and the scent of wool and silk. "I'm glad you're here," she said.

He chuckled. Anna felt it rather than heard it, and when

he pulled back, she saw the twinkle in his eyes. "I bet you are." With a wink, he let her go.

Louise clapped her hands together. "Well, I think I'll call around and find some volunteers to man the museum for the day, and then we can all go up to my house for a nice get-to-know-you visit. Why don't you all sit down and let me steal Anna for a minute?"

Olive and Salvatore nodded. Anna knew from long experience that this was simply the calm before the storm, and she kissed each one. "I'm so glad to see you," she said. "I'll be right back."

But if she thought she was escaping, it was only from a bed of thorns to a bed of nails. Louise walked silently to the front of the museum, and abruptly turned the corner to go upstairs. "What are you doing?" Anna asked, confused.

"Come on."

In one of the bedrooms, Louise closed the doors, then turned to face Anna. It was only then that she saw the rare, dangerous fury in the older woman's eyes. "Honestly, child, if you weren't pregnant, I'd whip you within an inch of your life. What were you thinkin'? Did you think they'd never know? Were you planning to cut yourself off from them completely?"

Anna bowed her head. "I don't know."

"Well, I *know* you're in big trouble. Oh, Anna. How could you do this? Everything was working out so well, and now this."

"You see them, Louise. I didn't know how to break it to them. I mean, pregnant, then married? And not only that, he's not Italian, or even Catholic. You haven't even begun to see what a mess this is. Trust me."

"I'm not real worried about you at the moment, you'll forgive me." Her blue eyes blazed, and she crossed her arms over her ample bosom. "I've spent the past few years wondering if I'd ever get my Tyler back. He was so lost, and you've brought him back. I really didn't know if it would happen, Anna. And it did."

Anna felt bewildered. "I'm not going to leave him just because they showed up, Louise. I mean, they'll be mad, and there will be endless lectures until they go back home, but nothing else has changed."

"That's where you're wrong, darlin'." Agitated, Louise paced toward the window. "Think about how this is going to look from Tyler's perspective. He isn't going to trust you to go around the block after this, and I don't blame him. It really looks like you hedged on the commitment you made there in that courthouse."

Anna frowned. "I don't think he'll take it that way. I didn't mean it that way."

But, with a sinking feeling, Anna realized that she had. She hadn't told her family because she hadn't been sure it would work out and there was no point to them knowing if she and Tyler parted ways.

Winded, she sat gingerly on a rocking chair. "Louise, you know I love him."

"Funny way of showing it."

"That's not fair. I didn't want to show it. I didn't want him to feel obligated to me. I wanted to see if he could fall in love with me on his own. And I didn't want to humiliate myself with my family." A jolt moved in her middle as she realized anew that they were waiting for her. "And this isn't even the tip of the iceberg. They'll all be out here before we're finished with this, examining everything, making judgments on the way I live, scolding me, teasing me, acting like I don't have a single brain in my head." She gave a low moan and buried her face in her hands. "I love my family, Louise, but they are a serious pain in the neck."

For a moment, Louise said nothing. "Well, it's out now. We'll just have to make the best of it."

Anna raised her head. "Do you really think Tyler won't understand if I explain it to him?"

The cornflower eyes were troubled. "His problem has always been that holier-than-thou attitude. He wants everybody to be honest and true and noble, and he's not very forgiving of human foibles."

When it was put that way, Anna knew exactly what Louise meant, and her heart plummeted. She wanted to break down and cry, but really, it was her own fault.

Louise put a hand on her shoulder. "I'm here for you, honey."

Anna gripped her hand fiercely. "Thank you."

"Come on. Time to face the music."

Louise herded everyone to her house and got some coffee started, then called down to the construction yard to get Lance and have him fetch Tyler from the renovation job he was doing. For a moment, she wavered over how to handle things, but then she blurted out, "Lance, you might let Tyler know—gently—that Anna hadn't told her family about the wedding or the baby."

"Oh, brother."

"Yeah, brother. Try and break it easily, will you?"

Lance sighed. "It won't make any difference how I break it. He's going to be upset."

"Do your best. Maybe he'll get over it before he gets here."

"Yeah, that's possible. Like he got over Kara being pregnant in a day or two, right?"

"It is what it is. We'll have to just go forward from here."

"I don't know how such a good-natured woman raised such an uptight man, Mama."

Louise knew. Tyler clung to his almost impossibly high standards as a way of keeping the world at bay, of keeping his very private self as private as possible. If he held others at arm's length, if they fell short of his expectations, they would never hurt him. The more worried or hurt he was, the more he cloaked himself in the protective code of honor.

That lofty code was both his most admirable virtue and his most devastating character flaw. When he was a boy, Louise had despaired of his righteous indignation over world affairs, over the intrigues of government, the lack of faithfulness and honor in leaders. She'd tried to help him understand that human beings were simply flawed— they did their best, but they faltered.

But Tyler didn't. Not often, anyway. And when he did stray from the path, he owned up to it. He took responsibility. He did not lie. He did not cheat. He did not take lovers.

Listening to the tone of the voices coming from the other room, Louise sighed. The real reason for Tyler's code went deep. She knew his reasoning was very simple: If he held himself to that knightly standard, he could never be mistaken for his father, whose philosophy could be summed up as "Go and sin some more." In the end, his excesses had killed him.

For the twentieth time that week, Louise wished Alonzo were here to lean on. But their relationship had cooled after the argument the night Anna found out she was pregnant. Oh, not from Alonzo's side, at least not at first.

He'd hurt her more deeply than he realized that night, and she had retreated. Better to have her simple, calm life than to risk the sorrows she'd known in her first marriage. When she told Alonzo that she thought their relationship had gone as far as it could, he had simply looked at her for a long moment with those luminous Hershey-bar eyes and nodded. Two days later, he'd announced he'd found an apartment in town and would no longer be needing the guest house.

She'd seen him at the wedding, and they'd been excru-

ciatingly polite, but that had been the last time. Through
Lance, she heard he was still working at Forrest Construction, and he'd been seen dancing with a woman much
younger and prettier than Louise, a divorced teacher who'd
come to Red Creek in the fall.

Standing there, staring at the phone, Louise finally admitted to herself that she missed him. Missed his company
and his gentle teasing and the way he touched her, as if
she were precious, and beautiful, and desirable.

But it was too late for her. She vowed it would not be
too late for her son. By all she held holy, she vowed she'd
do everything she could to make things right with Anna
and Tyler.

Anna sat on the couch in Louise's living room, half
listening for the sound of Tyler's truck in the drive. With
the other half of her mind, she filled herself with the chatty
gossip of her family, like an arroyo after a rain. Louise
brought in coffee and cookies and sandwiches, and although she lit for moments at a time, chuckling over the
anecdotes they told, she never sat down for long.

Which meant she was nervous.

About Tyler.

Resolutely, Anna made up her mind to stop worrying
and let herself enjoy the moment. Soon enough, one or
two of her family would take her aside to some private
corner, and the lectures would begin. Another would join
in, or maybe they'd do it one at a time, each lecturing
about some new angle. Soon enough, Tyler would be here
and she would be faced with his reaction.

So she focused on the moment. On her mother, vibrant
in her green wool, her nails freshly manicured, the diamonds flashing on her fingers. Her father, looking pros-
perous and clean in his carefully tailored suit, his hair
neatly combed back from his face to show off the gorgeous

high forehead and Roman nose. What a handsome couple they were, Anna thought.

She'd forgotten so much about them, about their relationship. Her mother, like Anna, was a talker, while her father was a rather silent man, who only roused himself to make the odd teasing comment or wickedly ironic joke. But always they were quietly attentive to one another. Olive put chocolate cookies on a napkin and passed them to her father without missing a syllable in her tale of another of Mary Frances's displays of prodigious vanity. "Four hundred dollars for a blouse!" she exclaimed. "Imagine!"

"She can afford it, Ma," Jack said from his corner.

Which wasn't the point. Anna smiled.

In his turn, Salvatore touched his wife's hand, reminded her of a detail she'd forgotten, patted her leg. They knew each other so deeply, so intimately, Anna realized. She wondered with a sense of vague sadness if she and Tyler would ever interact like that. If they would ever know each other that well.

When she heard his truck in the driveway, she started so badly that she almost spilled her tea. "Oh!" she exclaimed, flustered, trying to smooth her hair and her blouse and catch the tea, all at once.

Jack rescued the tea before disaster struck. "He must really be something," he commented quietly.

She met his curious gaze. "Do I have any food on my mouth?"

"Nope." He grinned. "It's been a long time since I've seen such a happy newlywed."

Anna nearly choked on that. She was spared the necessity of answering by Curtis, hurtling himself through the front door. "Mommy, do I really have another grandma?"

Thank the saints for children. Anna bent to scoop Curtis into her arms, a shield and a comfort all at once. "Yes, you do. Remember I told you about my mama, how she had eight children? This is her, and look how healthy she is.''

Olive blinked a little, but she immediately moved around to greet Curtis properly. ''Well, aren't you a handsome young man!''

''Mama, this is my stepson, Curtis. Curtis, say hello to your grandma Olive.''

To her delight, he stuck out a hand. ''Pleathed to meet you, Grandma Olive.''

Olive beamed. ''Such nice manners. Oh, you're a sweet boy.'' She turned and gestured toward the couch. ''That's your grandpa Sal, and Uncle Tony, and Uncle Jack.''

''Jack?'' Curtis echoed. ''Hey, I have an uncle Jake, too!''

Tyler came in, carefully cleaning mud from his boots on the mat. Anna looked at him, trying to find some sign of his mood. It was so hard to know what he was thinking behind that natural reserve. ''Tyler,'' she said as calmly as she could, putting Curtis down. ''I'd like you to meet my family.''

Next to her, Olive slipped a hand around Anna's upper arm and squeezed. ''Anna,'' she whispered urgently into her ear, ''he's as handsome as a prince!''

''Yes,'' she said. Her heart still pounded painfully in fear. She just couldn't see what Tyler thought of all this, if he was angry with her. Anything. He simply moved into the room in his loose-limbed way. ''Hello,'' he said.

''Mama and Papa, this is my husband, Tyler Forrest.'' She realized it was the first time she'd said the words. ''Tyler, these are my parents, Olive and Salvatore Passanante.''

Sal stood to shake Tyler's hand, and Anna watched them take each other's measure. Her father looked underwhelmed, but Tyler bore the scrutiny well, with the dignity of a man who had nothing to hide. ''It's good to meet you at last, sir,'' he said.

Sal relaxed marginally. From the corner of her eye, Anna saw Jack ducking his head to hide his expression, and she knew he was silently laughing. She wanted to throw something at him.

Olive was less suspicious. She moved forward with her trademark charm. "Oh, my Anna's found herself a very handsome husband," she said, and kissed his cheek. "Welcome to our family, Tyler."

Tyler smiled. And, with amazement, Anna saw that it was his full, unguarded smile, complete with dimple and twinkling eyes. "It's easy to see where Anna gets her beauty."

He still had not looked at Anna, and she didn't think her heart would stand the suspense much longer.

At last he turned to her, his eyes opaque, and said, "Can I talk to you for a minute?"

Anna swallowed. "Sure. We'll be right back."

He waited for her to navigate the furniture, then took her hand, lacing his fingers between hers. A good sign. To the others he said, "We'll be right back."

He led her toward the dining room, but then took a turn into the hallway that led to the bedrooms, and Anna's heart plummeted. She tried to think of some excuse, something to blunt his disappointment in her, but for once couldn't even think of anything to babble about. Silently, he led her into the spare bedroom, at the very end of the hall, then reached behind him and closed the door. Quietly.

Anna looked at him. "Tyler—"

"Later," he said in a raw voice, and, with a swift gesture, pushed her against the door and kissed her. Not a sweet little kiss, either—a deep, hungry, erotic kiss. For a split second, Anna was stunned, but her body quickly recognized the proper course of action, and she flung her arms around his neck, standing on her toes to reach him better.

He pressed his body against hers, all of him against all of her, and she felt the fierceness of his arousal, nudging her stomach. Then his hands slid down her buttocks, holding them even tighter together. His breathing was hurried as he broke the kiss to look at her, and Anna thrilled at his need of her, feeling valued and womanly and as sexy as a Victoria's Secret model.

His eyes were a mercurial color, blazing and unmistakable. "I've been thinking about this all day, Anna," he breathed, and pulled her skirt up in back. "All day, I've remembered how you felt, how you tasted, and I couldn't wait another second to touch you again."

She felt his hands against her bottom, felt him slide her panties down, and he kissed her, openmouthed, without closing his eyes. It was insistently intimate and unbearably arousing. Anna felt her knees weaken, thinking of everyone in the house. "Your mother is sure you're yelling at me," she whispered, and put her hands under his shirt.

He knelt to push her panties down her legs, and lifted one foot then the other. "All the better," he said, pushing her skirt up, his hands sliding up the front of her thighs, his thumbs making an impossibly erotic trail on the inside, a trail that alarmed and excited her in equal measures.

"Tyler, do you think—"

He tucked her skirt into the elastic waist, holding her still, pressed against the door, and Anna looked down to find him looking at her nakedness, and for some reason, it made her dizzy. She let her head fall back as his mouth fell on her thigh, following the same trail his hands had made, only his tongue rose higher, and plunged into the secret heart of her, and Anna clutched his head. "Stop, Tyler!" she gasped. "I can't do this and go— Oh!"

He nudged her legs apart, and with skillful hands and his even more talented mouth, he did things she had never even imagined could feel so good. It ceased to matter that her family was on the other side of the door, or that she would look like a Kewpie doll when they finished, or anything else. It only mattered that it was Tyler giving her such riotous, unbearable pleasure, that he was as out of his mind with need of her as she was with need of him. When she started to shiver uncontrollably, on the verge of release, he stopped. Anna made an involuntary sound of protest.

Wickedly, Tyler untucked her skirt to let it fall around her legs modestly once again and stood up. "I think we've spent too long in here."

"Oh, no," she whispered. "Fair is fair."

She reached for the buttons of his jeans, but he caught her hands with a smile. "No, you don't. For one thing, I seriously doubt I could hold out. For another, I think you should suffer a little, the way I've suffered today."

There was such thickness in her blood that Anna felt almost drugged. She moved a little, and her foot touched the edge of her panties. An idea bloomed in her mind, and she smiled. "Two can play this game, Tyler Forrest," she said, and bent over to pick up her panties. Neatly she folded them into a very small bundle and then, with a grin, tucked them neatly into her pocket.

"Anna!" he said with a choked sound. "You can't tease me like that."

With a smug smile, she opened the door and flounced out, exaggeratedly swinging her hips as she walked down the hall. Once, she glanced over her shoulder and saw him standing there, staring after her with a most unmistakable expression on his face. She laughed softly.

The evening would prove to be interesting indeed.

Chapter 17

Tyler stared after Anna with a dry mouth. Her hair had been tousled by his fingers and fell in glossy gypsy curls against her neck. She sashayed provocatively down the hall, perfectly aware of his attention. And did he ever give her his attention—he couldn't tear his eyes from the round rear end swaying with exaggerated swings from side to side, swings that made her skirt slide sweetly, suggestively, over the flesh that he knew all too well was naked beneath the linen.

She'd had to buy new clothes, but although this skirt had an elastic waist, the back was nicely tailored to show off one of her best qualities.

He would die before he could get her back to the cabin tonight.

Die.

His skin felt flushed, and he closed the door against temptation, trying to rein in his raging hormones. He'd been able to think of nothing but Anna all day, a naked Anna, an Anna stoked to wildcat hunger by his touch.

He'd forgotten, in the months since she was stranded at the cabin, just how intense the connection was between them. He'd forgotten how fierce she got, how incredibly, intensely sexy it was to have a woman respond to him with such uninhibited delight.

It had been doubly hard to remember because in daily life, coming and going in her routine, that secret, wild gypsy was well hidden—like the purple glitter nail polish she'd worn on her toenails, below wool socks and snow boots.

"Tyler!"

Louise. Hastily, Tyler straightened, tucked in his shirt and prayed he didn't look as rattled as he felt. "In here, Ma!" He opened the door and nearly slammed into her.

"What are you doing?" She scowled. "I hope you aren't going to make that poor girl suffer all night long. She's been on pins and needles waiting for you to get here."

Suffer? Oh, she'd suffer, all right. Just like he was suffering—in the most delicious sense of the word. "I was—" he glanced over his shoulder "—just thinking about something."

Her eyes narrowed. "Sulking, I suppose."

"Sulking? About what?"

"What did Lance tell you?"

He was anxious to get back to Anna, and he impatiently took his mother's arm to lead her out. She resisted. "He said Anna's family flew in to surprise her." He chuckled. "And, boy, were they ever surprised."

"So he told you they didn't know about the wedding or the baby or any of that."

Tyler shrugged. "Yeah."

"And that didn't make you mad."

"Well, maybe a little." Truth was, he'd felt injured more than angry, but it had only lasted a moment. He'd remembered everything she had told him about her family and her place in it, and understood immediately how poorly the whole mess with him would make her look. "It's not too hard to understand, really." He paused. "Were you upset?"

Louise gave him a puzzled expression. "Only because I was worried how you'd take it."

And suddenly Tyler understood. She had been afraid he'd use this an excuse to distance himself from Anna. "She had a good reason." Just as he had good reason to hide the existence of Kara's house from her.

"There's something not right here, Tyler Forrest. I don't know if you're lying to yourself, or lying to me, but this just doesn't feel right."

A twinge of guilt touched him, but he brushed it away. "Don't borrow trouble," he said lightly, and dragged her into the living room with him. So that he could lust after his wife properly.

And lust he did, all evening, just as she'd meant him to do. Her father insisted on taking the whole crew out to dinner at one of Red Creek's finest restaurants, and when he announced it, Anna shot Tyler a mischievous expression that sent his blood boiling all over again.

And aside from the arousal their secret kindled in him, Tyler also found himself feeling extremely protective. He took her arm from the car into the restaurant, unwilling to let even the maître d' near her. At dinner, they sat side by side, and Tyler was barely aware of a single syllable of conversation. It seemed the only light in the world was seated placidly to his right, her black eyes glowing with passion, her cheeks rosy with color. When she leaned forward to pick up her water glass, he caught a lovely, discreet glimpse of the lacy edge of her bra and remembered all over again how sweet she'd tasted to him this morning.

About halfway through the first course, he remembered that his aim was to put her into the same wildly aroused state she was managing to keep him in, and when he finished eating, he put his hand on her thigh, under the table. She gave him an amused smile, much like her gloating poker smile, and he was all the more determined.

He turned to listen to the conversation on his left, an anecdote told in a hilarious manner by Anna's mother. He laughed easily, thinking it was obvious where Anna had gotten her storytelling abilities, but under the table, he eased up her skirt, a quarter inch at a time, until he touched the bare skin of her thighs and heard her suck in a breath. He removed his hand before she could grow alarmed.

She stood up. "Excuse me a moment," she said, and headed toward the ladies' room. Tyler stared after her, knowing she was teasing him again.

Her brother leaned close. "The Passanante women, they really get a glow when they're pregnant."

Tyler straightened with a grin. "Am I that obvious?"

"Hey, brother, that's what I've been waiting for all these years, for someone to look at my little sister the way you do."

The twinge of guilt struck him again. There was a falseness to all of this, after all. He'd been lusting over Kara in his dream, and it had only been Anna when he woke up. Was that wrong?

He really didn't know. Somehow, the lines between right and wrong, moral and immoral, were not as clear-cut as they once had been.

And not for the world would he let her down tonight. Ruefully, he lifted a brow. "She's one gorgeous woman."

Just then, she came out of the hallway at the other end of the room, and Tyler realized it was true. Anna was drop-dead gorgeous. He wasn't the only man in the room with his mouth hanging open—waiters and customers and even some of the women stared openly as she passed. He felt a queer, sharp twist of possessive pride in that.

His wife. His woman.

Taken one by one, there was not a single feature that

set her apart particularly, with the possible exception of that lush, sexy mouth. But the whole was unbelievably sexy. The black hair, the dancing black eyes, her shoulders straight, head high. She walked with a kind of loose, confident awareness Tyler had not noticed before, and, with a slight smile, he realized it was something he'd given her.

Tyler found his gaze on her thighs, lifting the skirt on one side, then the other, and could not help remembering—

"*Really* gorgeous," he said aloud, his mouth dry.

Jack chuckled and slapped him approvingly on the shoulder. "I'll make sure we don't keep you long tonight."

Anna thought the evening would never end, but at last they were all standing together in the parking lot, chatting cheerfully. Anna's mother slid up next to her and took her arm. "We'll talk tomorrow, all right? Your papa and me and you. Maybe we can have breakfast."

"That would be wonderful." Anna knew she would be grilled, but nothing mattered tonight. Except Tyler. She shot a glance to where he stood under the streetlight, a head taller than anyone else there, his hair shining in the darkness, and she felt a shiver of happiness.

Her prince no longer looked lost. At that moment, he was laughing at some joke her father had made, and the sound was deep and rich and full of life. Somehow she had helped bring that about—a peasant girl from Queens.

It could only be magic.

And that thought sobered her the faintest bit, for she had yet to pay a penny for the magic.

Silliness. Fairy tales were one thing, but this was real life. Sometimes, wonderful things just happened. They didn't have to be explained or examined too closely.

Curtis leaned sleepily on his grandmother. "Gramma, can I spend the night at your house tonight?"

"Sure, sweetie. What about your bear?"

Curtis yawned. "I don' need him. I have an angel mommy who watches over me all the time."

"Oh!" exclaimed Anna's mother, softly. "Is Tyler a widow?"

She glanced at her husband, a twinge of dread in her, but he hadn't heard the exchange. "Yes."

"Poor little boy." Olive touched her mouth, and Anna knew her heart was going out to Curtis, and to his poor, departed mother, whom Anna would rather not have thought about just then. "I'm so glad you're filling her shoes."

Anna repressed a sigh. She knew it wasn't meant to be such a backhanded compliment, but it was. She tried not to mind. "So am I, Mama."

Finally, they all climbed into their cars, Curtis going to his grandmother's house, Anna's family to the hotel rooms they'd reserved. Anna and Tyler stood next to his truck in the nearly empty parking lot, watching them drive away.

Now that they'd been waiting all night, Anna felt overcome with shyness, as if they'd never made love before. As if she'd been extremely silly by teasing him with her underwear in her pocket. She ducked her head. "Well, I guess we can go."

Tyler nodded, and she wondered if he felt funny, too. "It's a really nice night. You smell that? It's almost spring."

Anna lifted her head and inhaled the loamy scent of wet earth. "I do.

Unexpectedly, he took her hand. "Do you mind if we take a short walk? I'd like to show you something."

"Sure. What is it?"

He winked. "A surprise. It isn't far."

Without speaking, they walked to the edge of the parking lot and along the blacktop. "Here it is," he said, and pointed out a narrow path between thick trees.

"What if there are bears?" She'd been hearing a lot about bears lately, and they scared her.

"There shouldn't be any this early, but if we see one, we'll run." He tugged her hand, a light shining in his eyes. "C'mon. I promise it'll be worth it."

And because she trusted him, she followed, surprised to find railroad ties laid into the mountainside as steps. The snow had melted this far down, and the ground smelled rich and fertile and spicy. After a short climb, the ground leveled off in front of a bubbling spring. Standing sentinel was a big pine with widespread branches, and a small grove of aspens. Illuminated by a three-quarter moon, the spot was faintly mystical and silvery. "It's beautiful," she said with a sigh.

"I thought you'd like it. It's a shrine to Saint Blaise, established by some German settlers a hundred years ago. The waters are supposed to be healing."

"Saint Blaise. I don't know him."

"He was a healer." He turned to her, and she sensed a hesitance about him. "Will you drink the waters with me?" He cleared his throat. "Just to be on the safe side?"

Anna, touched by his worry and his faith, nodded.

"It's not too muddy this high, but be careful."

"I don't mind a little mud." She knelt next to the spring with him, and together they bent to cup their hands and drink of the water, which was cold and delicious and faintly flavored with minerals. It was so good, Anna bent for another drink, and when she straightened, wiping her face on her coat sleeve, Tyler was looking at her very soberly.

He lifted a hand to her hair. "Thank you, Anna."

"My pleasure." She stood up and brushed off her knees, then put a hand down to help him up. He waved it away and stood on his own, then took her hand and pulled her close.

"Now, I think we have some unfinished business."

"Oh, I thought you'd never ask." She stood on tiptoe to kiss him, kiss his beautiful mouth, setting free the passion she'd kept tamped down all night.

Stumbling a little, they moved to brace themselves against an aspen, kissing deeply, piercingly, hands roving. Tyler unbuttoned her coat, and she unbuttoned his. Then his hands were on her blouse, and Anna stilled, allowing him to unbutton each button in turn, until he sighed and pushed it away, then covered her breasts with his big hands. "You fit my hands exactly right, Anna," he whispered.

She swayed at the pleasure he gave her, closing her eyes against the silvery moonlight, simply accepting the loving attention he gave, his hands against her breasts, and over, and on her tummy, his mouth on her lips, then her chin, her ear, and her mouth again. She found her breath moving far from her, and heard his, hungry and low, against her ear.

Slowly, he pushed the cups of her bra downward, until her breasts were uncovered in the moonlight, brushed with his fingers and the cold, and then his hot mouth was upon the tips, until her body trembled with the sensation of heat followed by the sudden lack as he moved to the other side, leaving the moisture of his mouth to cool the abandoned one in erotic contrast. Anna gripped his shoulders fiercely, crying out softly.

His nimble hands moved to her hips, and Anna felt her skirt begin to rise, felt the air touch the backs of her knees, then higher, on her thighs, then blow across the most sensitive part of her, and his hands were on her naked buttocks, his mouth upon her breast, and Anna clutched him to her. "Tyler!" she gasped. "You have to let me touch you, too. I can't stand it."

He raised his head, his eyes burning. "Touch me any way you want, Anna." He kissed her.

She slid her hands under his shirt, at last putting her

hands on that smooth, supple flesh she had so long admired. She brushed her hands over his waist, and up his back, and slid them around to the buttons of his jeans.

And this time, he did not protest as she unbuttoned the worn denim, or when she slid her hands inside and found his hot and rigid flesh. It was his turn to still, to cry out softly as she stroked him. His turn to fall, lost in pleasure, as Anna touched him, and kissed his chin, and his neck, and his mouth, feeling his hands tighten against her bottom, then grow more hurried, stroking urgently.

With a soft, wicked laugh, she let him go, and put her arms around his waist. "It's too cold out here," she whispered. "I think we have to go home."

He made a wordless noise of protest, and captured her mouth, kissing her into a trembling frenzy. Anna eased away, pushing her skirt down. "Fair is fair," she said, laughing, and, clasping her coat around her unbuttoned blouse, slipped away.

His low chuckle told her he was following. At the truck, he said, "I'm going to torture you for that, Anna."

"Oh, I sincerely hope so," she said, and climbed in, sliding across the seat to open his door for him.

He stood there looking at her for a moment. "God, Anna, you should see yourself. You look like Venus herself."

She only smiled.

Tyler felt drunk. Dizzy and alive and vividly happy. The drive up the mountain was too curving to take with anything except the utmost caution, but he managed it in record time. And at last, at last, they were home, and inside, and shedding clothes the minute the door was closed behind them.

Tyler grabbed her, holding her head with one hand to kiss her while he fought her coat from her willing shoulders with one hand and she fought his from his body. They stumbled and turned, and he tore her blouse in his hurry, unable to bear another second of waiting. She unhooked her bra, he discarded his shirt, their tongues and mouths joined. He kicked off his shoes, and she tossed away the bra, and they fell together on the bed, chest to chest, in an agony of want. He didn't bother with anything else, only shoved up her skirts, and freed himself, and plunged.

Deep.

He cried out at the same moment she did, both of them shocked at the pleasure of the joining. His breath caught in his throat, and he gripped her shoulders, looking down into her beautiful, vividly colored face. The luminous black eyes opened, and held his gaze as he began to move. He kissed her, and she clutched him tightly to her, and then there was only the furious power of their need, rocking and intense, limbs and lips and bodies entangled in the deepest, most intimate joining of his life.

And it was not only bodies, but hearts and souls and minds, too, all melting into some blazing, illuminating, light-filled melding. He felt himself nearing release and captured her face in his hands, feeling the sweat and heat and need between them. She opened her eyes and met his gaze, and he let himself go, shuddering and kissing and looking deeply into her soul, and he watched her eyes a moment later when she followed, her body arching, her head flung back, and he kissed her throat and felt her come apart.

And he knew that he was forever changed, from this moment forward.

Anna lay in Tyler's arms limply, letting her heart rate slow, and her breathing return to normal, floating in the glorious sense of communion she felt with him in this moment, an attunement so pure and clean and satisfying that she felt no need of words. He shifted, pulling her on top of him, and they sighed together at the small aftershocks of pleasure it sent through both of them.

"Oh, Anna," he breathed, his hands stroking his hair. "You're one hell of a woman, you know that?"

The words came through his chest, into her ear. "Mmm..." she said lazily, smiling.

His hands moved from her hair down her back. "I love the way you feel. Your skin feels like rose petals, and you smell like heaven. Like the way the ground smells when it's been really hot, then it rains."

Anna lifted her head to look at him, amazed at the words pouring out of him. As if he did not realize, he touched her cheeks. "I love your coloring. Those black eyes and red cheeks." His fingers grazed her lips, then slid down her chin. "And your breasts." His gaze followed his touch, skirting the round of one bare breast, cupping the weight in his palm, and Anna found herself growing aroused by the simplicity of that touch and gaze together. "Your breasts are so sinfully sensitive. All I have to do is slip one finger, right over the top—" he did, and the tip rose to meet him eagerly "—and there it is, ready for me, again." He spread his hands around her rib cage, and helped her into a sitting position straddling him.

Anna tried to adjust her skirt, but he grabbed the fabric, and began to draw it over her torso. "Lift your hands," he said, and Anna complied, feeling deliciously pagan and amazingly unshy as he drew the skirt over her head and tossed it away, leaving her naked. He dragged his hands over her body. "You're so gorgeous." He touched her round belly, and slid his thumb between her legs, and Anna simply allowed it, taking pleasure in the sensual abandon that was on his face, making him look like a sleepily dangerous lion. "I think maybe now I'll torture you."

Before she could react, he had turned her on her back. His jeans hindered him, and he held her still while he shucked them from his long, long legs, then straddled her. "What do you like, Anna, my sweet?"

"You, Tyler."

He bent to kiss her neck. "You like this," he said, suckling the tender flesh there. "And this." He flickered his tongue over her ear. "But I wonder...do you like this?" He tasted her shoulder, her biceps, her inner elbow, her inner arm and wrist. He kissed her belly button and knees and bent to her toes.

And all of it, all of it, was exotic and rich and wonderful. He teased her unmercifully, with dancing tongue and clever fingers playing over her body in usual and unusual places. At last, he bent between her legs and let that skillful tongue rove and flicker and lave until Anna was shivering all over, arching against him with low, panting cries.

Then he halted and straddled her again, and Anna pulled him close, to take him into her mouth, and she teased him the way he had teased her, until once again they fell together, shouting in triumph at the eventual joining.

And the whole night passed in that way. They made love on the bed and in the shower. Standing in the kitchen, braced against the counter, lying on the floor in front of the fire in splendid, unashamed nudity. Tyler spilled brandy over her breasts and belly and licked every tiny drop away, and Anna spread him with chocolate, and they made love in sticky, laughing joy, requiring another shower.

Finally in exhaustion, they slept tangled in each other's arms, only to awake and make love one more time as day crept into the room, tenderly, slowly. Sore and still hungry, they simply lay together afterward in silence, as birds brought in the morning.

Chapter 18

"I almost forgot," Tyler said as they drank coffee the next morning, sitting on stools in the kitchen. He reached into his duffel bag and pulled out a sheaf of papers. "Yesterday, I spent some time with a friend of mine and we drew up a rough plan for the cabin."

"Really?" She smiled happily. "Show me."

"Well, I was just about to do that." He unrolled the blue-and-white sheets on the counter, anchoring one end with a heavy stoneware pencil holder. "This is the original plan," he said, tracing the outline. "And this is our lot. Plenty of room, as you see."

"Wow. How much land do you have up here, Tyler?"

"Almost five hundred acres." He lifted his brows. "Enough to make our grandbabies rich, if they ever have a need. By the time they grow up, this land will be worth about ten times what it is now." He drew his finger around the lot. "The meadow we sit in is about five and a half acres, but I put the house against the trees for wind protection. That means—" he unrolled a second sheet

"—we'll have to add on through the front. I thought maybe we could make the main room now into our bedroom, with the baby's room where Curtis sleeps now, and we'll add on this way." He pointed out the generous dimensions to the front of the cabin. "A big main room, and a bedroom for Curtis."

He felt as if he were babbling, and he hated the lump of guilt in his gut. Still, he reasoned, Anna would better like having a home of her own, not something that had been built for another woman. He would give her a house she could love in her own right.

She bent intently over the plans, and asked serious questions about the placement of windows and doorways, then finally leaned back on the stool. "It looks wonderful, Tyler. Will you be able to finish it before the baby gets here?"

"Easily. Once the ground thaws, I'll get Lance on the ground work, then I'll do the rest."

She smiled. "Really? You're a pretty talented guy, aren't you?"

He lifted one wicked eyebrow. "Very."

"Indeed." She crossed her arms and leaned over the plans again, sucking on her bottom lip in a way he recognized as meaning that she was biting back her words.

"What's bothering you about the layout?"

She took a breath. "I don't want to interfere with your life-style choices, Tyler, but do you think we'll ever have electricity? I can live without a lot of the comforts of the world, but I miss being able to watch movies. And I'd like to have music sometimes."

"Fear not, my lady," he said, lifting a palm. He pointed at notations at the bottom of the plans. "This means we have to hire someone to lay the lines from where they stop, about three hundred yards down the mountain, all the way up here to our humble meadow."

Her happiness tugged at him. "Oh, Tyler, that's wonderful!"

"I'll let you give me my reward later."

She chuckled. "Gladly."

The birdlike screech of the cellular phone went off, and Tyler picked it up. It was his mother. "Just thought you might appreciate a little warning," she said. "Anna's family is on their way up the mountain to see where she lives."

"Are they driving on their own?" He didn't like to think of them on that road.

"No. Lance is bringing them."

He hung up. "Showtime, kid. Your parents are on their way to examine your abode."

Anna groaned, covering her face. "Now I have to be reprimanded. Ugh."

"You'll get through it."

She rolled her eyes. "I guess."

With a sense of surprise, Tyler realized he felt completely comfortable with Anna this morning. And more than that, there was an odd, light sensation in the region of his chest that, upon examination, proved to be simple happiness. It made him smile, and he leaned forward to plant a kiss on her mouth. Not a kiss of hunger or need or anything else remotely sexual. Just a kiss. Just because.

"That helps," she said.

"Yeah?" He did it again, and put his hand on her belly. "How's my girl this morning."

"Never better." She covered his hand with her own. "You know, if you keep up this grinning and laughing and joking, you're going to completely ruin your reputation as a grizzly loner."

He lifted his brows and kissed her once more. "It was getting to be an old song anyway."

Anna heard the truck on the road a half hour later and, wrapping herself in a light sweater against the cool wind, stepped out on the porch to wait. Tyler, never one to waste time, was using a metal tape to set stakes in the softening earth in front of the cabin. He straightened and waved as they drove up. Lance and Anna's brothers both ambled over to him, and they fell into the manly discussion of foundation requirements and construction materials.

Curtis, too, had returned with them, and he ran to his father's side. "What ya building?"

"A new bedroom for you, Slick."

"Oh, boy! Can I help?"

Olive, dressed sensibly in sturdy walking shoes and jeans and a layering of coats, followed more slowly. "Anna, this is beautiful!" she cried, gesturing around her. "You must be so happy!"

Anna relaxed. She ambled down the steps to give her mother a hug, realizing that all she ever really wanted was their approval. "I am, Mama."

"Good." She nodded. "It would be better if he was Italian, but he's a nice man, Anna. You found one who will take good care of you."

"Now, Mama, look at that man and tell me he would be better as anything but exactly what he is."

Olive made a show of looking Tyler up and down, her lips pursed approvingly. "Like a movie star."

"I always thought he looked like a prince," she said. To her mother she could say all that she had kept to herself, all the foolish things that had moved her, and Olive would understand. "Like a lost prince, who was bewitched by some evil spell."

Olive's eyes glittered. "And you rescued him," she said, smiling.

"I think I did. Imagine that. Me—a princess."

"I need to walk. Can we? I get so stiff when I don't get my walks."

"Sure." She gestured. "It would be best if we stuck to

the road, but most of the snow is melting now." She called out their intention to the others, and pointed down the road.

"Why don't you show her the point?" Tyler suggested.

The point was the place where they'd seen the wolf, and Anna shook her head. After a few days, her mother would adjust to the lower oxygen levels in this air, but until then, the altitude would be too much for her. "Too hard right now. We'll just walk a mile or so down the road and back."

He hesitated. Anna thought he was going to add something, but he did not. Curtis broke away from the group. "Can I come, Mommy?"

Anna looked at her mother. "Do you mind?"

"No, no. Please come with us."

The boy ran forward and then back up the road, always in sight, but always on his own private quest, too, so they were free to talk. "Go ahead and get it all out now, Mama," Anna said when they were out of sight of the cabin. "I know you have some things to say."

"No, Anna. Yesterday, I might have. But today, I see you found the life you wanted all those years when we didn't listen to you, and it makes me happy." Her eyes held a suspicious sheen of moisture when she looked at her daughter. "It makes me sad, too, because I'm not going to be seeing you the same way I see everybody else, and I miss you. My grandbabies won't know me so much, you know?"

Anna took her hand. "I know. I'll do my best, I promise. We'll visit as often as we can. Money isn't a problem."

"It's a good family," she said. "But it's not the same."

"I know." But there was no changing certain facts.

The sun was fierce on their heads, and Olive pulled off her hat. "There's one thing, Anna."

Anna watched Curtis fall to his knees in the muddy mess off the road, putting his face very close to something on the ground. She chuckled. "Wonder what he's looking at."

"Anna."

"I know. We didn't get married Catholic." She sighed. "There wasn't time right then, but he has promised to take classes with me, so we can have a real wedding in the church."

"When are you going to start?"

Anna looked at her. "Good question. The sooner the better. I'll talk to him about it. I promise."

"And you're going to raise the baby the way you should?"

"Yes. Curtis, too."

"Oh, that's good! Very good."

Curtis had been right in front of them, but Anna glanced over and didn't see him. Unalarmed, she said, "Where did Curtis go? Did you see?"

"No."

"Curtis! Where are you?"

No answer. A fist hit Anna's gut. She let go of her mother's arm and rushed forward. "Curtis! Answer me right now."

Still nothing. Sometimes he played the "invisible" game, and she'd warned him repeatedly that it wasn't to be done outdoors, or when she called his whole name. Remembering, she called, "Curtis Forrest, answer me right now."

He popped out of the trees, a blond imp. "I found my angel mommy's house. Come see."

Angel mommy? Anna frowned. Was it a tomb or something? "Maybe we'd better not. Let's just keep walking."

"No. It's pretty."

Anna looked at her mother. "Hang on. I'll be right back."

There was a faint path in the dry grass, and Anna followed it to where Curtis stood. "How far is it?"

He took her hand. "Not very far at all."

The path snaked through the forest for about fifteen yards, and ended at a meadow. "See?" Curtis said, pointing. "Mommy's house."

Anna simply stared. She recognized Tyler's craftsmanship immediately, in the carved wooden shutters and the elegance of line and the thick half-log siding that matched the cabin on the hill. She tugged on Curtis's hand. "Who lives here?"

"Nobody," he said, as if it were obvious. "But I got the key. You want to see?"

"Let's go back and get Grandma first."

"Okay." They hurried back the way they had come, and Anna called, "Mama, you have to see this!"

They waited for her to catch up, then went back to the meadow, with its astonishing view of Red Creek. "Oh, my goodness!" Olive gasped.

"Come on!" Curtis cried, running ahead. He clomped up a wooden deck that faced southeast, a direction Anna recognized would provide optimum heating and cooling. Such things were important in the mountains.

He reached under a rock and came up with a key. "See? I remembered."

"Have you been here lately, Curtis?" Anna asked. There was a strange sense of warning in her gut, something that she should be noticing but was just out of reach.

"Gramma Louise showed me it." Sticking his tongue out, he struggled to put the key in. His voice dropped to a whisper. "My daddy wasn't s'pposed to know."

Anna took pity and took it from him, squatting down to his level. "Did your daddy build this house?"

"Yep. It's his bestest house ever."

"Are you sure he won't mind if we go in?"

He looked unsure, and Anna made her decision. "Maybe we should just look in the windows until we ask him."

"No. Please? I wanna go in."

Olive nudged her. Sotto voce, she said, "We don't have to tell him. I want to see."

The truth was, Anna was dying to see the inside, and she allowed herself to be persuaded. She fit the key in the lock, and the door swung open easily, without any telltale creaks that would mean no one had been here in a long time. Her heart pinched.

She stepped inside, a hollowness deep within. With sorrow she saw how beautifully designed it was for comfortable family living, and for minimum ecological impact. The windows on the south wall were enormous, and Anna was sure the site had been selected with both the southern winter sunlight and the view of the valley in mind. The windows to the north were small and high. A generous kitchen, with cutouts for a stove and fridge, and the outlets behind them illustrated plainly that it had been wired.

Curtis ran from room to room, his feet clunking on the plywood subflooring, and the sound struck Anna's nerves with thuds of doom. Wandering blankly from room to room, she saw in every loving detail the grace of Tyler's wood art.

It was not especially large. A big central room with big windows and access to the deck, the efficiently planned kitchen, a bathroom with a tub, and three bedrooms. The largest also faced the valley.

But she halted in a room that was very nearly finished. The walls were paneled in warm varnished pine, and a carpet of plush dark blue covered the floor. Curtains, once pressed and starched, hung at the two windows, and it was by their pattern, cheerful blocks and teddy bears in clean primary colors, that she understood what this room was to have been.

"This is my room," Curtis announced. "I think it'th real pretty, don't you?"

"I do, Curtis."

"It's Mommy's house, though, so we don't live here."

"I see."

She turned slowly, thinking of the woman who had hung the curtains and chosen the color of the carpet, and she touched her stomach with a sharp, almost physical sense of sorrow. Kara must have been full of joy and anticipation, making preparations for her child and her new home. Anna could almost see her here, her blond hair pulled back from her face into an efficient ponytail, her big tummy covered with something sensible, like a cotton smock.

Poor Kara.

Instead, she had given birth only to give her own life in return. Anna wondered how she would feel if she knew Tyler had not finished the house, had not brought the son they'd made to the room his mother had prepared for him. Tears rose in her eyes. How awful that he'd made it a tomb, instead of the love-filled place it was supposed to be.

Just as he'd made his life a tomb.

Creeping anger filled the hollowness she'd been feeling. This very morning, he had stood there at that counter and showed her plans for additions to the cabin, and all the time he'd known this house was here. Looking around, she figured it would take about one-tenth the money and less than a quarter of the time to finish this place than it would to build and finish the addition.

She suddenly remembered hearing him leave the cabin the night Curtis had been worried about losing his new mommy to childbirth. He'd left and come back much, much later, and when she innocently curled up to him, he'd turned away almost violently.

And she'd awakened later to him making love to her.

"Anna, is something wrong?" Olive asked. "You look funny."

"I don't know," she said, and walked away, her arms crossed, to stand out on the deck that overlooked the storybook village spilling down the mountain. She breathed in the cool air, trying to calm her racing thoughts, but there were too many.

She thought of the morning after the wedding, when he had stopped her attempts to make love to him by saying he'd been dreaming of Kara. Had the same thing happened yesterday morning? Had he come here in his grief and then returned home to dream of Kara, but expended that energy on Anna?

It wounded her to think that it might be true. That she had been foolish enough to believe a real connection was growing between them, that he might truly be starting to love her. Last night had been achingly beautiful and real and deep. And she knew in her bones that it was Anna to whom he had made love last night, Anna who had reached through his sorrows and touched his soul.

But all along, he'd known this house of his hands and heart was sitting here empty, and rather than move his new wife and new family into it, he'd chosen to leave it as a tomb to a woman he had still not let go of.

It made her furious. "Mama! Curtis!" she yelled into the echoing rooms. "Let's get back, now!"

Tyler knew the minute Anna came over the hill. She'd found the house.

And she was mad.

"Uh, you know, I think Anna and I are about to have a serious discussion," he said, putting down his hammer. "Why don't you guys go in and have some coffee. Lance?"

"No problem." Lance glanced over his shoulder as he put down the tape he'd been using.

Quietly, they moved inside, and Anna had evidently given the same instruction to her mother and Curtis, for they broke off and headed toward the house as Anna approached Tyler. Against the vivid blue of the Colorado sky, she looked like some rare, exotic bird, passing through on the flyways, and the image gave Tyler a lump in his throat.

"You found the house," he said when she stopped in front of him.

"I did." She stared at him, her arms crossed. "Did you think it would never come up?"

He took a breath, touched his chest, looked over her shoulder. "I don't know. I didn't really *think,* you know." He shrugged, unable to think of anything to add.

She kicked the stake he'd driven into the earth only moments before. The gesture pained him, but he said nothing. There was nothing to say, no defense he could offer except the truth, and that he would not say.

"You know, Tyler, I've pretty much been in love with you since the first moment I saw you."

Her small chin jutted upward, and he saw the effort she exerted to keep her voice even. The thickness in his own chest grew more dense.

"I saw you, and I saw the sorrow in your eyes, and you were just like a prince in a fairy tale."

"Anna, don't."

"No, for once you're going to listen to the whole thing, Tyler Forrest. All of it." She took a step forward. "I haven't asked one thing of you. I let you live in that glass tower of yours, safe from everything, from feeling things and loving people and participating in the world you live in, because that was what I thought you needed."

A small, tight kernel of anger ignited somewhere amid the thickness in his chest. Tyler straightened. "Are you finished?"

"No. I thought you were lonely and grieving," she said, and now tears of pure silver anger welled up in her black eyes, "and I know that's what you think. I know it's been Kara in your heart all this time, and I was willing to let you get over it in your own way, in your time."

"Then what—"

"How could you just let her house sit there that way, with no life or laughter in it? How could you kill her dream like that?" She dashed away the tears on her face. "When I saw those curtains that she hung so carefully for her son, I wanted to kill you, Tyler, because you were so selfish you couldn't even let her have that one thing. Because she had the nerve to live her own life, her own way."

Of all the reactions he might have expected, this was one he'd never anticipated. It cut to the quick of his long-buried anger and guilt and hurt. "I was the selfish one? I begged her not to have that baby. We had a perfect life."

"There's no such thing as a perfect life. And she had a right to try, Tyler. She had a right to feel that baby inside of her. Don't you see? She was willing to risk her life—she gave her life—to give you a son. And she did it because she *loved* you, you arrogant son of a bitch!" Tears washed over her face. "And in your heart, you know you were wrong. You were wrong to have a vasectomy, and you were wrong to be so angry with her, and you were really, really wrong to make an empty tomb out of the house you built together with so much love. You *cheated* her."

With a distant part of his mind, Tyler realized her grief was raw and deep, and for a woman she had never known. He stared at her, unable to move or act, frozen by shame and sorrow—not only for Kara, but now for Anna, too.

She bowed her head for a moment, then lifted it again, and she was calm. "I've done all I can, Tyler. You have to make a choice now." She lifted her shoulders. "Either you wake up and live, or spend the whole rest of your life waiting for someone else to come along and break down those walls." She tossed her head. "As much as I love you—and I do love you, Tyler—I'm not willing to martyr myself to save you."

"Martyr yourself?" he echoed, just this side of sarcasm.

"Please don't bother. I told you when you first came here that I wasn't some lost prince. You've always had this fantasy about me that doesn't have anything to do with who I am." Dangerous emotion welled in his throat. "Now you see who I really am, you see what a mess I made of my life, and what do you do? Run away!"

They weren't the words he had intended to say, weren't even close. But he felt a choking panic at the thought of her driving back down the mountain, leaving him alone again. He closed his eyes. "Anna, please don't go."

"I have to. You'll never sort it out as long as I'm here to lean on." Her voice quavered, very near, and he felt her head against his chest.

He wrapped his arms around her fiercely, as if he could will her to stay.

For one aching moment, she allowed it. Then she shifted, and Tyler reluctantly let her go. She patted his chest, then backed away. "For your sake, Tyler, I hope you'll do some serious soul-searching. It's time."

Then she walked away, and Tyler let her.

But in the deepest part of his heart, a wolf howled, low and long, silent and alone. Again.

Chapter 19

Anna asked quietly if she could ride back to town with Lance and her family, and they wisely asked no questions. The one thing Lance did that Anna had not, in her numbed state, considered, was call to Curtis, "Hey, kid, you want to come with us and go play with Cody?"

Oblivious to the adult undercurrents, Curtis leaped off the porch. "Sure!"

In the car, Anna's mother took her hand silently, and squeezed, but even when they dropped her off at Louise's house, Olive didn't pry.

There was a first time for everything.

Louise let her in with a frown. "Is there something wrong? Is someone hurt? You look terrible, child."

"Would you mind if I stayed here for a few days, until I can make other arrangements?" Anna raised her chin. "I don't really have anywhere else to go."

Louise, eyes troubled, nodded. "Of course, Anna. You know my home is open to you."

"Thank you." She took a breath. "If you wouldn't mind terribly, I'd like to just be alone for a little while."

Wordlessly, Louise embraced her, and Anna fought hard to maintain her self-control for just a few more minutes. There was a great gaping wound in her heart, and she didn't think she could bear much sympathy just yet. Stiffly, she drew away.

"Let me get you settled." Louise led her to one of the back rooms, and turned back the covers and drew the drapes. "You just lay down and have yourself a good cry, honey. Sometimes, it's the only thing in the world that helps." At the door, she paused. "If you need me, I'll be here."

Anna nodded. Louise quietly closed the door, and Anna followed her advice. Pitching herself face-first onto the mattress, she gave in and let herself cry. They were tears of genuine grief—for the barely budded love that had been growing between she and Tyler, for the beauty of the days they might have had. She wept for poor Curtis, who would never understand that it wasn't his fault that this had happened.

And she wept for Kara, because she really had understood her in those moments in that lovingly decorated bedroom. She wept because she could not be there for her little boy, not the way she would have liked to be.

And finally, she wept for herself, for the love she had found and lost, wept for the loss of her dream. Wept because there was, after all, no magic in the world to save lost princes.

At last she quieted, and fell into an almost drugged sleep, where no dreams dared follow.

Louise paced the kitchen, unable to even calm down enough to cook. She didn't intrude on Anna's grief, but twice she heard her faintly, weeping as if her heart had shattered into a zillion pieces.

She paced out to the deck and breathed deeply of the fresh air. What had she done when she put this in motion all those months ago? It had seemed such a good idea—two wildly romantic people who genuinely deserved the kind of passion each was capable of delivering, who were both pure and good and innocent in ways the world could never change. She had thought, somehow, that they might protect each other.

Instead, she'd only made them hurt.

In bewilderment, she wondered what had happened. Last night, they'd seemed to have finally reached that luminous place of lovers who were truly in tune. She'd never seen Tyler look as radiant as he had then, and Anna had made her think of nothing so much as a ripe plum, ready to burst with sweetness.

What could have gone so terribly wrong in so short a time? She resisted calling Lance to get the details. She would let Anna tell it in her own way, in her own time. Or Tyler, if he showed up, which she doubted very seriously. At this moment, he was likely skulking and brooding.

A knock sounded at the back door, a quiet knock that seemed to recognize the need for gentleness in this house. Louise looked at the door for a moment, her heart leaping in sudden hope. Then she shook her head. The romantic tangles of her children this past year had addled her wits. She'd even thought *she* might find true love.

But maybe someone had brought news. She hurried forward to answer it, and stopped cold, her hand on the screen door.

It *was* Alonzo. Standing there on her back steps, looking hale and tanned, his black hair freshly cut and shining in the bright day. He wore her favorite shirt, an improbably colored cotton stripe in tones of green and blue and purple.

"Hello, Louise. Is she okay?"

Of course. He'd come to see about Anna. It had nothing

to do with Louise. But it was so good to see him, to have him here at a moment of crisis, that she swung open the door anyway. "I don't rightly know."

He stepped inside, politely standing just inside the kitchen while she closed the door. While her back was turned, Louise tried to remember if she'd bothered to put on any lipstick this morning, and how long it had been since she combed her hair. Resisting an urge to lift a hand to her head to make sure it was neat, she gestured to the table. "Sit down. I have coffee, if you like."

"That would be nice." He settled in the chair he favored, one that put his back to the wall and gave him a view of the window and the kitchen.

Taking a mug from the cupboard, Louise said, "I think she's fallen asleep now." She gave him the cup and sighed. "I think I have some—"

"No food, huh? You just sit. I no like the way you look right now."

Louise frowned, not at all pleased by the comment, but she had to admit she felt a little winded by this new development. "Did Lance say what happened? They were so happy together last night."

"It happens that way sometimes, no?" His dark eyes met hers, and Louise thought she caught a glimpse of melancholy there.

"I suppose it does."

Silence fell and roared between them, the only sound the ticking of the cuckoo clock in the dining room. Louise smelled the spicy aftershave he used, and the clean scent of starch in his shirts, which—judging by the knife-sharp crease in his sleeves—had been done by the commercial laundry.

"I saw Tyler yesterday, you know," Alonzo said. "He was like somebody I never saw before, all happy and laughing. I never saw him laugh, never, in all the time I been here."

Louise raised her eyes.

"Maybe," he said, "it's not such a bad thing to push somebody you love a little bit, so they see what's good for them."

"Well, I appreciate you trying to make me feel better, but I reckon I was still wrong to be such a busybody."

"Louise."

She stared at her cuticles, thinking that maybe sometime she ought to get a real manicure so they didn't look so raggedy all the time.

He reached out and took her hand. Still Louise did not look at him, afraid he would see how desperately she missed him, how much she wanted to undo the damage they'd done each other.

"*Lo siento mucho,* Louise. I am so sorry I did not understand how much you wanted for your children, for that girl in there and your son, who was dying a little every day." He tightened his hand. "I hurt you. And I am so sorry."

In more than thirty years of marriage, Olan Forrest had never seen Louise cry. She would not give him that satisfaction, and though she managed still to keep her tears contained, she could not still the roughness of her voice. "Thank you," she whispered, tightening her fingers around the heartbreakingly familiar length of his.

"Is there any chance you will allow me to maybe take you to supper again one day? Not to rush, not to ask too much, but I will tell you the truth, *mi amor,* there are not too many women who laugh the way you do."

And finally, she raised her eyes and let him see what was in her heart. For too many years she had hidden her true self, let others' needs come first in her life. She had learned to not even ask for anything. "I miss you," she said clearly. "Almost every minute."

He sighed, and closed his eyes, and for a minute, Louise thought he hadn't meant what she thought, that he'd only been kind. Then he pulled her hand and pressed his mouth fervently to the palm, then her wrist, and she realized he had only been overcome. "Me, too," he said quietly.

At that, Louise really did cry. And for once, she didn't even mind.

Tyler sank down on the porch steps as they drove away, all of them, leaving him alone. He felt dizzy with the sudden upheaval in his life. This morning, everything had felt so calm and easy and good. How could that have changed so quickly?

It was utterly silent on the mountain, and he tried to tell himself he didn't mind. Once, he'd longed for the silence of these mountains, away from the noise of cars and people chattering.

His father blustering.

Tyler picked up a piece of wood and idly began to whittle, his mouth twisting bitterly. His father. That had been the real reason he wanted to be away from town. He'd known his father would never come up the mountain, and he never had. Which sometimes wounded, but mostly satisfied Tyler just fine.

His brothers had each handled their father in different ways. Lance, of all of them, had been the only one who genuinely loved him. And in some ways, maybe Lance was the only good thing Olan had ever done. Even he had been unable to resist the steadfast faith Lance put in him. Lance had turned inward the damage that unrewarded faith had caused, but all in all, he'd turned out all right.

Jake had become an overachiever, who damned near overachieved himself to death, trying to live up to some unreachable standard Olan had set for him.

Tyler liked to think he'd escaped. His mother had been older and wiser by the time he was born. She'd protected him to some degree. But he'd been a skinny, peaceful child who wanted nothing to do with the macho things his father enjoyed, and it had enraged his father.

His knife slipped, and he sliced his finger neatly. Blood spurted out from the cut, but, lost in his memories, Tyler didn't feel it. Mechanically, he put the cut to his mouth, then went on with the whittling.

Tyler and Olan had been openly at war from the time Tyler was nine and made up his mind that he hated his father. People had always frowned when he said it: "Oh, you don't really mean that."

But he had. And still did. The more his father pushed and blustered and browbeat Tyler, the more stubbornly he'd adopted ways that were sure to inflame him. He'd eschewed the material wealth his father so valued in every possible way, and moved off to this high meadow to live without electricity with a vegetarian herbalist his father thought was a crackpot.

Blood welled up in the cut again, and Tyler lifted a shaking hand to his mouth.

But what had he done? He'd become as autocratic and arrogantly certain of his own way as his father had been. His methods of browbeating and punishing those around him were less blustery, less emotionally violent, but in the end, the actions were the same.

My way or the highway.

His vision filled with a picture of Anna—beautiful, loving Anna—so furiously angry with him, and grieving for a woman she had never met. And at last, all the emotions that had been breaking free, one by shattering one, over the past few months, swelled over the dam and rushed through him, wild and fierce and painful. His head filled with a hundred images, a thousand, all at once, folding in over each other in a whirl of color and sound and smell, all of them Anna: appearing out of the snowstorm with her black hair and dancing eyes; her purple glitter toenail polish; her pleasure at seeing the wolf on the hill; her determination to show him she wasn't a tenderfoot by driving down the mountain in a blizzard; the sweetness of her curled asleep on his couch when he came in from the storm.

And more, the rush and fury of the passion he had conceived for her, and the generous, heartfelt way she responded, and the taste of her mouth against his. And the way she made him laugh, even at himself.

He thought, too, of Kara, in the first moments after Curtis had been born, and how she'd wept with happiness at the beauty of her son. He had never, in all the years he'd known her, ever seen her as happy as she was in those moments after Curtis was born.

Overcome, he let the knife and wood fall at his feet, bowing his head in defeat and acceptance. All the visions coalesced into one: Anna and Curtis in Curtis's room the night the boy had been afraid Anna would die. He saw them, Madonna and child, with the yellow light all around, and that swath of transparent white that he'd seen for one single second.

Tyler finally bowed his head and wept, because he knew all the things he could never undo, and all the moments he'd thrown away, and all the things he wished he could right.

And when he was finished, he knew what he had to do. He'd been given a second chance, a chance to wipe the slate clean and begin again. He could never undo the sins he'd committed against Kara, but he could make sure he did not repeat the mistakes of the past—both his own, and those of his father. Olan Forrest had been given dozens of chances to turn over a new leaf, and he'd scorned them all. Tyler had a son who needed him, and another child on the way, and a woman who had somehow, by some miracle, found a way to love him in spite of the clarity with which she saw him.

Humbled, he stood and went to find the keys to his truck.

Anna slept for hours, a long, deep, healing sleep that knit some of the torn places in her heart, and gave her strength to stumble from the dim bedroom into the vividly bright late afternoon.

She found Louise with Alonzo, the two of them sitting close together in the kitchen, talking in low, earnest voices. Louise saw her and straightened instantly, a faint blush on her cheeks. "You're awake!"

"Maybe," Anna said, blinking. "I'd kill for some coffee."

"Well, I just happen to have some made," Louise said, and gently pushed Anna into a chair. Sleepily, Anna leaned over and kissed Alonzo's cheek. "I guess you heard about the big blowout, huh? Thanks for coming over to check on me."

"You look okay. Are you?" he asked, patting her hand.

She considered. "I think so." She sighed. "All you can ever do is try. I did my best."

Louise put the coffee in front of her, and Anna drank it gratefully, aware of the questions they both wanted to ask. As caffeine and sugar entered her bloodstream, she felt capable of giving them at least a little background. "The bottom line is, he hasn't ever worked through his grief over Kara, and I suddenly realized he never will as long as I'm there to lean on."

"Are you going to go back to New York with your parents, then?" Louise asked nervously.

"No way, Louise. It'll make it harder to stay here in some ways, but this is my home. I love my job. I love the mountains, and I'm not going anywhere." She reached out and covered Louise's hand. "Your grandbaby is safe."

Louise smiled. "I'm glad."

The doorbell rang, and Louise went to answer it. Anna

touched Alonzo's hand. "Looks like you two are working things out."

He winked.

Louise returned to the kitchen, and by the expression on her face, Anna knew instantly that Tyler was here. "He wants to know if you'd like to go for a drive with him."

Anna looked at her, closed her eyes.

"If you want to wait, I'll tell him to come back later."

But Anna was already standing. "No. I'll go." As if in anticipation, the baby kicked, much more distinctly than it had before, and she closed her hand over the place.

Taking a deep, steadying breath, she walked into the living room, where Tyler stood uncomfortably. As if it had been a long time since she saw him, she realized he'd gained a little weight lately, and his lanky muscle was more balanced. She said nothing.

"I was wondering if you'd go for a drive with me," he said. "Talk."

She nodded. "Let me get my coat."

When she had fetched it, they drove through a part of Red Creek unfamiliar to Anna. "Where are we going?" she asked finally, realizing he wasn't going to just drive and talk, but had a destination in mind.

"I'd rather just show you, if you don't mind."

Anna nodded.

He pulled under a bank of trees just as the sun sank behind the highest peak nearby. Anna knew it would be back, reappearing twice more as it set lower and lower on the horizon, but it gave her a shiver, because they had stopped at the graveyard.

Carefully, she emptied her mind of expectations as she stepped out of the truck. From a carrier in the back, Tyler took a bunch of mixed flowers, of the sort that could be purchased at the grocery store. Against the gray day, they were startlingly bright—sprays of orange freesias, improbably blue carnations, a handful of roses in different colors, a little baby's breath.

Carrying the bouquet, Tyler led the way into the graveyard. The world was washed with the soft gray of twilight, and within the wrought-iron fence, the air felt moist and cooler. Some hidden wrens whistled in the trees, but there was no other sound.

A grove of aspen enclosed it, with the mountains rising in giant blue splendor all around, and Anna thought it was an exquisitely beautiful, serene place, and would be no matter what time of year.

The headstone was simple, with Kara's name and the dates of her birth and death, with a quotation from Omar Khayyám:

The Moving Finger writes; and, having writ, Moves on.

"She picked this plot herself," he said. "The quote, too. She made all the arrangements for her death the day before we got married. I didn't know until she died."

Anna had often been jealous of the threat Kara represented. Now, she felt only a poignant sorrow that moved through her with swift, piercing suddenness. "It's as if she knew."

Tyler lifted his head, as if he were trying to hold back tears. "I think she did. I think she always knew." Taking a breath, he divided the flowers and gave half to Anna. "But I think she was more sincerely grieved this morning than she has been since she died. I thought—" He stopped and his jaw went hard. "I thought you would like to see her grave." He lost his struggle to keep his voice even. "I thought," he said raggedly, "that she would like to meet you."

Anna let the tears come, and could only nod.

"She loved flowers," he said, fingering the freesias,

"but not very many of them grew well on the mountains. I brought them to her whenever I could. She liked these because they smelled good."

He put them on the grave, and Anna bent down to do the same. It felt like a healing act, somehow, and her deep sense of loss evaporated.

Tyler simply stood there, looking at the flowers in their brightness on the grave, and Anna waited. He touched his chin, then raised his head, and his eyes seemed to borrow light from the twilight sky. "This is hard for me, Anna. I don't say what I mean very well."

She said nothing.

He took a breath. "You were right about what I did to Kara—and I knew it. I don't think—" His brows drew down in puzzlement. "I don't think I really believed she would die. I wanted to punish her for making me hurt and worry, and I was really furious when she died." He met her gaze apprehensively, as if waiting for censure. "I'm not proud of it, but it's the truth."

"Grief isn't rational."

"No." He crossed his arms. "The thing is, Anna, it really did hurt to lose her. I really did love her."

"I know."

"So it seemed like the only way I could make it up to her, make it right with her, was to keep myself away from other women for the rest of my life. It was the only penance I could think to offer."

He looked at the grave. "Then you came bursting in, like those flowers, so bright, and made my life look so gray, and I wanted you, and I hated myself for it."

A faint spark of hope lit in Anna's heart.

"I didn't want to fall in love with you. I really didn't want to find something that wonderful, something that made what Kara and I had seem like kid stuff." He swallowed. "But it happened anyway."

At first she didn't really understand what he was saying. Blankly she stared at him.

"When you wept for her this morning," he said, his voice going rough again, "I realized I'd gotten over Kara. Maybe a long time ago, and I was just waiting for a magic kiss from a gypsy to wake me up."

He let out his breath. "I love you, Anna. I want you to be my real wife. Is that possible, do you think? Can we start again?"

Anna lifted her chin. "What about the house?"

"You were right," he said. "It needs to be lived in. I was selfish."

Anna closed her eyes to be sure he wasn't going to disappear, that this wasn't a dream. When she opened them, he still stood there, a prince of the forest, who'd conquered his dragons. "Oh, yes! I love you," she whispered, and moved forward to fling herself into his arms.

He made a noise of surprise and gratitude, and clutched her in an embrace so tight Anna could barely breathe. "It killed me to have you walk away, Anna. You're a part of me now."

"I love you, Tyler," she said, and her wild sense of dizziness carried her away. As he kissed her, she thought she felt the faintest brush of love over her face, and a sense of a woman's soft sigh of relief—and then it was gone.

"Let's go tell the crew, huh?" Tyler said.

She smiled. "Yes."

Epilogue

Seven months later

A thick wet November snow fell from a low, heavy sky over the little Spanish church in Red Creek. Its pews were overflowing for the double wedding as the music started. Anna waited in the anteroom nervously for her father's signal, and when the music swelled through the aisle, her heart soared.

Her mother had been scandalized that Anna would wear the medieval dress Tyler had given her, but Anna had insisted. Tyler, too, wore his tunic, and he'd let his hair grow out again at her insistence, so it hung in a long, shining braid down his back. He looked proud and happy next to his handsome brothers and Alonzo, and she gave him a radiant smile as her father handed her to him.

Then she turned and waited for the second bride. Louise wore a simple green dress that flattered her ample figure, and on her head was a simple hat with netting that had belonged to her grandmother. Anna saw that the flowers she carried trembled a little, and she had to suck in a quick breath to keep her sentimental tears in place.

Through the mass and the sacraments, Louise held up fairly well, but when the priest asked them all to turn, Tyler and Anna, Louise and Alonzo, and introduced her as Mrs. Alonzo Chacon, she made a strange, strangled noise, and the whole church started to laugh.

And even above the laughter, Anna could hear her baby cooing and crowing in her grandma Olive's arms. She grinned at her beautiful, dark-haired daughter, then turned to Tyler, her prince, and whispered, "I think Kara is going to love church."

He squeezed her hand, and then, even though it wasn't in the rehearsal, he bent down to kiss her soundly, passionately, eliciting a cheer from the pews. "What do you say we get right to work on another one?"

"I hope you aren't expecting me to have eleven children, Mr. Forrest."

He grinned. "No, we can stop at say...six?"

Anna laughed. "It's a deal—if you have half of them."

He kissed her again. "Thank heaven for second chances."

Anna smiled up at him, thinking maybe there was magic in the world, after all, good magic, powerful magic.

The magic of love.

* * * * *

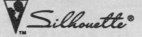
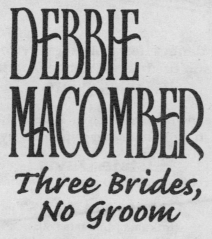

TRINITY STREET WEST

where danger lies around every corner—
and the biggest danger of all
is falling in love.

Meet the men and women of Trinity Street West
in the compelling miniseries by

Justine Davis
continuing in September 1997 with

A MAN TO TRUST
(Intimate Moments #805)

Kelsey Hall was hiding secrets and needed
someone to trust, and Cruz Gregerson, the one man
she desperately wanted to trust with her secrets *and*
her heart, was the one kind of man she knew she
couldn't—a by-the-book cop. But this time, he wasn't
thinking with his badge....

INTIMATE MOMENTS®
™ Silhouette®

National Bestselling Author

MARY LYNN BAXTER

"Ms. Baxter's writing...strikes every chord within the
female spirit."
—Sandra Brown

LONE STAR
Heat

SHE is Juliana Reed, a prominent broadcast journalist whose
television show is about to be syndicated. Until the murder...

HE is Gates O'Brien, a high-ranking member of the
Texas Rangers, determined to forget about his ex-wife. He's
onto something bad....

Juliana and Gates are ex-spouses, unwillingly involved in an
explosive circle of political corruption, blackmail and murder.

In order to survive, they must overcome the pain of the past...and
the very demons that drove them apart.

Available in September 1997 at your favorite retail outlet.

MIRA The brightest star in women's fiction   MMLBLSH

Look us up on-line at:http://www.romance.net

MATERNITY ROW

the street where little miracles are born!

The exciting new miniseries by

Paula
Detmer
Riggs

continues in September 1997 with

BABY BY DESIGN
(Intimate Moments #806)

Morgan Paxton returned home to find Raine, his estranged wife, pregnant with twins—after a trip to the sperm bank! Although he hadn't been the best of husbands, they were still married, and even if they didn't share his blood, these were *his* children. He wouldn't give up Raine without a fight, not when he had finally realized how much he loved her.

INTIMATE MOMENTS®
Silhouette®

Share in the joy of yuletide romance with brand-new
stories by two of the genre's most beloved writers

DIANA PALMER

and

JOAN JOHNSTON

in

LONE STAR CHRISTMAS

Diana Palmer and Joan Johnston share their favorite
Christmas anecdotes and personal stories in this
special hardbound edition.

Diana Palmer delivers an irresistible spin-off of her
LONG, TALL TEXANS series and Joan Johnston crafts an
unforgettable new chapter to **HAWK'S WAY** in this wonderful
keepsake edition celebrating the holiday season. So
perfect for gift giving, you'll want one for yourself...and
one to give to a special friend!

Available in November at your favorite retail outlet!

Only from

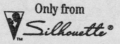
Silhouette®

Bestselling author

JOAN JOHNSTON

continues her wildly popular miniseries with an
all-new, longer-length novel

The Virgin Groom
HAWK'S WAY

One minute, Mac Macready was a living legend in
Texas—every kid's idol, every man's envy, every
woman's fantasy. The next, his fiancée dumped him,
his career was hanging in the balance and his future
was looking mighty uncertain. Then there was the
matter of his scandalous secret, which didn't stand a
chance of staying a secret. So would he succumb to
Jewel Whitelaw's shocking proposal—or take cold
showers for the rest of the long, hot summer...?

Available August 1997
wherever Silhouette books are sold.

Silhouette®